Iban Journey

Golda Mowe

monsoonbooks

Published in 2015
by Monsoon Books Pte Ltd
www.monsoonbooks.com.sg

Editorial / Sales:
No.1 Duke of Windsor Suite, Burrough Court,
Burrough on the Hill, Leics. LE14 2QS, UK

Registered office:
150 Orchard Road #07-02, Singapore 238841

ISBN (paperback): 978-981-4625-21-0
ISBN (ebook): 978-981-4625-22-7

Copyright©Golda Mowe, 2015

The moral right of the author has been asserted.

All rights reserved. No part of this publication may be reproduced, stored in a retrieval system, or transmitted, in any form or by any means without the prior written permission of the publisher, nor be otherwise circulated in any form of binding or cover other than that in which it is published and without a similar condition being imposed on the subsequent purchaser.

Cover design by Cover Kitchen.

National Library Board, Singapore Cataloguing-in-Publication Data
Mowe, Golda, author.
Iban journey / Golda Mowe. – Singapore : Monsoon Books Pte Ltd, 2015.
pages cm
ISBN : 978-981-4625-21-0 (paperback)
1. Fathers and sons – Fiction. 2. Iban (Bornean people) – Fiction.
3. Borneo – Fiction. I. Title.
PR9530.9
M823 -- dc23   OCN906994277

Printed in Singapore
18 17 16 15   1 2 3 4 5

monsoonbooks

IBAN JOURNEY

Born and raised in Sarawak on the island of Borneo to an Iban mother and Melanau father, Golda Mowe has always been interested in the culture and traditions of Borneo's indigenous people. After graduating from university in Japan and enduring ten years of corporate life, the author found herself yearning for childhood evenings spent in the longhouse, sitting in a pool of lamplight, listening to her great-aunt tell tales of jungle animals or her father recount his hunting adventures. *Iban Journey* is Golda's second novel and is the sequel to *Iban Dream*. Learn more about Golda and her writing at *www.gmowe.ws* and chat to her at *alpha@gmowe.ws*. For updates and news of author events, follow Golda Mowe on Facebook at *www.facebook.com/IbanDreamByGoldaMowe*.

Praise for Iban Dream

'This is exactly the book I've been waiting for – a fantasy novel that draws on the legends of our land. This exciting story draws on Iban mythology as well as the old ways of life that have all but disappeared.' *The Star*, Malaysia

'Mowe, of pure Borneo ancestry, is a great talent, a mistress of the English language, who has accomplished what no one else has done. Dash and craft at once inform her novel. *Iban Dream* is an ensera, or epic, written in English. The heroic register of Iban language differs exceedingly from that in English, yet Mowe has succeeded in recreating the Iban feeling–and even hinting at Iban literary glories–by English means. She's a skilled and learned prose stylist.' Otto Steinmayer, *Borneo Research Bulletin*

Also by Golda Mowe

Iban Dream

Chapter 1

Nuing kept his head bowed, his brown eyes staring at the pair of callused hands he clasped over his crossed legs. He was too tall and fair-skinned for an Iban, like a highland Kenyah who lived in the cool ranges of the hills. Yet the eyebrows arching over his eyes were thick, and his sideburns bristled dark down the side of his cheeks before fading into the shadow of a beard on his chin. His long black hair which he tied into a bun just above his nape was unkempt, like an old man's. The loincloth around his waist, like him too, looked tired and threadbare. Anyone who saw him would have assumed that he was in mourning.

In contrast to him, his father Bujang Maias was a picture of the perfect Iban. His long black and grey hair was combed and his eyebrows and sideburns plucked clean, making the tan face completely free of hair. But his expression was harsh and sorrowful as he repeated the message that was passed to him only that morning. "*Apai* Gupi does not want you to see his daughter. He says that if he ever catches you in their room again, he will strike you with his machete and kill you."

"But I have no quarrel with him, Father," Nuing said, looking up with blazing eyes under a frowning brow.

A cooling breeze blew in through the veranda door in front of which they were both sitting. Bujang turned his gaze away from his son's to look out to the horizon beyond the river. Dusk was setting behind the house and far off in front of them, the faint light of a star could be seen clearly shining just above the tree tops. He stared at it, wishing that he could find an answer to his son's predicament. There was nothing more that he could wish from his youngest child Nuing because he was already the perfect son. How could he explain to the young man before him that no matter how hard he tried, he would never be a good enough man for the other fathers and mothers in the house. The day was reaching its end, smelling and sounding much like all the other long humid days of the rainforest.

Bujang then turned to look at one particular pillar within the gallery of the longhouse, the one in front of his *bilek*. The three skulls of Tama Ramun, the bear-warrior; Salang, the hornbill-warrior; and Burak, the python-man were abnormally large compared to the heads of the Bruni soldiers and sailors hanging with them. He had hoped that their strong presence would persuade the people to accept Nuing as a child of his loins, but the fact that Nuing was Upa's bastard son was a knowledge too steeped with taboo for them to ignore.

A young woman crossed the gallery of her family room and went out to the *tanju*. Bujang watched her slide out one medium-sized basket from a pile just inside her veranda door. This woman too had rejected his son. Even now as she scooped drying illipede nuts from a mat into the basket, she kept her back to them so she would not accidentally look up and catch either of their eyes. Bujang then turned his face to scan the open gallery under the roof of the longhouse, lingering on three other single women, who were either pounding rice in wooden pestles by the door of their family quarters or sweeping under her bachelor brother's bed with a broom made of coconut-leaf spines bundled together.

None of them were kind to Nuing. None of them looked his son's way to try to catch his attention the way they would the other bachelors in the longhouse. Bujang's heartache increased when he recalled that not even Upa was willing to pluck her son's eyebrows and sideburns for him. His thoughts returned to Gupi, the young woman who lived only five doors away from his family room.

"You must not see her again," Bujang said.

"Did her father say why?"

"You are my son. He is unwilling to be part of my family. Maybe he thinks that becoming my *ihsan* will bring him too much grief." After a moment of silence he continued, "You are still young, just over twenty harvestings. There is still much time for you to choose a wife."

Nuing again bowed his head, for he knew the reason he was rejected by Gupi's father. The women spoke of him being a cursed seed often enough, and did not care if he was within earshot or not. All maladies, bad harvests, and ill hunts were blamed on him. Though he proved himself over and over of being worthy to be called the son of Bujang Maias, his efforts always fell short and he had grown weary of trying. His harvest basket was as large as his father's, his hunting spear as true, and his heart as brave in the dim silence of the jungle, yet no man or woman in the longhouse considered him worthy for any of their daughters.

Without looking up, he said, "I am going hunting tomorrow, Father."

"There is still much meat in the home."

"I think it is best I go out."

The older man watched his son try to wring the frustration out of his hands for a moment then he said, "Very well, but come home before dark." Sensing no reply forthcoming from his youngest, Bujang stood up and strode back into their family room.

Inside the longhouse all was quiet, the gallery now empty of people. From the bank of the river the squeals of children, and the calls or laughter of adults reached him. How he wished he could laugh and call aloud too like them, but even as a child he was not allowed to squeal because every loud sound he made was treated as a sign of bad omen. According to his sister Lanai, the first two months of his life went well. Then one day he started crying each time the river tide went up. It went on for a week. On the day that he stopped crying, a man called Ampi failed to return from his fishing trip. Every able man and woman went out to search for him the following day. Though they soon found his boat two miles away from the longhouse, they only found his lower arm three days later. He was recognized by the distinct tattoo of a crayfish on the appendage. Ever since then each cry or shout from Nuing, whether it was due to sorrow, pain or joy, was treated with fear. Children were often reminded to keep their distance from him, so from the moment he learned to crave for friends he also learned, through threats of a sound beating, to stay away from them.

Through the door closest to where the common ladder was, a group of young women and their mothers came in, shouldering baskets holding bamboo tubes filled with water for their kitchen. Though Nuing kept his eyes turned away from them, they hurried past him as though he was a predatorial animal or demon who was lying in wait for them. The first aromatic smell of cooking food reached him but Nuing shut his desire for them because he knew that he would never be invited to a meal by a head of any of the families living in the longhouse. He might live in the same community as they but he knew that he was no better than a hunting dog that was tolerated and kept at a distance. To them he was useful for nothing, but for the provision of food, and even the very food that he provided with his hands would be portioned back to him meagrely. That evening, Nuing had heart for neither bathing in the river nor cooking at the hearth. Instead he stared at the constellation of the Pleiades, telling the seven stars all his longings for a different life, a life away from this place and this people who had disdained him since his birth.

***

It was still dark when Nuing woke from his restless sleep. Outside, a thick mist hung over the gardens and the river like a cloud. Inside the longhouse the air was cold but stuffy, for the ember beneath the trophy heads were producing more smoke than warmth. Though the bachelor plank-bed was warm from his body heat, Nuing felt restless, like a visitor who had overstayed his welcome. He sat up on his wooden bed, rolled his well-worn blanket and stuffed it into a travelling basket he had hidden inside a large *basong* basket under his bed the night before. He pondered over what to do with the hunting basket, for his father would expect him to carry it with him.

The condition of the still-dark common gallery was well-ordered and had no obvious hiding place Nuing could use. Then he remembered that *Apai* Kalong was still working on the repairs of the walls of his part of the house which he started well over a month ago. After looking about the gallery to make sure that the other bachelors were not astir, he picked up the hunting basket, trod lightly to the *ruai* of the last family room and hid it under a pile of wood bark. *Apai* Kalong was a lazy man, so it would be days before he would resume repairing the wall of his family room and notice the basket lying there. Nuing expected that by then his father would have given up trying to find his tracks. Then he crept back to the door of his family's *bilek* and unhooked a machete from the wall next to it. Just as silently he walked out to the veranda then shouldered a bamboo ladder leaning against the wall outside. He walked to the edge of the veranda and lowered the ladder to the ground.

After climbing down it, he walked under the house between the raised pillars of straight columns. The pigs grunted in their pens and the hens clucked then just as quickly settled back to their rest. The dry clay ground was cold, but the scent of animals in the air was warm. Nuing re-emerged on the other side. Among the feathery palmate leaves of his mother's tapioca plants he stood for a moment undecided. His skin cringed under the mist of dew, and his heart listened for his father, whom he had half-hoped would come after him. But all was silent of human sound. So he turned his ears to the sound of the jungle about him, and to the silence of the sky above him. This sound he followed as he wound his way down the back garden along the length of the longhouse then into the wild foliage that grew at its edges.

***

Bujang had heard his son moved to the door. He wanted to go out and beg him to stay for breakfast but then decided against it. Nuing was now a man after all. He had caught his first wild pig while all the other boys his age were still learning how to throw their spears. Since no one else would play with or teach Nuing,

Bujang was forced to give him his full attention. It was a natural thing to do, but Bujang's behaviour had created strife with the rest of his children. Except for his daughter Lanai, they had all wanted him to punish Nuing for existing, and they could not understand why Bujang would spend so much time with a boy who obviously was not of his own blood. Bujang did not know how to explain, and his lack of eloquence had caused his son Patas to deliberately pick a woman from a distant longhouse for his wife, and thus moved there. The burden of trying to uphold the customary laws against his own paternal instincts weighed heavy on Bujang's mind that morning as he listened to Nuing's movements.

Maybe he should have done a proper adoption ceremony, but if he had done so, he would have had to admit that Nuing was not born of his loin. Then the problem of Nuing being a bastard would again rise. Bujang had hoped that he could stay the community's judgment by his will and reputation alone, but Ampi's relations had never allowed people to forget that the man was eaten by a crocodile which Nuing had called with his ceaseless crying during the high tides. On the day they found Ampi's arm, Bujang was even swayed into believing that he had gone against the will of the gods by calling Nuing his son. But when he thought of abandoning the boy like his own father had abandoned him, his spirit had weakened and his arms and legs had become numb until it was easier for him to just sit and do nothing. Since that day, he had never allowed himself to again consider forsaking the boy.

Bujang now sat up and watched the door, ready to release its lock the moment he sensed a hand against its surface. But the door remained firmly in place and the thin wall next to it barely sighed as the machete was lifted off its surface. Then he felt Nuing's tread move away, and he smelled the coolness of the breeze coming in from the veranda as the door there was opened just long enough for a man to pass. When it was closed, his senses lost his son.

***

Nuing pushed aside an outspreading arm of fern that brushed against his face then looked up to the dark canopy. He had walked east a whole day and night without stopping and, as the area was dimly lit by luminescent moss and mushroom, he could see that he was now in an unfamiliar place. He climbed the bent and sloping trunk of a lindera tree. Using the fork between its thin branches and trunk like step ladders, he stealthily made his way up until he could see the clear sky between breaks of the taller emergent trees. He gazed towards the horizon, looking for a sign to show that he was going in the right direction. Far ahead lay the morning star, unattainable. He tried to return to the ground but his stiff muscles could only manage a few branches down. Pain shot up his ankle and calf as he tried to bent either leg. The harder he tried to fight the stiffness the more he shook like an old man shrunken to bones.

Finally he sat and leaned back against the grey tree trunk while keeping his eyes gazing east. The day slowly brightened and faded the light of the star in its glow. He began to weep, for life was hard and all his choices were hard. In his exhausted state, he would have fallen immediately into sleep, but his faithless heart momentarily turned to home, and at the threshold of that place he stopped, his mind imagining his father repairing a fishing net and his mother pounding rice grain in a wooden pestle. No sleep came to him as his mind fantasized that the smile his mother gave to Patas was one she had given him, or that the rice she fed by hand to Lanai had been the mouthful tasted by him. Over and over he went through the fantasies in his head, filled with brothers who took him hunting and fishing, and sisters who plucked his eyebrows and washed his blanket. Yet his heart knew that the thoughts were all lies, because it was his father's voice that fell out of their mouth and it was his father's scent that sat close to him.

As his thoughts slowly returned to the present, the smell of standing trees, sprouting leaves and unfurling fern enveloped him, a perfume that he was all too familiar with, for he had spent more time in the forest than in the longhouse. Self-pity washed over him, and he began to weep like some women he had seen weeping over their dead children. Yet he wept not because of loss, but because he felt that no one else would weep for him. Then reminding himself that he was a man, he wiped his face and swallowed back his sorrow. He had no one now, he told himself. If he could not be useful to himself then he would be useful to no one.

As his mind returned to the present, he soon became conscious of a sweet vanilla-like scent. He looked about him until his gaze fell on a large-leaf tall grey tree bearing brown head-sized *terap* fruits. His belly cramped with hunger, but when he tried to stand up from his rest, his muscles shook and he again fell back against the tree. He un-slung his basket and pulled out the blanket with which to wrap himself, for he suddenly felt both hot and cold. He began to shiver and sweat until he eventually fell into a restless sleep. The tree swayed in the breeze as though rocking him to slumber like a mother her babe. As the day brightened, it began to warm in conjunction with the rising tone of insects and birds that had grown bold in the light.

It was to this din that Nuing woken to three hours later.

Feeling refreshed, his gaze fell once more on the adjacent fruit laden tree. He eyed the many layered branches of the artocarpus plant, and judged that they were strong and flexible. He flexed his sore calf muscles a little then pushed himself to a stand on the bough before looking down its whole length. He stuffed his blanket back into the basket which he then slung onto his shoulders and checked that the strap of his machete was tied securely to his waist. After deciding that the bough was sturdy enough to carry his weight, he edged his way to the end, one hand holding onto another branch above him. In response to his light jump, the bent bough under him lifted a little higher than its resting attitude and when his weight came down again, it responded with a higher bound. Twice more Nuing repeated this motion, and when he sensed that the counter-spring was strong enough to help him jump clear, he released his hold and stretched his arms out, reaching for a thin branch stretching from the fruit tree. The branch he caught snapped and as it swung down, Nuing grabbed a lower branch which bent low under his weight. Once he had a firm footing on the branch below it, he let go and light-footed his way to the tree trunk.

Though he had done this many times before with his father, it still sent his blood pumping. After he calmed down from the adrenaline rush of dread, he unsheathed his machete, reached up and cut the long stem holding a *terap* fruit. The soft, spiny jacket of the fruit yielded instantly to his gentle handling. Little white fragrant globes lined the inside and at first he grasped them in fistfuls before stuffing them into his mouth. After cleaning this fruit of its sweet flesh, he cut down a second and third fruit which he relished with less haste. Thus nourished, he again looked to the east and decided that he would continue his travel therewards.

For days he sustained himself on wild fruits and young leaves. He dared not light a fire, and travelled with so much haste that anyone who saw would have thought that he was running from an enemy. He did not care where he went, for he had nowhere to go. Even the hope that he had poured into the stars was nothing more than a dream in his waking mind now as the reality of the jungle began to set the pace of his life. To the east, a wall of mountain appeared and he decided to follow its course northward. For days he found no community, and came across no traveller, but on the sixth he heard the approach of a troop of silent men, so he climbed the vines of a strangler fig tree and hid himself in the thick foliage.

Below him they passed, with proud tall feathers bristling from their crown and tough skin of fierce animals covering their chest and back. Their wooden oblong shields were carved in grotesque patterns of hungry demons, some with turfs of human hair, many without. In twos they went, winding their way through the path chosen by their leader like a giant serpent on the prowl.

After the last man had passed, Nuing climbed down and followed them.

***

Bujang scanned the jungle edge along the back of the longhouse. He guessed that Nuing had gone by that path because he had not taken the boat. Upa, bent and old in contrast to her still straight-backed husband, from behind him said, "Why do you worry about him so much?" She pulled out a tapioca plant after digging through the soil around it, exposing the fat tuberous roots which would be cooked for their meal that night, in place of rice.

"He is my son."

"He is not," she said, looking up. "He is my curse and my shame. Let him die."

Bujang turned to look at her bowed form for a moment before turning back to the jungle. They had had the same argument so many times since Nuing was born that Bujang had grown weary of it. He recalled how Upa would not care for the baby with the excuse that her breast was dry, so he could not suckle on her. Bujang then boiled rice in water and fed the milky gruel to Nuing. She let him go naked even beyond his seventh year, so Bujang had torn up his own loincloth to dress him. The more Upa rejected her son, the more dear the boy became to him so that his face now began to flush and his eyes to tear when he again saw that the bright sky had faded into a grey light.

When Upa returned to the house, he did not go with her. Another layer of painful concern fell on his recollection of the day when *Apai* Kalong had returned the hunting basket he found beneath his building materials. Suddenly Bujang felt tired, like an old man with no spirit left in his bones. He wondered then hoped that his spirit had indeed left him and had gone out searching for his youngest. Maybe this way he would dream about Nuing tonight and learn how to find him. A rustling reached his ears and he hurried to the source of it. At the fringes, just beyond the patch of field where his wife plants the *taya* cotton bush, he found a small bony man with matted lanky hair and shrivelled legs dragging himself across the ground.

Bujang was surprised, for the old man was a stranger to him. "Who are you and why are you here?" he asked, though not with the usual vehemence that he would have asked a younger traveller.

The old man looked up from the ground with a joyful smile

that revealed his near toothlessness. "Greetings to you, Friend. My name is K'lansat. I am old, alone and hungry."

Pity filled Bujang's heart and he said, "Please come up to my house. There is plenty of food."

"You are kind, but I think it is better if I stay here, at the edge of your field."

"You will be more comfortable and welcomed in my home."

K'lansat shook his head. "I will not be, for I am a curse. I dare not repay your kindness with sorrows to your household."

Bujang stared and a sudden pain filled his chest. And because he was thinking of Nuing at that moment, without giving his question much thought he asked, "Have you seen my son?"

K'lansat studied his face for some time then nodded. "I met a young man some days ago. He told me to come here because he said his father is kind."

"Can you show me where you met him?"

"Of course I can, gladly."

Bujang turned to go back to the house. The old man called, "Where are you going?"

"Back to the house, to bring you some food and water. And a blanket, if my wife can spare one."

"But we will miss your son. Let us hurry now."

"What about you? You are hungry and must be travel worn."

"Do not worry about my needs. I have had my food. Anyhow I prefer eating a different kind of food from you." Seeing Bujang's hesitation he said, "He is not far."

Bujang's worried face immediately brightened and he looked into the jungle hopefully. "Which way should we go?"

The old man mumbled and grunted a few times as he tried to propel himself forward then he said, "Well, I know the way, but I cannot travel fast because I have no use of my legs."

Without a second thought, Bujang lifted him onto his broad shoulders and asked again, "Which way, old man?"

The wizened fingers pointed and, seeing it, Bujang hurried into the jungle, towards the direction it indicated. What he did not see was the awful smile and the terrible change that came to K'lansat's face. He had smelled Bujang's sorrow from afar, and it had taken him two days to find him. The spirit of a great chief would make a great meal, and even now, K'lansat's mouth was watering from the thought.

Chapter 2

For days they travelled following a trail in K'lansat's memory, climbing up and trotting down slopes yellow or grey with clay or trudging through sparse jungle floor thick with dead leaves and wood. Wearily Bujang trudged on, not willing to stop even for a short rest because each time he did K'lansat would call out 'There he is! There he is!' Every time he heard the old man's call, his strength would rise anew and he would go to the place indicated. Though it happened many times, not once did he question K'lansat's call because he felt numb and unable to think. A strange kind of desperation soon clung onto his spirit, like one of a starving man who believed that there was food just a little farther along the way. The need to find his son was so strong it eventually became the only nourishment that sustained him. Onwards he walked, obsessed only with the thought that his son was just behind the next bend or up the next hill. And then he crawled. On the day he started walking like a beast, K'lansat led him to a cave at the foot of a limestone hill.

As Bujang approached the cave mouth, he saw more men and women like K'lansat coming out of it. A sense of danger suddenly broke into his consciousness. He tried to get K'lansat off his shoulders but the old man would not budge, his legs clinging around Bujang's neck like a tight vice. The people, if they were people, crawled out of the cave and grabbed Bujang's arms, dragging him after them. Only then did K'lansat got off his shoulders, and Bujang saw that the pair of legs which he had thought were shrivelled and deformed were actually long and sinewy, and could be folded twice like the front raptorial legs of a mantis. He tried to break free from the hard pincer-like hands that clung onto his arms and legs, but his exhaustion was no match to the creatures' fervour. With shouts of glee and whoops of joy they pulled him, belly down into the cave. Then they clawed on his back with their sharp nails until he got up on all fours and went into a tunnel no larger than a hole that a man could crawl through.

The way was pitch dark and the air so rank that soon Bujang was wheezing and out of breath. On and on they drove him, screeching and scratching, some pulling, some pushing until finally he felt himself fall down a steep incline onto a stone floor peppered with rough rocks. He moaned when the rocks scratched and cut into him. Then again he got up and crawled where they led him. Some of the creatures stayed behind and started to lick the ground where he had spilt blood.

***

Dark night fell swiftly but the line of warriors ahead did not stop to camp. Nuing moved in closer because he was afraid of losing them. After a while he stopped, turning his face from side to side, to listen and to smell. But he sensed nothing. Not even the sound of insects or night birds. A chill filled his chest as he wondered if he had been found out. With body bowed close to the ground and knees bent he began to move backwards, retracing his steps as silently as he could. After about two yards he stopped, for his nose caught the moist scent of dew mingled with sweat. The chill in his heart spread to the rest of him, so that he became unable to move as though his spirit had been caught in an invisible snare.

The smell of men drew closer. Nuing's trembling hand went to his machete but before he could pull it out two pairs of hands grabbed him from either side and threw him down on the ground. A hard kick struck his back and he twisted his body to one side to try to free himself. Blow after blow rained down on him and the more he struggled, the harder they fell. He stopped struggling, his breaths coming hard and heavy. Then he felt himself being dragged by the hair to his feet, and his machete and basket stripped off him.

They pushed him forward, growling impatiently each time he stumbled. Then they threw him down and a man kick him in the stomach making him double over in pain. A voice said, "Who is this?"

A man behind him replied, "A spy, *Tuai* Aso. He has been following us."

"Bring me some light," the apparent leader said.

A hidden ember was brought out, laid on some dry moss and leaves then blown upon. The tinder over it began to smoke and tongues of fire leapt out. A low pile of twigs were placed over it, and a circle of men formed a tight wall around this fire to hide the light emitting out of it. In that light, Nuing found himself face to face with a middle-aged man whose bristling eyebrows was dark with contempt and whose hands looked as hard as the spines of an ironwood buttress. The man said, "Where do you come from, Spy?"

"I am no spy."

A man kicked his back, making him fall on his hands. The man said, "Why are you following us?"

Nuing scowled at the man behind him then turned with equal ferocity to the leader. "I wish to join your expedition, and was looking for the right time to approach you."

"He lies," another man in the crowd hissed in a low voice filled with great vehemence.

"Who are you that I should give you a place among my warriors?" Chief Aso asked.

Nuing straightened his back, squared his shoulders and said, "I am the son of Bujang Maias. The war leader of Pantu."

"The son of *Tuai* Bujang?" Aso said. "I know him. He is a great warrior."

Nuing said, "Yes, my father is a great man."

"Why are you not with him?" the man behind him asked.

Nuing again turned to glare at the man for a moment then returned his gaze to Aso. "My father has no interest in war expeditions since his last foray at the mouth of the Batang Lupar."

Aso nodded. "I have heard songs of that expedition many times, and it is still a wonder to me. It was more than twenty years ago?"

Nuing said, "That is so."

"Which son are you?"

"I am Nuing, the youngest."

A murmur began to rise among the listening men, some of whose eyes began to harden as they studied Nuing anew. One of them said, "We know you. Your people call you a curse."

Nuing's scowl deepened and he replied, "I have come to prove them wrong."

"Spoken like a proud man," Aso said, "And we have great need of proud men."

"He will be the cause of our death," another warrior said.

Aso turned his head a little and said, "Kuti of Bukong, your words are a curse. We have already obtained good omens for this expedition. If anyone would bring ill, it appears to be you."

The man addressed as Kuti scowled and turned his face away. Aso again returned his gaze back to Nuing. "You are welcome to join us." Then he raised his head and said to the rest of the group, "We rest here tonight. Tomorrow we make ready to smoke out the Kantus from their house."

Though the chief had the final say in letting Nuing joined their group, Kuti was not convinced that it was the right decision. After all, a matter of such serious nature as a curse should be discussed properly among the men, and their opinions gathered in the proper manner. He began to move among the groups of men to complain about Aso's conduct of ignoring their feelings, and his words soon turned to predictions of bad fortune for if they were to continue their march to the Kantu longhouse. He reinforced his dark premonition with stories that he had heard about the youngest son of the great war-leader Bujang Maias. After he left their midst, the men of each small group discussed the new stranger in hushed voices. Many recalled rumours they heard about the bad things that had happened at *Tuai* Bujang's longhouse, and about how they were always preceded by cries uttered from his youngest son's mouth. The stories grew, and soon the death of one fisherman became two or three depending on who told the tale. Though they too had experienced bad harvest due to unfortunate weather, *Tuai* Bujang's longhouse was reckoned to experience it more often because of Nuing's presence. Before the men retired for the night someone came up with the true reason why Nuing was cursed; in that he was fatherless and that Bujang Maias had committed a great taboo when he claimed the boy as his son. If he had not wanted to exile his wife, they said, he should have abandoned the boy in the deep jungle where a wild animal would have finished the work for him. No man in his right mind should eat fruit planted by his enemy, for it would turn bitter in his belly and make him ill.

The following day when the chief called for men to give him their final word to either follow him or not, many cited bad dreams or bad omens, and thus declined. So it was that *Tuai* Aso, who started with eighty-six men, was now down to forty-five including himself.

"Maybe it is not wise to attack, *Tuai*," his eldest warrior Jantan said, "after all, large numbers of our men have received warnings from their guardian spirits."

The chief scowled. It had been many years since his father passed away, and he had been unable to cut the spiritual ties between them. The sacred jar that held some of his father's possessions was still sealed because the binding ropes could only be opened with the blood from the head of an enemy. His family had been living under the shadow of mourning for far too many planting seasons. They were not allowed to be joyful, nor could they participate in celebrations, and it pained his heart to think that he had not seen his daughters or wife dressed in their best for many years. Many times he longed to put on his brightest loincloth, shave his sideburns, and pluck his eyebrows clean of hair but he dared not because that would bring death and disease down on his people. The spirit Puntang Raga had taught Sarapoh the death rites for a reason, Aso reminded himself, and he was now on this warpath so he could do the proper thing for his family. With a vehemence that could only come from a man whose righteousness was being tested, he said, "The augur has divined success for us in the liver of the pig. We will go, and we will come back victorious."

Jantan bowed his head to indicate his submission to the decision but his brow frowned, for though he did not doubt his leader's courage, he was unsure that they could take a whole house of Kantu warriors with so few men. However, he kept his silence since a man who talked carelessly was a curse.

They chose for the attack a night when the moon was as slender as a reaping hook. Quietly they approached the slumbering longhouse, from the backyard where the palm-shaped leaves of tapioca plants and elliptical leaves of betel vine creepers hid them from alert sentries. A pig snorted. The men stopped advancing and crouched low in the pitch dark. The animal's restlessness spread to a few other pens. More snorts and shuffling feet were heard followed by a couple of barks from the house. A sleepy voice hushed the dog. Soon the pigs also began to settle and, except for the call of cicadas and frogs, the area fell silent once more.

Nuing resisted the urge to readjust the hastily made bark shield strapped to his back which was now scratching and pinching his skin. He sensed rather than heard his fellow warriors resumed their advance. Keeping his back low, he too moved forward as he gripped tight his unlit bamboo torch of wood shavings in one hand and a bamboo cup holding a smouldering ember in the other, excited yet terrified at the same time.

The grass-covered ground soon gave way to hard bare ground and the open airiness to a sense of closedness. He was under the house, he realized, and he moved forward slowly so as not to startle the pigs or fowls. This was his first expedition, soon to be his first kill. It seemed easy enough: Smoke the people out like insects, catch them by surprise then take their heads one by one. Nuing's stomach tensed, tightening itself like a spring and he knew that the moment the leader light his torch, the whole group would jump like a trap springing out on its victim, catching him, rendering him helpless. In the cold, he began to sweat in excited anticipation.

A shout went out and immediately he lit the torch. The resin and wood shavings caught fire almost instantly and began to smoke profusely. He could hear a riot of pounding feet and screams above his head. Then he felt a bamboo spear brushed past his shoulder. He planted the sharp edge of the bamboo torch into the ground because he sensed that its embers were helping the people above guess his position. Then following the chief's voice, he ran out to the front of the house with loud fey shouts, unstrapping his shield and pulling out his machete at the same time.

Torches were thrown down from above and, by the light they gave off, Nuing saw an endless stream of men sliding down bamboo ladders or slipping down ropes. Adrenaline rushed to his head as he imagined carrying home a large basket of head to rival his father's. Surely that alone would nullify his cursed existence. With demonic glee, he struck and cut down every man who charged him and each time a body fell before him he would give a shout as shrill as the call of a hawk to announce to the spirits and to his comrades that the head belonged to him.

All else was lost to his eyes, as he searched for the next victim to strike down after the one before him fell. A sense of invincibility filled his being as he imagined the songs that would be sung about him, a vicious pride grew on his head as he thought of the praise name that would be given to him after this night. His people might call him 'Mali Lebu', indestructible, or 'Rentap Menoa', world shaker. His fantasies of glory and victory eventually gave way to the reality about him, for the fight before him grew harder, and the men who struck back did not fall as readily. Soon he felt himself surrounded and, instead of meeting his enemy one on one, he was forced to twist and turn about in a desperate frenzy in order to fend off the sword-strikes coming towards him from all directions.

Then above the din of war cries and death throes, came the shouts and curses of women from above. They called to their men, demanding for this or that head, pointing out which attacker had struck down a husband, a father or a brother. Their hate and fury came down like rain, like the fey cries of crazed demons. The voices rose and fell, many ending with a high note of rage and despair. Nuing's spirit seemed suddenly frozen, his arm grew heavy and his feet began to stumble under their vehement voices.

A loud cry to his right made him turn in time to see *Tuai* Aso fall under the blow of a sword to the centre of his chest. The wall of men around the chief immediately turned their attention to Nuing. The cries from above grew louder and more incessant. Nuing swung his machete and the hastily made bark-shield about until his muscles began to scream. He could not find a way out, for the attacking men hedged him on all sides two to three men deep. Nuing fought his way to a pillar. A bamboo spear fell from above and cut into his shoulder, making him drop his shield.

A despairing fear suddenly washed over him like a swift tide and he felt as though he was drowning in a sea of shouts and screams of men, women and children demanding for his life, demanding that his spirit quail before theirs. The pillar behind him shook when the blade of an enemy's *ilang* struck it. Nuing knew then that his life was hanging by less than a thread, and he decided that it was a good day to die. He was going to show them that the son of Bujang Maias would not be easily taken. He would show them that his head would cost them a hundred men.

A savage shout surged out from his mouth and he swung his knife with renewed strength, turning, twisting and each time aiming for a kill point. The ground soon became slippery with blood and his enemies stumbled and slipped before him, giving him an open opportunity to strike them down. Nuing gave another shout to show that his spirit was still strong and very much alive and the warriors began to bend away before him like trees against a gust of wind.

He struck the last man in front of him and the way was suddenly opened. Nuing ran with all his might, followed closely by over a dozen enraged men. The thin moon was now hidden behind a cloud and, like it too, all the phantasmal lights of insects and mushrooms were hidden. Yet more terrified was Nuing of what was behind him rather than the formless dark in front of him. He plunged in, stumbling, tripping and getting smacked or scratched by unyielding and thorny branches. The men chasing him stopped just outside the edge of light. They were not willing to enter the realm of demons, yet the bloodlust in them was still too strong to deny. They hesitated a moment. Finally it was the shouts of victory and loud drumming to announce the failed attempt of an enemy attack that persuaded them to turn back to the longhouse.

None of the men who followed Aso to the Kantu longhouse survived that night. Their heads were taken and their bodies thrown unceremoniously into the jungle to be eaten by the animals and any spirit that fed on flesh. For after all, the headless body of an enemy had no consequence on the well-being of the house.

Chapter 3

The darkness was so blinding that Nuing was forced to crawl on all fours. He had lost his shield, his machete, and everything. He had nothing left except for the loincloth around his waist. His whole body felt wet and sticky but he could not tell if it was from sweat or blood. His left shoulder, which was stiff and numb before, now began to shoot bolts of pain up his neck and down his back. He bumped his head against a buttress root and was stunned for a moment. Then he rolled on his back, his breath heaving. The adrenaline of fear that had sustained him this far was soon overwhelmed by the tide of pain.

A stiffness began to spread over him and he wondered if he was about to die. To his left the sound of grunting and snuffling slowly approached. A wet nose touched his hand and a warm tongue licked it. Then it snuffled his chest.

Nuing pushed its face away with his right hand. It growled, revealing by its voice that it was a sun bear. Terror gripped Nuing as he imagined being eaten alive. He tried to get up but felt dizzy and breathless just from the effort of lifting his head. The bear began to lick his shrinking shoulder and Nuing's breathing came out heavy and fast as he wept. After some moments, however, the bear stopped licking and lay next to him. Nuing's heart was pounding so loudly in his ears he could not hear even the riot of cicadas and crickets in the night jungle. Slowly, he began to get use to the warm scent of the bear next to him and fell into a restless sleep. Every now and then he would wake up, feeling insects crawling on him, biting him then feeling the bear licking them away.

When grey daylight finally filtered down onto the jungle floor, Nuing woke and raised himself up on his right arm. He felt the bear get up but when he turned it was gone. He checked his left arm and saw that the bleeding had stopped. In fact all his scratches and bruises were clean and covered in a layer of dried saliva. He stared into the underbrush, in the direction of where the bear had disappeared, and wondered if the bear was a friend of his father's. He tried to recall all the times when he had seen his father speak with animals, but for all his effort he could not remember ever seeing a sun bear.

Nuing forced himself to a stand. The Kantu men would have found his tracks by now, for he had run sightless into the jungle and left behind a trail of broken branches, torn saplings and scrapped ground. He realized that if he did not move quickly he would soon be caught. The seriousness of his situation added a sharp pang of urgency to his being, and kept him going for an hour or so though his bruised body cringed with pain with every step he took. Each time he thought of giving in to the protests of his physical self, he would turn his gaze ahead, and told himself to reach for the next tree and each time he did, he would urge himself to go to the one after it. Always, at the edge of his earshot he could hear voices calling to each other. Whether it was real or imagined he could not tell, but it got louder and louder as he became weaker and weaker. The surroundings became hazy and the heavy smell of fern and moist decomposing leaves suddenly gave way to the smell of smoke and warming bones.

In front of him the land began to slope downward, and he became conscious that the trees here grew taller and wider apart. The sight of endless pillars of trunk holding up a forest canopy that was as high as the sky almost took the last breath out of him. But he was not about to give up. He ran to the next tree, and when he made to go to the next he suddenly found himself in the middle of a clearing. About him were dancing shadows of men and beasts that merged and separated among themselves like black smoke. The shadows all turned to face him, as though suddenly sensing an uninvited presence in their midst. Nuing fell on his knees and tried to crawl back to the jungle but soon realized with horror that all the trees were gone. He fell on his face and turned on his back. The last thing he saw were black faces and empty eyes staring down at him.

***

It was dark when Nuing woke from his enchanted sleep. He sat up stiffly and hugged his knees for he was shivering mightily from the cold. The dim land about him was empty and stretched in every direction for as far as the eye could see. Then he saw a fire and the dark form of a man sitting in front of it. He got up and with bent back approached the stranger. As he neared he saw that the small man sitting just within its ring of illumination was watching him with round marble-shaped black eyes. The man was covered in a cloak of black bear skin clasped loosely over his chest with a sheet of beaten gold in the shape of a crescent.

Nuing hunkered across from him. He swallowed away the dryness in his mouth then asked, "What is this place, and who are you?"

The man leaned forward. "This is the invisible world. I am *Bunsu* Jugam."

Startled by the unexpected answer, Nuing fell into a long silence. Was he in a dream, he asked himself, because that was the only explanation he had for meeting the spirit of the sun bear. Then another thought came to him and, with a quiver in his voice, he asked, "Am I dead?"

"No, you are not, son of Bujang Maias."

Nuing relaxed and sat down with his legs crossed before him. "Thank you for saving my life."

"I did not save you because I wish for you to live. I saved you for the sake of another."

"Who is this other?"

"Your father, Bujang Maias. His life is in danger."

Nuing's head snapped back and his eyes widened. Then a terrible realisation hit him, making him bow his head and scowl to hold back the tears of shame and regret stinging his eyes. "It was my fault. I should not have boasted about who my father was. I should not have tried to assert myself among Aso's warriors. They might all still be alive if I was humble and nobody would have taken revenge on my father."

"It was not they who took your father," *Bunsu* Jugam said as he rolled some shredded tobacco leaves into a square of dry leaf. He offered it to Nuing and rolled a second cigarette.

Nuing held the roll dumbly as he pondered the man's words. "Merchant-soldiers. Did the soldiers come up our river and attack my father? But he told me that they were all killed." He frowned. "Then it must have been those accursed villagers. I knew they could never be trusted."

Bunsu Jugam growled. "You are more accursed than they.

I am the one who knows who took him, yet you, in your haste would deem yourself wiser than me." He paused to study Nuing's young face. "I should have left you in the visible world and let your enemies kill you, for you are too quick to judge and are useless."

Another long silence followed. Then Nuing said, "My mother calls me a curse. Everyone calls me a curse."

"Not Bujang Maias. He is the curse breaker, the war expedition leader and the lone fearless traveller. If he says you are not a curse, you should listen to him."

"But no one else believes him."

"*Tuai* Aso did. The failure of his followers to believe the wisdom of their leader had cost the brave chief his life, in the same way that the failure of your people to believe might one day cost them their life."

Nuing looked up, his face red from grief and said, "Tell me where my father is, I must find him."

Bunsu Jugam lit his cigarette and started smoking. His eyes stared into the growing darkness beyond the light.

Too disheartened to insist on an answer, Nuing fiddled with his cigarette and eyed the ground. This time he did not hold back his sorrow, and soon his hands and the clay ground beneath it were spotted with tears.

A breeze began to sweep over the camp and the sound like that of many voices and rustling leaves reached them. When Nuing looked up, he again saw the shadow creatures and their black faces. Three were giants and others, a number he could not count because they blended into one another like smoke, were smaller and human-sized.

"You failed your father," one giant said, "You will fail him again."

Another hissed. "You and your people call you a curse. You will fail him."

The third roared. "You think yourself wiser and more knowing than your father. You will fail him."

Failure, failure, failure chanted the smaller shadows.

Nuing watched them danced in an ugly lustful manner around him. The whole time the sun bear remained sitting, sometimes gazing, sometimes dozing. Finally the dancing stopped and all was silent. Nuing looked up, his eyes blazing hate and death. He jumped to his feet with a loud shout and began to strike wildly at the shadows. With every swipe he took, the form whirled into smoke then formed again into its former shape.

"Stay and fight," Nuing shouted, spittle of rage coming out of his mouth. "Stay and fight me, if you would have me dead."

From the side *Bunsu* Jugam said to the shadows, "He is still alive. Far more alive than when he had stumbled into this plain."

The largest black shadow laughed and turned into a giant serpent that stretches its head far up into the heaven. Then it brought its head down again to Nuing, to just above the man's upraised face.

"You will do," he said and spat on Nuing.

The young man's skin burned, and he fell on his knees screaming with pain. The more he tried to wipe off the spittle, the more the burn spread over his body. Through the fog of pain Nuing could sense the glee of the shadow spirits. Pride began to wash over him and he pressed his lips shut and swallowed back every scream that tried to surge out of him. The pain was so intense that his body shook from trying to tolerate it. Then the pain released him and he collapsed face down onto the ground.

Nuing took quick shallow breaths, expecting the torment to return at any moment, but nothing happened. He tried to lift his arm which was pinned to his side, but it pulled his skin painfully. He turned his face to look and what he saw horrified him. His whole body was now covered in thick rubbery scabs that made him look like a deformed rhinoceros encased in armour-like skin.

The serpent shadow said, "You owe your father your life, as I owe him my servitude. I cannot go where he is, but you can."

"Why did you burn me?" Nuing asked hoarsely.

"Those demons know your man-scent. And even if you were scentless, they can know that you are human by the taste of your sweat."

"What are they doing to my father?"

"They have shackled him to a cave wall, and are drinking his spirit through his blood. And after all his blood is spent, they will eat his flesh."

"How could they have caught him? He is a *Tuai Kayau*, a great warrior."

The serpent brought its face closer to Nuing. "You will find, Boy, that even the greatest war expedition leader die. They die because it is in their nature to die."

Chapter 4

The dim path before him was made dimmer still by the layer of thick scab hanging over his eyes. Nuing stumbled along, his anxiety for himself overwhelmed by his need to reach his father. The exertion, however, made his body burning hot because he could not sweat like a proper man. He stopped to rest, to cool himself. After days of travelling he had learned that it was pointless to dip in a pool, for the thick layer of scab would not allow him to feel any coolness at all. Involuntarily his hand went up to wipe his face, but it was bone dry.

Nuing panted and coughed, for it seemed to be the only way to get any relief from the fever-like heat. After another deep breath, he got up and continued his journey. By now it had become so dark he had to crawl on all fours and to feel his way forward. The undergrowth grew thicker and soon enveloped him, making him invisible even to the night spirits. Nuing had no sense of how long he travelled or in which direction he had turned. He put all his faith in his spirit which he assumed was being led by the shadow snake to his father. When his panting and coughing finally reached an unbearable point he lay down then slowly fell into a deep sleep.

The call of morning birds woke him with a start, and he found himself lying on a bed of rotting vegetation under a roof of living leaves. He tried to stand, but the ever growing scab had fused the part of skin on the back of his thigh and calf together, while he lay sleeping in a foetal position. Since he had nothing sharp to cut them apart with, he was forced to crawl forward like a four-legged beast. As the day grew older, the soft ground beneath began to harden to clay and by the time the sun was low in the horizon, his hands and legs were covered in chalky limestone white.

A growl from above startled him. Then a voice demanded, "Who are you?"

Nuing tried to open his mouth to reply but immediately realized with frustration that it had been fused shut. The best he could do was form a mumbled plea for information about Bujang Maias.

The owner of the voice drew near, moving like a carnivorous insect that was approaching its prey. On reaching Nuing, he sniffed him like a wild dog. Then he said, "You look like a small rhinoceros, but you don't smell like one."

"He smells like a snake," said his companion who had crawled out of a hole under the roots of a shrub. "What is it? Can we eat it?"

The first creature jumped behind Nuing and beat him, forcing him to climb up the steep slope at a fast pace, until they reached a narrow hole, into which he was made to crawl. Down the tunnel they went, twisting and turning along it like the ancient stream that once flowed through.

In the darkness, Nuing could see nothing. Yet he dared not slow to a cautious crawl for the beating behind smarted so bad, it was like a brand being burned into his flesh. Suddenly the floor beneath him gave way to nothing and he fell. He rolled and flailed, grabbing hold of bits and pieces of sticks and bones that came loose, broke free, or splintered at his touch. The wall suddenly curved out into a slope and he found himself sliding down it.

Then the floor disappeared under him. He fell a short way but hit bottom hard. Debris rained down, soon followed by a hard kick from one of the creatures. Nuing grunted in pain, prompting loud squeals of laughter from his captures. Then he was again beaten until he got up, and beaten some more even as he crawled in the direction they were herding him towards. In the distance ahead he could see a dim glow, and from that distance he heard a high pitch call. This call was answered by one from behind him of equal pitch. There was light, but the air was thick and black with the smog of past fires. They moved him forward, towards the dense hard roots of a tree that had pierced through the limestone ceiling above. As he neared it, a rough gate covering the wide gap of this root ensemble was swung open and smashed into his face. While his head still reeled from the sting, he was shoved inside. Then he heard the same wooden gate being dragged back into place.

He remained still, listening to the noises about him. He could not understand anything the creatures were saying because they spoke with clicks and squeals like a cross between crickets and howling monkeys. In between clicks and howls they laughed. Gradually they moved away and soon the sound of their voices faded.

"Have they caught you too?" a weak, raspy voice asked from a dark corner of the cage.

Nuing would have jumped to his feet with joy if it were not for the pain caused by his fused skin. He recognized his father's voice and he tried to speak but he couldn't because his mouth was fused shut. Instead he went towards the sound of the voice and grabbed his father's arm.

Bujang Maias groaned with pain. "No, Friend, don't grab me so hard. My wounds are still open and raw."

Nuing moaned with frustration at his own condition and with indignation at his father's.

"Be strong," Bujang said followed by a heavy cough. "You must be strong."

***

But Nuing was not strong, not the way that Bujang had intended him to be. When the demons came that evening to cut open more wounds on his father, the way a man would tap rubber from a tree, Nuing went berserk. The creatures beat him till he was unconscious, but when they tried to bleed him, they found that none of the flint knives they had could cut through the thick layer of skin covering him.

When Nuing finally came back to his senses, he found his father lying on his side with his eyes closed. Gently he touched the older man's shoulder, prompting Bujang to say, "I am still alive, Friend. Help me sit up."

Gently Nuing lifted his head then his back, but when he finally got Bujang upright, the older man begged to be lay back down on the floor. "I am sorry," he apologized once he was again on his side, "I feel drunk, and heady. My eyes cannot focus on anything. I feel as though I am falling, and I cannot stop myself."

Nuing approached the bars of their cage again, to try to find a weak point. His fingers worked on the lattice knots keeping the vertical roots in place but try as he might he could neither undo nor break them. He felt trapped, like an animal kept in a *basong* basket. This time, however, he would not give up. He growled at and shook the roots so hard, pieces of limestone broke off the ceiling above and rained down on him. A sentry came and beat his hands with a stick, but Nuing did not care. The more pain he felt, the more violent his shaking became.

Soon the sentry called out to others, and the gate was swung open. They beat Nuing, making him angrier and angrier, making him roar with a rage that set their hairs to stand on end. He roared and fought back with a desperation that cared not if he lived or died in the process. He only had one thing in mind, to keep that gate open, to take his father out of that cage. There were so many demons in the cage hitting and kicking him that he would strike a creature any which way he swung his arm. Soon his fist was breaking jaws and smashing heads onto the floor.

A bubbling, somewhat like the grunts of a wild pig began to be heard just below the din of shouts and high pitch squeals. Louder it grew and soon water was steaming out of the roots. Instinctively, Nuing threw himself over his father, ignoring the blows that fell on his back. Moments later a loud thunderclap and a flash of bright blue-white light burst through the roots, sending pieces of it flying like spears and knives through the air. Yells and screams followed then creatures that still had use of their limbs raced out of the steaming cavern in terror.

Nuing was bruised, but otherwise unhurt. He lifted his gaze and saw lying about the area a number of demons who were either killed or mortally wounded by pieces of shattered root. He looked up and thanked the god or spirit who had struck the tree above them with lightning. Then he picked up his father, slung him over one shoulder and ran out of the cage on threes. Though the cavern was now empty, he could hear the creatures calling for one another inside the tunnels. They would soon return, he sensed, but he could not tell where the noises were coming from because of the echoes. Then he saw a pair of cave racer snakes crawl out of a basket that had fallen on the side. Their pale grey body lined with a single white streak down the back stood out against the black of the cavern floor.

Nuing chased after them, over the expanse of the cavern, away from the voices that had now grown into a hysterical tumult. Soon the reach of light gave out and he panicked when he lost sight of the snakes. Yet he could not return the way he came because behind him was certain death. In the formless dark ahead was the unknown, and in it was his opportunity of escape. He took a deep breath to still his quacking limbs then moved forward. After a few yards, he let out a startled grunt when his hand dropped into a shallow stream. The sudden drop made him lose his balance, and he fell in. Bujang rolled on his back, coughed and started to pant heavily, for the water was ice cold. Nuing again lifted Bujang up on his back and, after making sure that his father had his arms wrapped firmly around his neck, followed the watercourse. The noise behind him began to fade as the water grew shallower and quicker. Then the way before him began to slope upwards. He reached to the side, and felt dry stones. He climbed out of the stream then he resumed following the sound of running water. A few twists and turns later, he felt a breeze on his face. Though the air smelled of bat guano that was rank and rancid, Nuing welcomed it as it meant that there was an opening nearby. Sure enough, after he passed a mount of guano and scattered off a few dozen bats, he reached the narrow mouth of a cave.

He listened and with his gaze searched the sparse vegetation outside. Other than the bats he heard and saw nothing else. Away in the distance the light had begun to rise in the horizon. The ground outside was drenched while saplings and the leaves of large trees were all bent to one side, evidence of a heavy storm. Once out in the open, he looked down one side of the slope and saw halfway down a tree that was shattered and broken into all directions. That was their cage, he realized, because it had been struck by lightning. The proximity of the tree meant that the creatures were still close so, after hiding his father behind a thicket, he immediately searched the surroundings to find a safe way off the limestone mountain. The slope was bare to one side, and he could see a dozen or more creatures moving about, going in and out of their many tunnels. If the creatures were everywhere, Nuing decided that he would have a better chance of escape if he were to go down via the slope covered in dense undergrowth. Once more he prayed that the shadow spirits would hide them from the creatures and continue to guide them to safety.

Chapter 5

Other than his father's heavy breathing behind him, the dark was silent. Not even the insects were chirping their usual symphony of the night in this world of the K'lansats. Nuing realized that if they must travel slowly then they need to travel quietly, but his father's breathing was too heavy and harsh for them to remain hidden for long. Once more Nuing wished that he had free use of his hands. He cursed his scab-covered body and wondered why he had not thought of finding a sharp stone while they were in the cave. If he had found one, he would have cut some of the fused skin free, so he could stand upright and carry his father on his back, with or without the elder's consent.

After a while, Nuing realized that Bujang was no longer behind him. He retraced his steps, and found his father a few yards away, lying on his back. Bujang coughed as quietly as he could then said, "I have no more strength left in me. You must go and leave me."

Nuing moaned, his fingers grasping Bujang's shoulder and pulling it hard, trying to turn him, to move him. Bujang said, "No," and turned on his side, pushing Nuing's hands away. "You must go. Both of us don't have to die."

Nuing began to look about him frantically, for something that he could use to strap his father to his back. About twenty yards away he saw rattan vines snaking between the branches of trees.

He hurried on all fours towards them and began grabbing the portion of thorny rattan vine that was closest to the ground. The thorns were so long and sharp some managed to cut through the thick scabs. His hands began to bleed but Nuing ignored the pain because the knot in between his chest and stomach was sharper and more acute. He wrapped the length of vine he managed to rip off around a thick tree trunk and pulled, breaking off the thorns. Then he ran the vine round the trunk again, to get at the remaining thorns. After coiling the vine around his abdomen, he hurried back to his father.

On reaching the spot, however, he stopped and stared. Then his surprise turned to horror when he realized that he was staring at the patched tanned patterns of a large clouded leopard. The leopard was standing next to his father and growling down into his face. Nuing gave a shout from behind his fused lips, pushed the leopard away and began to pummel it with both hands. The head turned to face him, and he was startled into moving two steps back because he found himself staring into the face of an ancient demon who had two long canine teeth projecting down to his chin. The face hissed and a long tongue trailed out of his mouth as he said, "Go away, Boy."

Nuing moaned and begged as best as he could for the leopard to leave Bujang alone, to go and find another meal, to take him instead, if that was his wish.

The leopard growled, "This man is dying. If I leave him now, he will die."

Surprised by the answer, Nuing moved back another step and sat on his haunches, his body shivering with grief and with anxiety. All his instinct told him to kill the leopard, but another part warned him that the animal may be a god, and that if he killed him, he would go mad. He watched the side of the spirit's face, as the other returned his gaze to an unconscious Bujang. A forepaw pressed down on Bujang's chest then moved to his throat, to the shield-shaped tattoo there, and began to purr and growl by turn. Nuing saw that the expression on the spirit's face was both harsh and commanding, like stone carved and re-carved by many hands, until the idea of perfection of many hands had turned it into a shape so strange it was beautiful.

Bujang's arms and legs began to move about, as though having a will of their own. On the ground in front of the leopard was a round black fruit that looked like polished metal. He moved his paw away from Bujang's throat, and instantly Bujang's body became stiff. The cat then glared at the fruit, snarling at it and demanding it to do his bidding. He clasped it in between his teeth then his eyes rolled back and he went into a trance, his body jerking every few minutes as though his soul was fighting a nightmare. When the night had reached its blackest moment, he woke with a roar and crushed the fruit in his mouth. A shard of iron fell out of it. After spitting the fruit out, he picked the iron up with his stickly tongue and placed it on Bujang's brow. Then he pressed his brow against the iron shard and began to sing a lullaby. Try as he might to keep vigil, Nuing began to nod, and soon he was lying on his side having fallen into a deep sleep.

***

When Nuing woke, he saw that he was lying next to a fire and that his father was gone. He jumped to his feet, his eyes searching the surroundings wildly. The undergrowth suddenly rustled and coming through them was Bujang with a fistful of wild rose apples still clinging to their branch in one hand and a head-sized green breadfruit in the other. Circling each of his upper arms was a woven band of palm leaves, amulets meant to protect the soul in his body until he became physically strong enough to hold it in place on his own.

"Good morning, Friend. I brought us some food."

Nuing sat down next to the fire with a sigh of relief. He smiled and nodded. Then he raised one hand palm up in a questioning manner and looked Bujang up and down. Sensing the nature of his question, Bujang explained, "I was blessed by Ribai, the river god. He came in one of his many forms and called my soul back into my body, thus curing me. It seems that a powerful spirit had told him about my trouble, and he decided to look for me." Bujang placed the food down on the ground between them then studied Nuing's face and asked, "Can you eat?"

Nuing touched his mouth and shook his head. Then he ran one finger over the ridge between his lips, indicating to Bujang that he wanted to cut it open. Bujang reached to the side of his loincloth and, from the folds, pulled out a newly formed flint-knife. He passed this to Nuing, and watched with a frown as Nuing pulled apart his lips then began to carefully cut the skin apart. As the opening became wider, Nuing began to taste air and gulped it down with relish. He had expected pain but felt nothing. After he had cut open the skin to the edges of his mouth, he yawned wide.

Bujang's frown turned to a smile and he offered a handful of the watery rose apples to Nuing who received them thankfully. The young man was about to speak but a sudden shame washed over him. What if his father recognized his voice? How could he explain his condition to the old man? He started eating, keeping his eyes down, afraid that his father would suddenly recognize his face under the layer of scab-like skin. He was ugly, an outcast, and a curse. He was nothing that a father could be proud of, and Nuing realized then that he would do anything to hide who he was from his father, until he could find a way to make the old man proud. To every question that the old man asked, he would only reply with a hoarse growl or grunt, nodding or shaking his head wherever necessary, giving Bujang the impression that he was no better than a mute beast.

Bujang placed the breadfruit in the fire. After turning it a number of times, and pressing the browning skin after each turn, he took the fruit out and broke open its now soft flesh with his hands. The white flesh had a starchy sweetness with a soft hint of salt which was very satisfying to the hungry men.

After their meal, Bujang said, "You are a strange one, Friend. I can understand the language of all animals and people, yet I cannot discern any word from you."

Nuing turned his face away, afraid that the hurt in his eyes would show. He took the flint in his hand again and began cutting free the skin that had fused part of his upper and lower legs.

Bujang looked up with wonder when his companion stood on both legs like a man. Not wanting to embarrass his rescuer with questions that he could not answer, Bujang turned his attention to the still burning fire. He leaned forward on his knees and began to pile wet soil and leaves on the fire to quench it. Then he wound the rattan vine Nuing had prepared the night before and secured it by wrapping the end over the loop twice before slinging it over his shoulder. After looking about him and sniffing the air to find a scent, he pointed to a westerly direction and led the way forward.

A sense of comfort came over Nuing as he followed his father from behind, a feeling that everything was now safe because his father was strong, wise and straight-back. The thick canopy above shaded them from the heat of day, while the ground below was bare and covered with a carpet of leaves. After about a mile, the ground began to slope downward and they had to move carefully because the snaking tree roots were covered with slippery yellow clay. At around noon, they reached a crag that dived into a milky-hued river.

Using the flint knife that he had made, Bujang cut into the bark of a tree by pounding against the blunt side of the knife with a fist-sized stone. First around its circumference at the base of the tree then at the farthest height he could reach. Finally he cut a straight line down. Nuing helped him ripped the bark off the trunk. Then using the same knife, Bujang pierced a line of holes into the edges of the bark. Nuing used a larger rock to beat the skin of the rattan vine and after the outer layer of skin broke open he stripped it off.

Once Bujang had finished cutting out the holes, he helped Nuing pulped the core of the rattan into one long but soft thick strip. Then he told Nuing to hold the folded bark together as he placed the soft strip in between them. Bujang strung a pair of rattan strips through the holes he had made and sew the soft rattan core inside as he bound the edges together. They repeated this process on the other side. They then cut two long canes of rattan and strapped these down to the rim of the boat, creating a frame for its gunwales. Bujang next cut a bamboo stem into sections and these into halves, tying them together in twos and threes with soft strips of rattan acting as the weft. Then he jammed these into the boat so that the soft fold of the bark would stay open. Bujang entered the boat to test his weight against it.

"Well this is the best we can do, Friend. Let's hope it is good enough for a few days travel."

Nuing grunted and smiled. He broke off two pieces of rigid bark from another tree, and offered these to Bujang as paddles. Bujang jumped into the river first. Then Nuing threw down the bark boat and the paddles before he too went into the water. Bujang held the boat steady as Nuing climbed into it. Water splashed in as Bujang rolled into the craft after him, and Nuing was quick to scoop the water out with his hands cupped together. The boat held, and soon both men were paddling it downstream, albeit unsteadily.

They travelled thus until the light dimmed. Then Bujang studied the banks to either side, finally settling on a rocky slope that was as high as his waist if he were to stand on the boat. "The tide will not reach us here," he explained, pointing to the clean grass and dry ground.

They heaved themselves up and pulled the boat out of the river, leaving it lying on its side. Just as they were about to turn towards the jungle, Nuing noticed a temporary shelter that had been built under a low bough and pointed to it. The slopping roof of palm leaves was browning but the space under it was dry. Bujang grunted his approval. He looked about him for more leaves to add to the shelter while Nuing went looking for firewood and dry moss for tinder. After successfully sparking his flint a few times against a rock, Bujang started a fire. The dark sky above began to rumble and flash intermittently. When Nuing returned again from the jungle, he carried on his back a long stem with about half a dozen green bananas and flowers still cupped in a red heart-shaped inflorescence.

Milky sap oozed out of the skin as Bujang cut the green

bananas from the stem. He placed them over the fire to cook. Then he peeled away the layers of red skin covering the tiny banana flowers. He placed the white blooms on the skins before putting them over the fire. It did not take long to cook the simple meal, but the nourishment was well received by both men, for the bitter green fruit was sweetened and the tart flower made fragrant by the fire. The rain began to pour, and though much of the onslaught was blocked by the canopy of leaves above them, it still managed to soak through part of their shelter and almost put out the fire.

Bujang quickly put up a cover of leaves over the fire and, with a stick, dug a drain around it to flow the water away. Then he offered to take the first watch. While Nuing slept, he stared into the blackness in front of him, wondering where his rescuer had come from and who he was. The rain slowed to a drizzle, and the insects began a noisy symphony to worship the night. A change in the call of the insects shook him out of his thoughts. His senses were suddenly on high alert. He shook Nuing's shoulder and they both picked up a stick each. It was the only weapon available to them.

A war-cry broke out from the darkness, and the form of four men wielding a sword or a spear jumped into the circle of firelight. Bujang turned his back to Nuing, who instinctively did the same, and as one they faced their assailants.

"Who are you?" Bujang demanded, "That you should come into our camp unannounced."

The leader of the gang laughed. "This is not your camp. It is our trap. We lure people here, and we take from them."

"We have nothing you want," Bujang said.

Another man chuckled. "You have heads. They will make a

nice ornament for my pillar."

Nuing gripped the stick in his hand hard. He had fought monsters to save his father, and now mere men had come and were trying to get his head. He was not about to allow that to happen. He dug deep into the core of his body, looking for strength, seeking for courage that would be stronger than their iron. A man with a spear lunged at him. He dropped his stick to the ground and twisted his body to the side, away from the thrust, then reached out to grab the base of the spearhead. The moment he had a gripped on the spear, he jumped and kicked both his legs at the abdomen of the other man. The man fell back and released his weapon with a yelp of pain. Nuing slid his hand down the shaft of the spear, rolled to his side and jumped to his feet. From the corner of his eye, he saw his father struggling with two other men who had their swords close against his face.

Nuing pierced the spear deep into the side of one of his father's attacker then pulled it out again to aim the weapon at another. The man, whose spear he took, lunged at him from behind with a shout, wrapping both hands around Nuing's neck. Nuing bent his knees backwards and threw himself down on his back, crushing the attacker beneath him. The man's grip tightened. Nuing turned the spearhead towards himself and plunged it down into the man beneath. The man shrieked and released him. Nuing then got to his feet, pulled out the spear and struck it down again, into the man's throat.

He then turned his gaze towards his father and was relieved to see him still on his feet and gripping a bloody machete over the body of a third man at his feet. The youngest attacker now faced them alone, turning his sword from one man to the other by turn. He had not attacked either of them, being only a boy who was brought along to learn from his elders. His frowning terror-filled eyes pleaded with them for mercy and his sword shook in his trembling hands.

Bujang watched him but made no move to attack. Seeing his hesitation, Nuing dashed forward and struck the spear into the boy's chest. Rage and disappointment against his father washed over him, making him pull out the spear and plunged it down again and again into the boy's chest. His father's courage was a legend, how could he have given in to cowardice when victory was assuredly his. As he again tried to pull the spear out, he felt a hand on his shoulder and he turned to see his father's face. The older man was not afraid. He was calm as he shook his head and pointed down to indicate to Nuing that their attacker was dead.

"You have killed three men tonight, Friend," Bujang said. "You are far braver and more capable than your ugly looks made you out to be." He turned back towards the single man he had killed and cut off his head with the enemy's own sword.

Following his example, Nuing picked up a sword lying on the ground and began to cut off the head of the three he had killed. Bujang build a new fire some distance from the hut, and they roasted the heads over it. After that Nuing kept watch till morning.

***

The tide was high but receding when dawn broke through the thick clouds. Nuing climbed down into the boat first and held it steady as Bujang loaded in the heads which were now wrapped in palm leaves before stepping in. The river was fast flowing, and judging from its ripples in the distance, Bujang deduced that they would be hitting whitewater in less than a mile.

The water soon turned rough, and Bujang paddled the boat to the lower bank. With Nuing's help, he pulled the boat up with all their possessions in it. He explained, "We cannot survive the angry water in this boat. It is foolishness to risk our lives when no one is here to admire our courage. We will have to walk until the water clears." With a signal from Bujang, they heaved the boat onto their shoulder. Then they walked along the stream for about two miles. On reaching becalmed water, they again entered the river.

The rest of the journey was uneventful. When the light started to grey, they would paddle to a bank and made camp. Bujang would often disappear into the jungle for long hours then returned with leaves, fruit or meat that would last them till the end of the next day. As they huddled close to the smoke where mosquitoes would not torment them, Bujang would tell Nuing stories of his young days with the apes and his lessons with his orang utan father, *Tok* Anjak. He talked about Semaga the crocodile lord, and *Tuai* Laing the Kayan Chief. Then he reminisced about *Tok* Jakun and his eyes grew misty as he looked up to the sky. Nuing, on the other hand, wished that he would talk about the men he had killed, about the battles he had fought, but Bujang remained silent on that subject.

Chapter 6

After spending four blissful days with his father, Nuing was surprised when Bujang did not stop to camp as the light began to grey. He looked about him and soon recognized the stretch of river they were on. They would be home soon. He wanted the boat to stop, he wanted his father to leave him on one of the banks, but he could not bring himself to utter the words. Suddenly Bujang called a war-cry that startled him out of his thoughts. The landing place was now within sight and Nuing saw two men standing upon it, with spears pointing upwards. There was a whoop of joy from both of them as they echoed Bujang's call and in that way informed everyone within hearing range that the chief had returned.

Half a dozen hands helped them steady the boat as the two men got out of it, and two dozen men gawked at the wrapped heads that Bujang placed on the platform. Then they turned their attention to the ugly visitor he had with him, and their eyes either widened with wonder or hardened with suspicion.

Bujang said, "Tell my wife that I am home, and that I come bearing a fruit for her to hang at the principal column." Then he turned to Nuing and invited him for a wash in the river.

Nuing could hear the men discussing him in soft voices. He could not quite make out the words they say, but he could sense that they were laughing at him. Then Bujang said, "One of those heads is mine. The other three belong to the visitor. He helped me escape from demons and saved my life."

Nuing could feel his body flush with pride as the chuckles behind him subsided into respectful silence. When he got out of the river, his best friend Gunggu passed him a fresh, dry loincloth to put on, while Bakak his nephew passed a fresh loincloth to Bujang. Nuing picked up the three heads by the straps holding the palm leaves in place then walked next to Bujang as they made their way back to the longhouse. The sound of a drum shook the air, and it was soon followed by a loud clamour of noise as large and small brass gongs, as well as the war-cries of victory began to fill the air. *Tuai Burong* Ugap, the Chief Augur, led the procession of sword brandishing warriors into the house. At the top step Upa stood waiting with a winnowing tray which had been covered with a woven pua motifed with three trophy heads housed in their rattan holders. She received the heads as though they were babes and walked the length of the house with her husband and Nuing. Every woman in the house watched her past with envy and each wished that it was they who had that honour and blessing.

Ugap instructed a group of young men to catch the largest of Bujang's pigs. Once this was done, he went down to the ground and chanted over the animal which was now hog-tied and lying on its side. A man plunged a spear into the side of the animal and held onto the shaft until he felt the last of the pig's life ebb away. Then he pulled out the spear, and with the help of two other men, cut open the underbelly of the pig lengthwise. Carefully he searched for the liver and cut it free. Then he placed it on a wide leaf with the underside facing upwards.

He brought this up to the house, to the open veranda where now a group of elders was gathered. When the liver was placed in front of Ugap, he saw that the tip of the gall bladder was bent back and that the quadrate lobe of the liver was long. To Bujang, who was sitting next to him, Ugap said, "The gall bladder indicates that you have great wisdom. The lobe also promises wealth and good fortune for you and your family. However," he pointed to the bruised spot on the left side of the liver before saying, "your new friend is not so lucky. He will experience trials and tribulations."

"What of my family?" Bujang asked.

Ugap ran his finger over the right side of the liver. "The spirits say that all is well with you and your possessions."

Bujang wished that the divination was better for the stranger who saved his life, but he hesitated about asking for a second pig to be killed for his sake. What if the second divination nullifies the good fortune promised to his family in this first one? Would he then asked for a third sacrifice? He nodded, to show that he accepted the augur's interpretation. Then he got up and went into the common gallery. The body of the pig was cut, cleaned, and cooked so it could be fed to everyone in the longhouse. The house was a prosperous one hence there was no shortage of meat or vegetables. Many also brought fruit from their trees to add to the feast.

Early the next morning, and after a long night of singing and praising the gods in the *Enchaboh Arong* feast to welcome the new trophy-heads into their midst, all the men who had been to war joined Bujang and Nuing as they went into the jungle carrying the four trophy-heads. They trekked until they came to a small stream that was away from the longhouse and never used by the people for their daily activities.

Bujang placed the heads to one side, turned to Nuing and

said, "Find us some rattan and cut two pieces down to about the length of half my arm. Shred one end so we can use them for a brush."

Nuing placed the heads he was carrying down next to the one Bujang had brought. Then he went into the jungle to look for rattan. After cleaning off the thorns of two canes and shredding one end of each as instructed, he returned to the stream. He saw that his father and *Apai* Gupi were scrapping off the dry skin and hair off a head each. Bujang passed him a small knife and taught him how to cut into the dry flesh, stripping them cleanly off the bone.

Then Nuing was shown how to crack open a saucer shaped piece of bone at the back of the skull with the back handle of a sword. Once Bujang was satisfied with the hole Nuing had made, he told him to immerse the head inside the water. Imitating Bujang, Nuing thrust the bamboo stick handed to him inside the skull and began to scrap out the brain. The water became cloudy with the exertion of their efforts. Then they scraped out the eyes.

After the heads were thoroughly cleaned, they were wrapped in large wild ginger leaves together with their jaw before each was again bound with strips of rattan. The men returned to the yard in front of the longhouse then lined the bundles along a stick placed over a smouldering fire which had been built under Ugap's supervision. For three days they smoked the trophies, and more songs were sung as the people ate and drank.

The whole time during the festivities people looked upon Nuing with wonder. Many endeavoured to talk to him but after ascertaining that he was dumb they stopped trying to get answers to their questions. Instead they began telling him about themselves and their families. Many fathers even pointed out their single daughters to him, and if he were to look to where they indicated he would cross eye with a blushing young girl who would turned away with a smile. For days Nuing watched and was glad that he had not asked his father to drop him off by the side.

On the fourth night, when the heads were brought back into the common gallery and hung at Bujang's pillar, Nuing dreamed of a snake that had started to moult and was stripping off its old skin. When Nuing woke at dawn he realized that the scabs no longer clung to his skin but was slowly coming loose. He hobbled over to Bujang's partitioning wall and unhooked a small knife from it. Pulling up a piece of skin under his armpit, he cut. There was no pain, and he could see that his own skin no longer stick to the layer of scabby skin.

"What are you doing, Friend?" asked Gunggu.

Startled Nuing turned, one hand still holding onto the separated skin, while the other had lowered the knife.

"The gods be praised. You are human," Gunggu exclaimed with wonder in his voice.

Others came to see what the commotion was about and each and everyone became as excited as Gunggu. They urged Nuing to cut all the skin away, but Nuing was shy and would not do so in front of them. He indicated with signs that he would like to go into the jungle alone.

Bujang, who had by now come out from his *bilek*, said, "I will go with you, *Unggal*. We have had some trouble with the Serus this past week. They attacked *Apai* Chanda in his farm while he was clearing it. Luckily he is a fast runner and reached the sentries before their swords touched his neck."

Nuing reluctantly agreed. They had to walk for a fair distance to where the foliage was thick, for following them from behind was a group of people who were excited to see this magic unfold before their eyes. Bujang had to constantly remind them to keep their distance. Once Nuing felt that he was safe from prying eyes, he took off his loincloth and began to cut open the skin from his chest to his groin. Then he cut the portion up the front of his neck to the side of his face. He tore off the mask and stripped off the body suit.

Bujang stared, eyes wide and mouth gaping. Then his face crumpled and he sobbed. Disregarding the smell of sour sweat and grime of dead skin clinging to his son, he hugged him and wailed, with relief and with joy. The world was suddenly brighter, the birds sounded gayer and the air filled with the scents of fruiting flowers. Not a day had past since the day Nuing left for his hunt that Bujang had not worried about him. Yet his son had been with him the whole time.

A few of the braver men came up to see why their chief was weeping. They stopped and stared, some frowning others staring with rage. Gunggu came up from behind them and broke into a laugh, for like Bujang he too was glad to see that his friend had returned.

Nuing picked up his loincloth and wrapped it back on. Then he let his father and his best friend lead him to the river for a wash. It was a cheerful bright morning, and Nuing laughed and joked with his father and friend, telling them about his adventures, about *Bunsu* Jugam and his visit to the spirit world.

"What did he save you from?" Bujang asked, after he learned from his son that the sun bear spirit had helped Nuing escaped from enemies.

It was at that moment that Nuing noticed the group of silent sentries, frowning down at him from the banks, from the landing platform. He stammered, "I met some men in the jungle. They invited me to eat with them, but then they tried to kill me when they thought I was sleeping."

Bujang nodded solemnly. "It is good that you remember my lessons." He patted Nuing's back then invited him to get out from the river and return to the house for breakfast. By now, he reasoned, Upa would have heard that her youngest had returned home.

The house was quiet when they entered it. None of the families had gone to their farm, yet there was no talk between them as each appeared to be engrossed in weaving baskets or nets or in sharpening their tools. Bujang talked loudly to drown their silence, he laughed joyfully to overwhelm their fear. Then he sat down cross-legged in his portion of the common gallery.

"Tiong!" Bujang called. His young granddaughter poked her face out the door of their family room. "Tell your mother to bring out breakfast."

The young girl dashed to the back of the room. Bujang smiled to hear her high pitch voice giving instructions to Lanai, his daughter. Soon she came out again, struggling under a wide mat. Bujang laughingly took it from her, and both Nuing and Gunggu got up to help him unfurl it over the floor. Then they sat back down, on the mat itself.

Lanai came out with coconut shell bowls filled with fermented meat and boiled vegetables. She went back in and returned with a bamboo tube that had been stripped open on one side. Bujang scooped out rice from it onto three banana leaves. The men began to eat with gusto. Lanai sat with them and started to ask Nuing questions that he had to answer between bites. After they finished their meal, she collected the bowls and bamboo tube of rice and returned into the *bilek*.

Bujang waited a moment more for Upa to come out, but she didn't. Sensing that Nuing was starting to notice, he went to the wall where he hung his tools and began to unhook two machetes, an adze and a hoe.

"Let us go to the farm," he said to Nuing. "The bushes have not felt the sting of your machete for many weeks."

Gunggu got up and dashed back to his family quarters. Soon he returned with a machete tied to his waist and a large burden basket slung over his shoulders. Bujang smiled. Then he became sad again as he wished that Patas, Nuing's elder brother, had also been as close with him as Gunggu was. He wondered how Patas was doing in his bride's longhouse. He hoped that he was being well-treated there. Bujang had never meant to make his other children think that he loved Nuing the most, yet because nobody had wanted to have anything to do with Nuing, he was forced to spend more time with him. He didn't do it because he loved Nuing more; he did it because he loved Nuing as much as his other children.

* * *

Upa listened in a dim corner behind the closed door. She could sense that Bujang was waiting for her to come out and talk to her son, but something held her back. Was it shame? Was it stubbornness? She could not tell. One part of her was proud of her son, but the other did not want to acknowledge his existence.

She had bore a child that was not Bujang's, yet he had forgiven her. The other women in the longhouse, however, were not so forgiving. They blamed her for his existence, hence for the string of bad luck which they attributed to his presence. Most of all, they blamed her for their night terrors when Bujang disappeared for six months after he found out that she was pregnant with her rapist's child. Upa dropped her face into a hand, because her head suddenly felt heavy and the weight of shame was too much for her neck to hold up on its own. Even after Bujang told her that he had met the goddess Kumang and that she had advised him to be selfish, Upa still could not accept her son. How could Bujang say that he was being selfish when he insisted on keeping her and Nuing even after they had brought him nothing but trouble and shame? He would have been accounted as one of the greatest *tuai kayau* in the area if it was not for the fact that many believed him to be cursed by Nuing's presence. He would have been invited to lead many war expeditions but for the bastard boy he called his son.

"*Inik*," little Tiong called out in her high-pitch voice, "Are you ill?"

"I am only tired," Upa said with a smile to her granddaughter who had thrown herself down next to her.

"Let us go outside, Grandmother. Riti and Idah told me that their mother is going to teach them how to weave a mat today. They've asked me to come and learn with them."

"That is kind of *Indai* Riti. Then you must go and learn from her."

"Will you be coming outside to watch?"

"Not now, Grandchild. I have many things to do inside the *bilek*. After they are done, I will go," Upa said though she knew in her heart that she never would, for she had made herself an outcast from her people, and from her husband.

After her granddaughter left her side, she made her way to a shelf where all her sacred woven cloths were kept. Hidden among them was a piece that had never been used. She remembered how she was forced to work alone on it, because she was afraid that the other women would find out. Alone she struggled with the thread from her *taya* cotton plant. She prepared the oil from the *kepayang* seed, roasted salt and ash from the *nipah* palm, and golden juice from the *entemu* turmeric root. Then she fought the spirit of the mordant bath on her own in a secluded part of the jungle next to her farm. In fact, she had to spend many days away from her family while she waited for the thread to dry. She had to pull the thread over the weaving loom alone then transferred it to the tying frame alone. She could have asked one of her daughters to help her, but she was afraid that their spirit would be overwhelmed by the work.

On the night when she finally tied the first strip of waxy *lemba* leaf onto the thread to create a pattern on the three layers of panels, she thought that she would die from weakness. Only Bujang visited her during that time, and even then she did not explain to him what she was doing or why she would not return to the house with him. She was ashamed. She was ashamed to admit to him that she wanted to weave a cloth for Nuing, just as she had done for each of her other children. She only returned to the longhouse after she had tied the first layer of pattern in the dyeing process. It was only two months later when she finally added the indigo *tarum* to the thread, because her health had prevented her from finishing the design sooner. Nuing was barely six when she started weaving the *pua*, and he was fifteen by the time she finished. Many times she had wanted to stop, because she felt that the spirit of the cloth was sapping the life out of her. But she could not because she thought that if she finished it then it must mean that the people were wrong about Nuing and that the gods did not curse her youngest.

As the memories of those days went through her mind again, she held the cloth close to her chest, regretting that she had not used it to receive the heads that Nuing had taken, regretting that she had not received him in it when he had returned from the jungle with his father. She unfolded the cloth, and the claws of the sun bear clawing between bamboo shoots seemed to reach out to any onlooker who would dare to trace their zig-zagging lines. She refolded the cloth and returned it to its hidden place.

Chapter 7

The morning shone down bright and clear, giving the young leaves in the lattice shade above them a transparent glass-like quality. Bujang's eyes scanned the underbrush they were passing and his ears listened to all the sounds about them. No bad omen crossed their path, nor were there any warning coming from the branches. He was glad because it had been some weeks since he had cleared the bushes along the border of his field, and if a snake or a bird had warned him to return home then the work would have to wait for another day. A length of thorny vine, which had dropped from a broken branch, was now blocking the path to his field. Bujang took out his machete and slashed it down. Gunggu and Nuing started to jostle playfully as they each grabbed a part of the cut vine then pushed or pulled it to the side. The sound of their child-like joy brought a smile to Bujang's face.

He walked ahead of them but they soon caught up with him. As they drew nearer, he could hear Gunggu asking Nuing questions about his adventures away from the longhouse. Bujang frowned. Nuing's voice sounded strained and he seemed to brush aside many details of his story. This was unusual, Bujang felt, because every traveller would go through each single aspect of his adventures, from the sound and smell of the terrain he passes, to the manners and peculiarities of each person he meets. He would regale his listener with stories of even the simplest hardship as a means to air his skill, courage, and wisdom. That was the reason why Bujang had always reminded his children to look at the way a man live, at the fruits of his labour, and most importantly at how he treated his family, and how they treated him in return. Every man had a right to claim that he was more hard-working than anyone else alive, but if his family was hungry or his field unfruitful then he was either a curse or a liar, so his company should be shunned.

"What did the men who attacked you look like?" asked Gunggu. "Were they Kantus, Penans?"

"I don't really know. I did not talk with them. Maybe they were Ibans, they looked like us."

Gunggu scowled. "It is a pity you don't know who they are. This would have been a good reason to attack their longhouse. After all, we cannot have people like that living near us."

Nuing laughed nervously. "They are not near us. I came across them days after my travels."

"I wish I had gone with you. We would have brought back some of their heads."

"But if I had someone as brave as you with me, I would not have met the sun bear and saved my father."

Gunggu nodded solemnly. "Yes, you are right."

"Come now," Bujang said, "We must not linger on this trail. The day will not wait for us." He hurried them along because he had just come to the conclusion that maybe his son had met with a spirit or god who had given him a gift which he was not ready to reveal.

The cool tunnel-like path began to thin and they stepped into a field covered with green stalks of rice interspersed with weeds. Bujang looked about him for a moment then pointed to a part of the field where a tree at the edge was leaning over some *padi*, looking as though it was about to fall into them. The two young men made their way to it then started to cut the light branches, making sure to catch each before it hit the rice plants.

Bujang turned his attention to the creeper vines that had begun to overrun or climb onto the young rice. While he was rolling the vines into a bundle, he heard a succession of quick creaks in front of him. An omen bird, he realized. He put down the bundle and walked towards the sound. Before taking each step, he gently pushed aside the long padi leaves in front of him until he finally reached a burnt wood stump that was no higher than his knee. Looking up brazenly at him was a small orange bird with dull green wings.

Ketupong, the rufous piculet, repeated his message. "Nuing lies."

"You have no right to accuse him without proof," Bujang retorted, his face flushed from both the heat of day and sudden rage.

"He lies," the son-in-law of Sengalang Burong said. "I will send proof, if that is what you wish." Then he flew off with quick flaps of his tiny wings.

Bujang stared at the stump of wood, wishing with all his might that he had not seen the omen bird. Then after some thought, he decided that whatever lie Nuing might have been forced to say, it could not be anything that would be worse than death. He looked to the opposite side of the field, towards the two young men, and watched them start to work on the main trunk of the tree with a deep frown on his face.

***

The next few weeks continued to be bright and sunny, with only a short drizzle in the afternoon. The weather was so fine for ripening *padi* that the people began to feel comfortable and started to accept the idea that Nuing might have neutralized his curse after all. They were even discussing a date to give him the *entegulun* tattoo on his hand. He was a headhunter, like his father, and it was only right that he should be marked as one with a dark ring on his thumb.

One evening, as men were washing themselves after returning from their fields, a small dugout approached their landing place. Two Iban men were in it, and they called out asking for *Tuai* Bujang Maias.

"Come up," *Apai* Gupi invited them. "Our house is not under any taboo. Come up and bring us news."

The strangers moored their boats at the end of a row of boats then deftly stepped onto each boat as they made their way to the bathing platform. Their faces were solemn, evidencing that the news they brought was one of great sorrow. The older visitor said, "Good evening, Friends. I am Kuti of Bukong, and this is my brother Bugan. We have come to see your headman. We come because a dream demanded that we do so."

Gupi's father frowned. "The message must be dire indeed. Please come with me, I will show you to his family room."

Apai Gupi led the two men back to the longhouse, to Bujang's gallery, and behind him trailed a line of other men. Bujang was sitting in his *ruai*, repairing a torn fishing net while waiting for his dinner to be ready. Nuing was no where in sight.

On sensing their approach, Bujang looked up with a welcoming nod to the two strangers but the smile he gave them turned to a frown on noticing their grave faces.

"Welcome, Friend. Where are you from?" asked Bujang. "What news do you bring?"

Kuti again introduced his brother and himself then started to say, "We have come to tell you of something," but his voice trailed off, like a bird that could not finish its song.

"What is it you wish to tell?" Bujang asked and a sudden heaviness fell on his spirit, for their obvious reluctance had reminded him of Ketupong's message. He waited until they had sat cross-legged in front of him. Then he reminded them, "If the spirits had spoken then you are duty bound to warn us."

"*Tuai* Bujang, you must understand, it is not to create trouble that I have come. My heart is heavy because of the news it bears, and fearful because of the wrath that it may cause in you."

Bujang looked down at his own feet, studying the callused toes. Without looking up he said, "Speak freely, *Unggal*. I know that it is not by your own will that you have come."

The longhouse augur Ugap said, "You had a vision too, Chief?"

Bujang only nodded, without explaining.

"Then with your permission," Kuti said. He looked to his brother then with great reluctance returned his gaze to the floor in front of Bujang. "A little less than three full moons ago, Chief Aso of Lemanak led a war expedition to Batang Ai. He had done all the proper offerings and was promised a great victory by the spirits. Eighty-six men followed him, for the signs were good and Chief Aso was also well known as a great leader who could not be defeated." He paused a moment to see the effect of his words. "While we were yet two days away from enemy territory, we caught a man who claimed to have come from this longhouse. He was following us, like a thief."

Bujang looked up and, on noting the fear in Kuti's eyes, extended a hand to indicate that he should continue, saying, "My son, Nuing."

"Yes, *Tuai*. It was your son."

"Speak. I will not harm you."

"*Tuai* Aso welcomed him. But that night many of us received warnings from our guardian spirits about him. I warned the war leader not to continue with the expedition. But he would not listen. He insisted that the spirits had blessed him. He said that he would bring home heads to cut the bonds of mourning, for you see, his family has been mourning his father's death for five years." Kuti swallowed. "Your son's presence brought a curse to the expedition. And now, instead of cutting the bonds of mourning from his father, the people of his house will be doing a *ngerapoh* ceremony to appease *Tuai* Aso's wandering spirit."

"His body was never found?" Ugap asked.

"No," Bugan said. "Not a single man returned. But the families have reported seeing their restless spirits roaming aimlessly in the jungle."

Bujang closed his eyes and his breath caught in his throat, for he felt as though a knife had been stabbed into his side. Then he saw Nuing come into the house, with a burden basket filled with jungle fruits and vegetables straining on his back. Nuing recognized Kuti, and the smile he had ready on his lips turned to gaping shock.

The gallery was silent, as men after men turned their eyes away from him, in shame, in remorse. Then his father looked up, and their eyes met. Bujang said, "You have done well today, Nuing. Send your basket to the room. Your sister and mother will be pleased to see the fruits you have brought them."

Nuing did as he was told then without a word he walked out of the longhouse to the bathing platform. Even before he had stepped out of the house, the silence was broken by pockets of opinions from various parts of the crowd. Bujang, however, heard nothing but the roar in his ears, like the sound of waves brought on by the tidal bore, rolling against and over one another in their rush to hit the banks. Bujang heard nothing else, until Ugap touched his arm.

Then he looked up with so much pain in his expression that Kuti, who had leaned close to tell his tale, now moved his body back as far as he could without shifting from his seat on the floor next to the Chief.

Bujang turned to Ugap and said, "Nuing has taken three heads before he came home. Surely that must have neutralized his curse."

Ugap turned to study the face of the crowd, to see which way the wind of opinion blows. They had lost strong and good men and women because of Nuing, including Bujang's own son Patas who had moved to his bride's longhouse because he could not bear to live under another man's curse. None of them wanted to continue living under a cloud of despair, for that was what Nuing had come to represent to them. Crops failed, couples remained barren, and most times when a man left the house to either fish or hunt, the rufous piculet Ketupong would call with its creaking voice to warn him that his efforts would be in vain.

Based on their laws itself, the augur knew that Nuing was now free from the curse of his birth. But what of the failure of *Tuai* Aso's expedition? Was this in connection to his birth, or should this be accounted as a new curse on his head. Ugap felt himself in a bind, and the only way to ease out of it was to ask for time. Maybe a spirit would appear to him or to someone else in a dream and tell them what to do.

He turned his face sideways and avoided looking into Bujang's face because of the sympathy he felt for his chief who was being forced to admit this shame openly. "I am afraid that this situation is beyond my knowledge, for it is never mentioned in any law that I know. Allow me to go into meditation, so that I may learn what course to take."

Then he went under the house and brought up his prized rooster. After tying the bird to a post at the veranda outside, he went into his family room and took out a woven tray that he had laden with a handful of pop rice, shredded tobacco, slices of areca nut, a few betel vine leaves and a boiled egg. He took this outside, and after placing it on a mat, untied the rooster and held it tight in his arm. With a small knife, he grazed a small cut on the rooster's scarred cockscomb, letting a small amount of blood drip onto the offering. Then he waved the bird over the tray and its contents, chanting,

"I will not falter in my steps, I will not be chased away, I will see the face of spirit, god, or demon, and I will ask, I will learn in dreams, of ways pleasing to the spirits."

From the silence that followed, Ugap could sense that Nuing had returned from his bath. He set the offering aside, returned the rooster to its usual perch below the house then joined his chief in the gallery. That night, the visitors talked of many things but never once alluded to Chief Aso and his failed expedition. Nuing sat with them, for there was no where else he could go, he could be. Sitting next to his father, he looked hunched and old, his shoulders heavy with the unbearable weight of blame and judgment.

***

Though only the faint light of the embers of the fireplace lit the room and Upa was lying on her side, Bujang could tell that she was still awake. After lying down next to her, he said, "Nuing might have to go away."

Upa said, "We don't know that. The augur has not received an omen yet."

"Even if it is a good one, Nuing will still need to leave. The people have no place in their heart for him."

A moment of silence later, Upa said, "Will you go with him?"

"No. He is a man now. I have you, our children and grandchildren to protect here."

"You have always been dutiful."

"I am a man. I made the choice to be one even before I was born. I promised Selampandai that I would uphold all duties that the role of my gender requires of me. You made a promise to the blacksmith god too when you chose a spindle over a spear."

Upa put her arm around her husband, crushed her face in his chest and wept; noiselessly, for she would not trust the secret of her broken heart to anyone but Bujang. She had failed in her duty as a mother to Nuing. From the moment he was born, she was filled with disgust and horror at the sight of him, at the memory he evoked. Yet another part of her also longed to hold him, to suckle him at her breast like she did her other children. Once more she wished that Nuing was dead, so that her suffering under the hands of her rapists would become a mere memory instead of a living daily reminder.

Bujang held her, wishing to weep himself. He had watched her proud shoulders bowed under the accusations and insults of other women, and then of their grown up children. He was tempted to bow his shoulders too, but he could not, for he knew that she relied so much on him. Many times she had wanted Nuing dead, for Bujang's sake, and Bujang kept the child alive, for hers because he felt that if she was too weak to bear the burden of Nuing's life, then he would bear it for her.

He looked up to where the *nipah* roof was, imagining how it would look in the light of day though it was now enshrouded in darkness. In his heart, he called on the spirits, begging them to tell him what to do. The cicadas called incessantly outside, synchronizing their music like the sound of a throbbing heart. Slowly he began to feel himself floating in a sea of sound, like a babe in his mother's womb; listening to the sound of her heart, to the sound of blood flowing in her veins. The music was so familiar.

From a distance it seemed, he heard a series of knocking sound of wood pestle against wood mortar. He moved Upa's arm gently from his chest, relieved to find that she was now sleeping. He stepped over the feet of his daughter's young family quietly, as he made his way to the back. There he found an old woman, who shone like the moon, sitting next to the trap door leading to the back of the house. Sitting there, and pounding a large quantity of ginger.

"What are you doing, old woman?" he said, as he sat in front of her.

She looked up and smiled with her red sirih-coloured lips. "I am pounding ginger to prepare the bath."

"Whose bath is it?"

"Nuing's of course. Everything is ready for him."

Then a realization, a sensation of terror and hope, washed

over him as he recalled the words that Kumang had given him, that she soak her threads in the mordant bath to prepare them for the brightest engkudu red. Was Nuing to go through the fiery bath too? Despair mingled with hope filled his heart. He recalled the divination of the pig's liver and realized that Nuing must make his own way in the world, apart from him. When he looked up again, the old woman had started to change and was beginning to look younger by the moment. Soon before his eyes, she became the beautiful goddess that he had met on the slopes of Gelong Hill. She was perfect, without blemish, and with skin so fair that there was nothing in the world that could add more to her beauty.

"I will let him leave," Bujang promised.

She looked up and smiled, and the room was dark again.

The floor behind him creaked. Bujang turned and made out Upa's silhouette. She said, "You had a vision." He tried to explain, but she said, "I heard what you said. I understand." Then she turned and he followed her back to their sleeping mat.

***

Nuing listened to his father's decision with disbelief, as though he was still in a nightmare. He wished he could wake up, but then realized that he was already awake because the sighs of relief and congratulatory words of encouragement and support from the people around him were too common to be a dream. He kept his gaze down, staring at the floor, beyond the crevices between the planks. He heard everything, yet understood nothing. As the accused and as his father's son he knew that he had a right to speak and defend himself, but the sound of joy around him shrivelled his boldness and numbed his tongue. There was nothing else he could do but stare at the space between the floor planks.

A hand gripped his shoulder, making him looked up. Gunggu said, "I will go with you."

Finally Nuing found his voice. "But you cannot. What will your father and mother say?"

"They have my brother and his family. I have been nothing but trouble for them."

Nuing's chest tightened. He looked away and his eyes caught his father's. They were frowning and bloodshot. Nuing squared his shoulders, smiled and nodded, pretending that he felt nothing but pride for the chief's decision, for his father's belief in his ability to survive on his own. He turned back to Gunggu and said, "I will leave as soon as I can, even now if possible. We will have nothing with us."

Timban his brother-in-law, Lanai's husband, whispered from behind him, "You will not leave with nothing. Come to the farm when you are ready to leave." Then he slipped away.

Gunggu returned to his family room to say goodbye to his parents. The angry voice of an older man could be heard above the noise of cheer in the gallery, and conversation was hushed as all eyes turned to see what was going on. Gunggu's mother begged him to stay with tears and lamentations. He did not argue his case with them; he only stood there as they poured curses and accusations on him. He listened when they tried to bribe him with gifts and heirlooms to persuade him to stay, but he remained resolute. After perceiving that there was nothing they could say or offer to stop Gunggu from leaving, his father gave him a favoured blow-pipe, a thick machete that he had only bought a month before from a Malay trader, and a travelling basket that his mother filled with tobacco, areca nuts, betel-vine leaves, a fresh loin-cloth and a blanket.

The house was quiet as he walked out with Nuing. As they made their way down the common ladder, all eyes were on them, many scowling fiercely as though needing to make sure that if the two men ever thought of returning and begging to be accepted back into the community, they would remember those faces and realize that there was no mercy for them. Once on the ground, the friends turned aside and walked along a path that was familiar to them. While yet a short distance from the house, Nuing said, "You need not come. You are not the one being banished, I am."

"Did you not see how the people looked at me? I am as banished as you are."

They walked silently for the rest of the way. The morning shadow had shortened by the time they arrived at the chief's farm hut. Nuing started, for he had expected to see only Timban there, but with his brother-in-law were both his parents, his sister Lanai and her three young children. With hope he looked about for his other sister Utih, and his brothers Baling and Patas, but they were not there. Then he chided himself for being selfish. Why should they be there and become part of his curse?

"This is not much," Bujang said when Nuing's gaze fell on the large hunting basket he was holding. Stuffed to one side of the packets of food were his father's adze and a machete.

"It is more than enough, Father."

"Your mother and sister have prepared some food for you too," Bujang added.

Then Bujang got on his knees, and began to scrape the surface of the soil before him. He scooped handfuls of the earth onto two wide leaves that had been laid by the side. After wrapping the packages with twine, he passed them each a packet and said,

"These are for the hearth in your new home. Never forget your roots."

Nuing turned to look at his mother and for the first time in years, saw her watching his face. A strange fullness, a sense of well-being began to fill his chest. Seeing her look at him kindly made the feeling of being cursed seem insignificant. Suddenly, in that moment of quiet parting, the sobbing of a kingfisher could be heard coming from the edge of the field. Soon another sobbing was heard from the other side of the field.

"Embuas says it is time to say goodbye," Bujang said, and Upa began to weep. "But he also told me that even if I will never see you again with my living eyes, you will be a great man."

Timban and Gunggu helped Nuing lift up the basket as he inserted his arms into the shoulder straps then drew the crown strap over his brow. Though it sagged with the weight of packets of leaf-wrapped food, it hung light on Nuing's hopeful shoulders. His father tied the straps of his own sword, the *ilang* he had used to kill demons, around Nuing's waist and his brother-in-law put a hunting spear in his hand. Finally his mother came forward and gave him a piece of cloth that she had up till then wrapped over one arm while she listened and watched.

"I wove this specially for you. I hope it will bless you, and prove to everyone that the gods have not entirely abandoned you."

After they said their goodbyes and the two friends walked away, Nuing was tempted to turn back just about as much as Bujang wished to call him back, so they could spend another night in each other's company. However, neither man succumbed to his heart's desire as they each stared ahead through a veil of tears.

It was a bright clear day. Bujang could see all the way to

the other fields surrounding his, some sloping upwards, others winding round the hillock. He could see that they were all empty, painfully so because the people had decided to stay back in the longhouse and celebrate Nuing's banishment. Bujang led his family back into the hut. They would be spending the night there.

* * *

The jungle had not changed, Nuing saw. It was still the same as it was the day he returned with his father. Today's jungle was the same as yesterday's, even though Nuing now found himself without a roof to sleep under. Rays of light shone down from the high canopies, and the sound of birds and gibbons called from all around. The jungle floor too was thick with the call of invisible insects. There was such a cacophony of noise that all sound of omen, if there were any, would have been blocked out, so that even though both Nuing and Gunggu listened with hope and trepidation, they heard no omen to support either feelings.

They walked for days, following the westward trail. Gunggu's father had been to the coast and told him that the sea beyond the sand was like a giant river, except that it must be at least ten times as wide as the widest river in the world because you could not see the other bank even after you had paddled your boat two miles from the shore. For the first week, they did not worry about food because of the supply that Nuing carried with him. Once that supply was finished, however, they began to spend more time gathering edible fruits and vegetation. In this way their fast pace slowed until the day they reached the main river, the Batang Lupar.

"It will be many more days before we reach the coast," said

Gunggu scanning the horizon ahead with one hand shading his eyes.

"Or we can build a raft," said Nuing. He turned to look behind them, at a cluster of tall bamboos. "We can use those."

Gunggu grinned. "Let's do it tomorrow. I am hungry now."

"You are always hungry," said Nuing with a laugh. The farther he moved away from his home, the lighter his heart felt, for there was hope where they were going. Maybe they would find a longhouse that would welcome them, and marry the most beautiful women there. They could start a family, clear new farmland to plant the sacred *padi* of their wife's family, go travelling to new lands and meet new people, or join headhunting expeditions.

From his basket, Nuing took out the round casting net that his father had woven from the fibre of vines. He wound the rope attached to the centre of the net round his right hand then wound the rest of the net atop the rope then around the same arm. He climbed down the side of the bank and waded into the river until the water reached his waist. Gunggu followed him from behind. They studied the surface of the water for a while then Nuing nodded to his left. Gunggu threw a small rock half a yard away from them, in the direction his friend indicated. They waited some moments. Then holding to an edge of the net so it would open evenly, Nuing threw the net outward. It opened into a wide circle and, being weighed down by rocks tied around the hem, dropped straight down into the water. Nuing twisted the net as he pulled it towards him.

On their return to shore, they found that they had caught one medium-sized catfish and three other small fish. The young *tapah* catfish filled them with glee, for its white flesh was tender and its fat sweet and fragrant when cooked in the bamboo. Carefully they let it out of the net, being mindful of the two venomous thorns along its dorsal fins. Nuing remained at the camp to cut up and clean the fish, while Gunggu went into the jungle to collect tinder and wood. It was not long before he returned because the ground was dry and he did not have to get burning materials from dead branches that still clung onto the trees. They soon had a fire going, and while Gunggu tended to the fire and cooked their meal, Nuing began to cut the palms and branches about them so he could build a makeshift shelter under a tree.

They ate and talked merrily about the great adventures that they were going to have once they reached the coast.

"Father told me," Gunggu began for the tenth time, "that there are boats as big as houses, and that they need brave men to stay in them."

"They must have a lot of enemies."

"Yes, they do. Because my father said, one time he saw a man come out of one boat and he carried five heads in his basket. He told my father that he had fought a great battle against another boat at sea, and that they had won."

"It is strange that the water is bad for drinking."

"Yes, father said it is too salty, and that the more you drink, the thirstier you will become."

"What about the fish? Tell me again about the fish."

"Father said some fish there are as large as men, and that they have rows of sharp teeth. He saw one man being fed to them once, after he was condemned by the other men. He said that the fish, too many to count, came up to the body and tore it to pieces. Their teeth, he said are like knives."

"Knives," Nuing repeated dreamily. "I would like to make

knives with them. The thorns that crocodiles have for teeth cannot be turned into knives."

Like children they lay near the fire, talking when the mood took them and dozing when drowsiness fell upon them. There was no sense of danger, nothing could touch them, nothing would as they talked and dreamed and talked some more.

Early the following day, as the cold of the night turned to an even sharper morning chill they both rose, rekindled the fire and ate the leftovers from the night before. Then they turned their attention to the bamboo cluster. They cut down three thick poles then cut these into shorter poles along the line of a watertight septum. Once satisfied that they had enough bamboo to make a decent raft, they went deeper into the jungle to search for vines that they could use for rope. The rattan they found was young and pliable.

"Maybe we should look for something stronger," said Gunggu.

"This one here is quicker to make into a rope. It is still soft," said Nuing. "Working with an older rattan could mean an extra day or two."

"You are right," agreed Gunggu. "We are not keeping the raft after we reach the river mouth. A simple rope should be more than good enough."

They carefully cut the thorny vine at either end then ran its full length over a tree trunk to break off the thorns. On returning to the bank, and after hastily beating on the rattan to make it pliable enough to be tied into knots, they started to strap the bamboo poles together. Then they tied down pairs of poles across the raft, above and below at either end, to hold the pieces together. After shaping a long pole from a branch, and making a pair of paddle out of tough bark, they dragged their new raft into the water. They placed their baskets and weapons in the middle of the raft and got onto it. The raft sank a few inches, but stayed afloat. Though it was wet because the water splashed through the crevices in between the bamboos, the two friends did not care, for it was starting to be a warm day, and the water felt cool beneath them. They stayed close to shore, laughing and joking as they paddled along, more to steer the raft rather than propel it because the tide was taking them downstream at a good pace.

"Is this not the river with the tidal bore?" asked Gunggu.

"Yes," Nuing shouted back, "But the water only rises during the time of the full moon. That is still many days away. We are safe."

Suddenly, the water to the side splashed out violently and a pair of jaws jumped up then dragged Gunggu down. Nuing swung around and started to scream his friend's name. The water turned crimson. Then an arm and a sputtering face came out of the water. Nuing grabbed Gunggu's left arm and pulled as hard as he could. The water, the raft and Gunggu shook violently. Nuing pulled as hard as he could then fell on his back. Awashed with relief, he still clung onto his friend's arm as he sat up. He stared, and stared but Gunggu was not on the raft. It was as though he had disappeared. Nuing again looked down dumbly at the arm he was holding onto then turned his gaze back upstream. A crimson stream of ribbon trailed after him, from the snapping jaws of a large crocodile. He stared as though in a nightmare, for he could feel his friend's hand in his own yet he was watching him being consumed at the same time.

Nuing turned away from the sight, to face the setting sun and wept. The tide continued to carry him away, and though it began to get dark he had no heart to go ashore. Many times through the night he wished that he had swum back to the crocodile and killed it with his father's sword, yet each time he thought of it, a chill gripped his belly so that by the time a thick fog had formed over the river, Nuing was vomiting and shivering violently.

He rode with the tide for the next two days and night, not caring about food or drink. He held onto the hand, not willing to let go, for it felt as though his best friend was alive but just a moment ago. He rode until the tide brought him to a bent in the river, and stranded him there. That was when he looked up from the cold white hand, expecting someone to be there waiting for him but was surprised to find himself alone.

He got up painfully, his legs stiff and blistered from long hours in the water. He dragged the raft up to shore. Then he opened Gunggu's travelling basket and took out his friend's blanket. He wrapped the arm in it before carrying it deeper into the jungle. His tired and sore limbs would not let him walk far, and he was soon forced to drop on his knees. He laid the arm gently to one side and began to dig the soft peat soil in front of him with his bare hands. He dug as deep as he could then stepped into the hole and dug deeper. He dug until his hands began to bleed, and then he dug some more. When it became so dark that he could barely see around him, he groped for the arm, held it to his chest and sat down in the hole.

He knew that it was taboo. He knew that he was still alive and should not be inside a grave. But he did not care because he wanted to die. Then he began to sing a song of mourning for his friend, lamenting Gunggu's passing, lamenting his own cowardice. He sang until he was hoarse then continued with weeping. When the darkness became so thick that he had difficulty breathing, Nuing placed the arm on the ground then reached up to pour the soil he had dug back into the hole, over his friend and over himself. But when the hole was yet halfway filled, a sudden tiredness overcame him and he stopped to rest. He fell into a doze as his face rested in the crook of his tired arm which he had placed on the soil in front of him.

A loud voice calling out startled him from his sleep. In the distance he heard a man say, "We have it! We have that crocodile. Come see."

Nuing struggled to pull himself out of the hole. After he had managed to wiggle himself out he dashed in the direction of the voice. "Come see, come see," the man kept saying. He ran and ran until he suddenly found himself standing on a bathing platform upon a still river that was as black as coal.

An old man turned and asked, "Who are you, Child?"

Nuing said, "I am Nuing. I have come to see the crocodile you caught, Uncle."

"Oh, I have sent it up to the longhouse." On noting that Nuing was about to make his way to the house he said, "You must wash yourself first. Our chief will not appreciate a dirty visitor."

Nuing blushed, and wondered if his good manners had also gone with his senses. Without hesitation he slipped into the black river, unwrapped his loincloth and began to bath. After wringing the cloth as best as he could, he came out of the water with a hand covering his loin, then quickly wrapped the cloth over himself once more. He made his way towards the longhouse. He was surprised to find that the journey was of many miles for his loincloth was dripping wet when he started but by the time he reached the common ladder, it had dried. The strange sense of there being no time or distance in this place made him wonder if he was in a dream. And that in turn made him wonder whose world it was. He climbed the ladder cautiously.

Only three steps and he suddenly found himself on a wide open airy verandah. He looked down and saw that the floor was far above the top of the tallest tree in the garden below. He crossed the wide gallery to enter the nearest door in front of him. The courage in his chest sunk to his belly, for he was in a gallery so long that he could not see the other end of the longhouse. He walked down its length towards the centre, past a forest of enemy heads. This must truly be a house of great warriors, he thought to himself, for every family post is brimming with trophies and every family door was criss-crossed with war weapons and bird feathers of fierce colours. Fear slowly made itself felt in the chill in his toes and fingers, but he ignored them, focusing instead on the distant thronging crowd.

Even while he was yet yards away, the rearmost man turned to look at him. Nuing stopped. The voices of the crowd muted to a murmur as each turned to look at him. Then they parted, and he could see that a large crocodile had been hung upside down and cut open. His fears suddenly rushed out of him to be replaced by a need to see his friend again, so he hurried forward and stood in front of the beast. He could see Gunggu's head and body in jumbled pieces on the floor. He knelt and began to frantically arrange them into their original form.

A voice behind him thundered, "His arm is missing."

Nuing turned to face a fierce man with yellow eyes and long white hair so stiff they were like spikes. Nuing said, "I have buried his arm."

"Why do you bury it?" the man asked.

Nuing sat on his haunches. "Because he is dead." Then he

asked, "Please, may I have the rest of him to bury."

"If I give you the rest of him to bury, he will die."

Nuing frowned, thinking hard. He did not understand what the apparent chief had just told him. He was so confused he did not know what to ask.

"Show the arm you buried to my sister, Ini Andan. She will give your friend back to you."

The signs suddenly became clear to Nuing –the heads, the bird feathers and the chief's allusion to Ini Andan being his sister– he was in Sengalang Burong's longhouse. Immediately Nuing fell on his face and worshipped. "Great Grandfather, tell me, how do I find her?"

"She is in the place where you bury your brother-friend. Wait for her, she will come to you."

Again Nuing begged, "My father told me that we will never meet again. I wish to know if there is anything I could do to change that omen."

Sengalang Burong leaned forward from his seat and glowered at the man before him. "Fool. He is considered blessed to be still alive. He disobeyed me." The god leaned back. "I promise you this: No one will be successful in attacking him while he is still alive, because I have placed a curse on anyone who tries. However, after his death, the longhouse he built will be destroyed, and anyone who stayed behind will also die in the hand of an enemy."

Nuing raised his head with a snap, the sudden thought of his sister Lanai and her family had formed a plea at the end of his tongue but he found himself suddenly staring at a dark jungle carpeted with a soft green glow that seemed to enhance its darkness. He wept anew, this time for his sister and his people.

He started removing the soil over himself and lifted out Gunggu's arm carefully, as though it was a sleeping child. He placed it on the ground next to the hole then climbed out. He walked about, digging out patches of the thin-stalked, umbrella shaped luminescent mushroom, and placed them in a rough circle around the arm. He sat next to it and waited.

The cicadas called in a synchronized throb, masking all other sound. Sometimes a bat would fly past so close to him that he could feel the fan of its wings. He waited until morning but no one came.

The smell emitting from the arm was beginning to attract flies. Nuing built a fire and waved a burning stick over the arm to keep insects away from it. He was famished, but he did not dare to leave the arm lest it be taken, and he did not want to take it with him lest the shaman goddess comes. So he waited until night fell once more.

While the light was still grey, the cicadas began their song, and when the dark fell, the mushrooms began to glow. Nuing started to nod. Like in a dream he saw a yellow glow making its way towards him. Then he realized that the cicadas' chirping and the mushrooms' glowing had faded into nothingness. The light grew closer and the air turned colder.

Nuing began to shiver violently and the joints of his hands, arms, legs and spine twisted painfully, curling him into a ball like a pangolin hiding from its hunter. A woman, whose bare pale feet were the only things he could see, approached. He could not lift his head, nor turn his face to either left or right. He could only see what was within the limited field of how far he could turn his eyes in their sockets.

A white hand reached down to pick up Gunggu's grey arm

and Nuing struggled to lift his face or to sit up. His face turned red and pale with exertion, sweat dewed out of every pore and his veins stood out hot and angry. When he finally managed to look up, he saw an ageless woman who was gripping the arm by the hand and swinging it over her head. She swung it hard, she swung it fast and soon, through the haze of his pain, Nuing saw the arm growing ever longer. The arm started to grow a torso, and the torso legs and an arm. Finally a head grew out of the torso and it twisted from side to side. One last swing and the goddess dropped the body to the ground.

Nuing stared with unbounded joy, for he could see Gunggu in the flesh, lying on the ground. At first his breath caught in his throat because Gunggu was not stirring then he noticed the chest moving. The woman walked away and the yellow light faded. Soon the cicadas again called and the mushrooms began to once more give off their light. The arthritic stiffness left Nuing and he rose to sit next to Gunggu, covering him with the blanket, until the first light of dawn filtered down into the jungle.

As he studied his friend, Nuing realized that though Gunggu looked the same, there was a strangeness about him. The arm that he had saved was grey and dark but the skin of the rest of his body was pale, like a new born child's. Nuing picked up his spear and went into the jungle. He was hungry and he suspected that his friend would need food too when he woke.

Chapter 8

Dew still covered the jungle floor as Nuing stalked forward silently, watching the bushes, listening to any break in the morning symphony of crickets, and taking in the scents of the air. Soon his diligence was rewarded by a slight movement behind a thick clump of aged fern. As he approached it, a rattling noise issued like the hissing of many snakes. He moved back a few steps then threw the spear into the bush, exactly where it stirred. A loud squeak issued and thick black and white quills shot out in different directions. Two hit Nuing at the shin but he managed to pull them out without trouble.

Nuing then grabbed the handle of his spear and pressed it down some more. The squealing and twitching stopped. He pulled out his catch and was pleased to see the adult sized porcupine. He returned to camp. As he neared it his steps slowed because he could smell the smoke of a fire. He wondered if his best friend was still the same. Cautiously he approached the camp, until he saw Gunggu squatting before a small fire, feeding it with more fuel.

Nuing released a loud cough to let him know that he was there. Gunggu looked up with a frown then he smiled as though he had not seen Nuing for many years and had just recalled his face. He said, "I wondered where I was."

Nuing was relieved to see the recognition on his friend's face. He laid the porcupine to the side then sat before the fire. "How are you, Gunggu?"

"I think I am myself, but I feel not like myself."

"Do you remember anything?"

"I remember being dragged into the river and waking up by a grey bank. I couldn't find you anywhere though I searched for you along many rivers and over many hills. I saw many strange people in these lands, but not one of them had seen you. Finally I crossed a bridge that was so large, three men could cross them abreast." He paused and frowned, trying to remember as much detail as he could. "When I got to the other side, a dirty and ugly old woman invited me up to her house in the tree. I did not want to visit at first, because it was such a filthy place, but she told me that she knows where you were, so I climbed up. She offered me some fruits to eat, and I ate one to be polite. Then she threw me out of her house and I was caught up in a storm. When I woke up, I found myself here. Do you know what happened to me?"

Nuing began to fidget then he turned to the porcupine's carcass and began to cut it open. "Let us have some food first."

After cleaning out the entrails of the animal and burying in a shallow hole the faecal matter and clotted blood, they threaded the pieces of organs and meat on a stick and placed them over the fire. While they waited for their breakfast to cook, Nuing collected the quills, tying them into a bundle which he put in his basket. Their meal was quiet. Nuing dreaded telling his friend about the crocodile attack, but after the meal he began his story from the time he lost Gunggu and had given him up for dead to his visit to Sengalang Burong's house in his dream and to seeing Ini Andan revive his friend.

Gunggu's frowning face lightened and he said, "We should make our way to the mouth of the river as soon as we can."

"No, a raft is not safe. We have to make a proper *perau*. A dugout boat will be safer and studier."

Yes, Gunggu agreed, it would be far safer because a dugout could be paddled down a river faster, so that no crocodile would be able to overcome one. Therefore soon after breakfast, Nuing and Gunggu collected their travelling baskets and moved farther into the jungle, looking up and about them until they came across a straight bole tree that was more than their heights put together. The *lauan* was just starting to grow buttress roots, and when Nuing looked up, he estimated that the lowest branch was a little less than ten feet above ground. He unslung his basket then knocked against the trunk with the hilt of his machete.

The spirit of a macaque screeched down. Nuing said, "I would like this tree for my boat. There are many other trees in the jungle. There are many other homes. Let me have this one."

Above him the branches snapped and the leaves rustled, some dropping down in flutters, as the troop of monkeys scampered away from the tree. Nuing knocked again, and when nothing responded, he checked the slope of the ground. After ascertaining which side leaned downward, he unsheathed his machete and struck the first blow. Gunggu also took out the machete in his basket and went to the other side of the tree, hacking on the trunk too but about a foot higher from the cut Nuing was making. When the tree began to creak, Nuing went to stand across from Gunggu and took turns with him chopping away at the trunk. Soon the tree began to lean to the lower side and, after a few more deep chops, the log broke free, snapping branches as it went down.

Gunggu went to the lowest branch and began to cut the log at a point that was just below it. Nuing started to level the uppermost portion of the trunk as well as to chop off as much of the upper crusty bark as he could. Then he stripped off the lower red stringy bark to expose the yellow wood beneath. The deeper he cut, the redder the wood became. The moment that Gunggu's portion of the work was done, Nuing felt the log roll a little. Gunggu helped him continue to carve a flat level on the top facing them.

Then Gunggu stopped and pointed to a cluster of palm, saying, "I think I saw some young palm there while we were looking for wood."

Nuing nodded. He was hungry too. As Gunggu went to the palm cluster to collect the soft edible core, Nuing emptied his basket then slung it on one shoulder and retraced their steps to where he saw a small stream. He cut down a bamboo and made four bamboo tubes with it. He filled two tubes with water and put them next to the other two empty ones in his basket. In this way, he carried water back to the camp.

By the time he returned, Gunggu had built a fired and cut out the heart of a palm into bite-size pieces. Nuing was pleased to see that he had also collected some young *sabong* leaves. The elliptical leaves of the gnetum tree could be used to stop the bamboo opening, as well as make a fragrant supplement to the palm heart. The meal being prepared, though good, seemed unsatisfying to him. So leaving Gunggu to cook the first part of their meal, Nuing again returned to the stream. Just a few yards away from it, he found a group of wild banana trees that were in different stages of growth. From one he took a sparse fruiting stem of five plantains, from another he took a heart-like banana inflorescence that was made up of layers upon layers of red bracts sheltering tiny ivory flowers.

Gunggu had begun cooking the palm heart on his return. Nuing placed the starchy plantains in the fire, but the more fragile banana inflorescence he placed atop a stick over the fire.

"Will we be cutting into the log after this?" Gunggu asked.

"You can start first, if you wish," Nuing replied. "Father has given me his *beliung*. The adze is very sharp, so you will make short work of it. I will be going back to get one of the banana trunks. The fibres are strong. They will make good ropes."

Gunggu nodded to indicate his agreement with the idea. Just then steam and water began to pour out of the single bamboo tube he had placed over the fire. He poured the soupy contents out onto two wide leaves. Nuing used a sharp stick to take out the cooked plantains then, with his bare hands, reached for the now shrivelled and dripping banana heart. They began their meal, commenting and agreeing that though the palm heart was bitter and sweet, it would have been better if it had been cooked in brine. The wild banana had many seeds but was satisfying and best of all was the banana heart, for the moisture from the flowers was like nectar, and the white petals were fragrant.

Nuing stuck his hand into his hunting basket to take out the *beliung*, his father's adze, and the machete. After helping Gunggu turn the log onto its flat side, he again returned to the banana trees. Carefully he studied the fibre along the trunks. He picked the toughest looking one, cut it down and began to strip the trunk, peeling it down to the core. He wound the still green strips over his lower arm and shoulder then returned to camp. With the branches from the tree they cut, he built a tall stand and hung up the strings to dry.

Gunggu stopped his work for a moment to watch him. "Those will make good raffia ropes."

Nuing grinned then picked up the adze that his friend had put down on the ground. He continued where Gunggu had left off.

His friend did not stay idle for long because after taking a drink from a bamboo tube, he went into the jungle and returned with a back-load of firewood which he had tied together with vines.

For days they continued this activity, searching or hunting for food, collecting firewood and carving the boat. On the fifth day when they both agreed that the boat was ready for shaping, they build four cross-shaped braces which they tied together with rattan. They planted these X's into the ground in a row next to the boat. Then, holding onto either end of the craft, they lifted it onto the braces. They then used knives to scrape the side of the boat, to give it a more even surface. Nuing set a sturdy branch on fire then went around the boat, burning off any stray strands of fibre.

Early the following morning, Nuing returned to the stream to collect water which he poured into the boat. After he had filled it half-full, Gunggu began building a fire under it, making sure to keep the flames low. Nuing continued to add more water until it reached to about an inch from the top of the gunwale. While waiting for the boat to take form, he started slicing and cutting out sheets of leftover wood for the thwarts and seats of the boat. The wood of the boat began to bend because of the heat of the fire and weight of the water, making the middle portion flare outward. Towards evening, they poured out the water, put out the fire and, with blocks of wood, hammered the thwarts and seats into place so that the boat would maintain its shape after it cooled. Then they turned the craft upside down on the braces over smouldering embers and left it there to dry.

After breakfast the next morning they carried the boat to the river where they set it down. Nuing was pleased to see that it floated easy on the water but after they loaded their things into it, and as they were about to push out, they suddenly realized that they had no paddles. Gunggu laughed so hard his eyes teared up. Nuing frowned good-naturedly as he dragged the boat back up the muddy bank. He went in search of a thick branch and, on finding one, cut it down and split it in two. On his return he found that Gunggu had plaited some of the raffia strings into a sturdy rope. He placed the wood down in front of his friend then sat down with a forlorn sigh. Gunggu again laughed as he picked up a piece of wood and started carving the rough shape of a paddle. Thus they spent the morning; laughing at themselves and trying to imagine how they would steer the boat without a paddle.

"We should catch a giant *tapah* fish," Nuing suggested. "Then tie it by the tail to the bow of our boat. It will pull us upriver."

Gunggu chortled. "But that catfish is slow. We will be old by the time we reach the river mouth."

Nuing leaned forward, all the while trying his best to keep his mirth down as he said, "How about a *toman*? The snakehead is fast I should think."

"You will need more than one. The biggest of those is barely half the size of one of us."

A man's voice suddenly called from the upriver direction. Nuing looked up and his muscles tensed, for coming down towards them, following the receding tide was a flotilla of dugout boats of various make and sizes. He relaxed on seeing women, children and the elderly among them but he did not let down his guard. A boat with a man and woman separated from the group and approached them.

Nuing stood up and waved both arms over his head. "Where are you going, Friend?"

The man leaned forward on the bow and said, "We are following the river to its mouth. Then we plan to follow the coast where the sea people build their homes until we find another river."

"That is a great distance just to move house."

The boat stopped behind their craft. "I am Megong," the man said, "May we stop here for a time."

"Of course, Friend. No one lives here," Nuing said.

Megong lifted an arm and waved the others towards him. At his signal, the men and women set to their paddles and approached the bank. He turned back to Nuing and Gunggu. "This is not your land?"

"No," Gunggu replied. "We have been chased out of our longhouse."

Megong stepped out of his boat and pulled it up onto the bank then he squatted next to the two friends. "Why? What have you done?"

"My friend Gunggu here was not chased out," Nuing said, "I am the one who is a curse. Gunggu followed me."

"A true friend indeed. And you, what is your name?"

Nuing turned his eyes away to the bank on the other side, avoiding Megong's eyes and the looks of gratitude from the people who were now climbing ashore. "I am Nuing, son of Bujang Maias."

Megong let out a sigh. "I have heard of you."

"Then we will say farewell," Nuing said.

Megong lifted a hand to stop Nuing from getting up, "Wait, Friend. You don't have to leave. We are the trespassers. You were here first." Then he turned to face the waters. "I too am like you. My people also think that I am a curse."

"Why?" Nuing asked, turning full face to look at Megong with a frown of confusion on his face.

"Because I am the younger of a twin brother. The augur advised my father to abandon me in the forest after I was born, but my mother insisted that I stay. All was well, until about six months ago. My brother became ill with a fever and his wife accused me of eating his soul. I left, so that my brother will not die."

A baby cried, and a woman hushed it softly, holding one hand over its mouth to muffle the sound. Gunggu turned to look at her and said, "My brother friend and I have stayed here for many nights. This is a safe place." The woman nodded her thanks and hurried to join the group who were now starting to clear an area that was farther in, where they could build fires without being seen from the river.

"We found her wandering alone with the baby when we were hunting for food," Megong said with a nod to her direction.

"Did she say why?" Nuing asked.

"She could not name the father of her child because she was attacked by a stranger while looking for dye materials in the jungle," Megong explained. "So after the baby girl was born, her people banished them."

Nuing now turned to study the group of almost fifty people. "Are they all accursed?"

"Not all. Some are like Gunggu here. True friends and family. Only four of us are cursed."

"But there are so many of you," Gunggu said.

Megong looked at the activity being carried out in front of them. Then reluctantly he explained. "A few men are ashamed to return home to their families. They are unwilling to collect the heads of the wives and children of their enemies. So they lied to their families and told them that they are going on a long journey,

a *belelang*, and asked their love ones not to expect their return."
After a long moment of silence during which time some men had managed to build two large fires, Megong said, "Come join us."

Nuing's head snapped up, "Are you not afraid? My very presence has brought death and failure to many warriors."

"We are also curse bearers. How can yours be worse than ours? Many of the men in my group are either too young or too old to swing an *ilang*," Megong said, pointedly looking at the war sword in Nuing's basket. "You and your friend will make a wise addition to our group. Please, we need you both."

The young woman who was in the boat with Megong now approached them with a small basket of tobacco. "This is my sister, Nambi," Megong said. "She followed me when my family cast me out."

Nambi sat behind her brother shyly, and explained, "I have no one but my brother. After he leaves, there will be no one to help me farm or bring meat for my kitchen."

Megong looked down at his feet, and Nuing could sense his feeling of guilt. He suddenly recalled Lanai's face and quick smile. His sister was a semi-outcast too because she was kind to him, her accursed brother. He remembered how Timban had to go against the will of his own family to take her as his wife. The memory of his sister's sad plight went through his mind as he received the basket from Nambi's hand. Then he looked into her face and saw that she had kind eyes too, like Lanai. Shyly, he placed the basket down on the ground and took out a roll of dry nipah leaf and some tobacco for a cigarette.

Nuing then offered the basket to Gunggu, who also rolled a cigarette from it. After the three men finished their smoke, Megong led them to the campsite and introduced everyone to the new members. For the first time in his life, Nuing sat among men and women who welcomed him with genuine friendliness.

It was a strange group to be amongst, for though there were quite a few young people not a single person spoke carelessly or loudly as young men were sometimes wont to do. Nobody bragged, nobody made claims of great or brave feats, and most of all, nobody teased another by putting him down. Their demeanour was pleasant though their manner guarded.

While Nuing continued his conversation with Megong, Gunggu led a group of able-bodied men and women to a clump of sago palms that he had seen growing near a murky pool. Some of the palms had started flowering but there was at least two that had not and were of the right age. They started cutting down the bigger of the two palms and slashed open the soft trunks. Then with the same machetes they beat on the pith until it was a wet mashed mess. Two men striped a tree of its bark and sewed both ends shut with a young rattan vine to make a makeshift trough. The women collected the mash of sago onto wide leaves and, leaving the men to continue beating into the remaining pith, they started to knead the sago until a milky liquid oozed out of it. Then they poured water over the mash, and kneaded it some more before straining it with a finely meshed mat into the trough. This they continued doing until the trough was full then they waited for the starchy powder to settle at the bottom.

The more restless in the group began to look about them for materials and supplies to take on their journey. A man gave out a cry of joy, drawing the others to his side and sure enough, his find brought the same shout of delight from the onlookers. They began to carefully cut open the rotting trunk of the sago palm to extract crawling fat sago worms. The larvae of the palm weevil beetle were so large that one man claimed the smallest among them was as big as his toddler's penis. A basket was lined with wide leaves and the worms carefully put in it.

By the time they returned to the trough, they saw that the women were starting to pour out the top water carefully, leaving a sediment of white starch at the bottom. As half of the group made their way back to camp, some men followed Gunggu to a clump of banana tree, cut down one that had not flowered and cut open the core. Another man found rattan shoots and proceeded to extract the heart.

By the time they returned to camp, they saw that the sago was already cooking in wide mouth bamboo tubes over the fire. As the water inside began to boil, three women churned the contents with a long stick, to make sure that the white starch mixed properly with the hot water and turned into a transparent glue-like mass. After the supplementary dishes were also cooked, they all sat down for a simple meal. It was good company, and as the people became more relaxed around Nuing and Gunggu, there were many jokes and teasing. The sky above them suddenly flashed and a deafening thunder clapped over their heads. Instantly the group became silent; the young crouching next to a parent, and the elderly looking up into the darkness.

Megong said, "We have overstayed our welcome in this place. We must leave tomorrow."

The people nodded and went into their hastily built shelters, leaving only the sentries of the first watch by the dying fire. But the group could barely sleep that night because the lightning continually flashed and the thunder rumbled and roared in reply. To make their life more miserable, a heavy downpour began soon after they went into their shelters. Water hammered down on the roofs and puddle on the ground, soaking into everything that was dry. It became so bad that some men took their boats, turned them upside down over the studier frame of their shelters and lay or sat beneath them. Late into the night, the crack of a giant tree crashing down nearby woke even the deepest sleeper. The oldest man in the group came out from under his shelter and promised the jungle that they would leave come morning light. The thunderstorm soon abated and the heavy downpour slowed to a drizzle that lasted the rest of the night.

Morning was dismal but welcomed, for it brought with it the warming light that chased away any lingering mist and dew. Gunggu and Nuing got into their boat and rowed abreast with Megong at the head of the group. Since the flotilla kept close to the banks for safety reasons, the two boats had to scout ahead, to warn others of their approach as well as to keep a lookout for ambush.

For days they travelled down the river, going slowly for the sake of the elderly. But on days of the new or full moon, they would set up camp and rest for a day or two, always watching the water, dragging their boats farther inshore to avoid a sudden rise of the tide. Sometimes they would come across a village or a group of hunters, but they were never welcomed once they explained who they were. People were so afraid of them, all feeling of common courtesy were gone. Nobody was willing to offer them food or shelter. So most times if they do come across a community, they would move farther downriver, until they reached unoccupied land. But as they got closer to the coast, it became more and more difficult to avoid people. For that reason, only those who were not cursed would approach the people and exchange some rare jungle product for food such as rice or tapioca root.

The first day they came out to the coast was exciting because none of them had ever seen so much water in their life. Though they know from rumour that the water was salty, they still had to taste it for themselves to be sure that the stories were true. Nambi wondered if it was the tears and sweat of the world because the water tasted so much like her own tears. But then the wind came and the sprays hit their faces, and the waves rocked their boats and terrified the children. Food was difficult to find along the coast and they were forced to eat coconut and coconut cabbage day after day, because the other plants that grew along the coastline had thick bark and tasted bitter, like poison. Their round nets, though useful in river fishing, yielded them little from the sea. Most times they would catch fish that looked strange or deformed, and they would throw these back into the sea out of fear.

So it was that when they reached the mouth of a river two weeks later, the children let out a cheer that gladdened even the weariest heart. But on learning who they were the Saribas people living at its mouth would not let them pass.

"Please, Friend," Megong said. "We come peacefully."

The village chief looked him and Nuing up and down before saying, "The spirits you bring with you will destroy our life in this land. You must go."

Behind the village chief, the number of men standing with their hand on a machete or spear continued to grow. Though they all lived in the same fishing village, their attire was different one from the other. Some men wore loincloths, others wore trousers. Most had long-sleeved jackets but a few wore vests. A number had turbans, some only a ring of cloth on their head, and two men had long braided hair. All of them were burned dark by the sun but a handful of men were so dark, they looked as black as gods.

Nuing turned his gaze back to the waterline of the beach, to where the children and elderly were now sitting. It was with a great effort that he held back his tears when he said, "May we at least look for food and drinking water for the next day or two."

"No," the village chief said firmly. "You will poison everything you touch. You must leave now." He added gently, "I am sorry."

A long despairing silence followed. Neither Nuing nor Megong had any fight left in them, no fight for the men before them or for the elements ahead. For the first time, Nuing wondered if it were better to bring their boats farther into the sea because they had no hope for living. But then a new fear shook him, for he remembered stories from travelling Kayans of how the souls of those who committed suicide would be tortured by the demon fish Patan for all eternity in a lake of suffering.

The sky above them began to darken and rumble. "You must leave now," said the village chief with a hint of anguish in his voice. A man touched his shoulder and whispered into his ear. The chief shook his head to disagree, but his face was lined with indecision.

One of the black men suddenly said, "We will bring food and water for you. After that, please leave."

Megong nodded. "Thank you," he said. Then he and Nuing returned to the beach and told the group the result of their discussion with the village men.

"It is good that someone in the village still remembers the customary law," said *Akik* Bada, the oldest man in their group.

"What is that law, *Akik*?" asked his grandson Bada.

"It is the law of hospitality. No man or woman is to deny a traveller food or shelter if he requests it." Then with a serious frown on his face he continued, "You must remember that law. It is so important that when a longhouse in the Sebuyau River ignored it, the gods became angry and turned the inhabitants into stone."

By evening a handful of village men started to approach them and gave them a supply of both cooked and uncooked rice, vegetables, meat, fruits, and fresh water. They were allowed to stay the night, giving them an opportunity to rest and to eat a proper meal for the first time in days. Early the next morning, they resumed their journey north.

Chapter 9

It was another week of cold and wet; of braving sharp rocks that suddenly loomed from the shallow waters, and of battling surfs that dashed against their boats. Seven more days of battling the elements had to pass before they finally reached the mouth of another river. Nuing and Megong were the first to see it, and on noticing the blue clearness of the salt water turned murky with the ochre colour of alluvial mud, they called out gladly to the people behind them. Everyone was in good spirits when they turned their boats into this river. Their gladness, however, quickly turned to caution on spying a small village just beyond the border of sand and ground creepers. Nuing and Chaong, a young warrior who was ashamed to return to his community, climbed into Megong's boat. Then the three of them made their way to the bank, while the others waited some distance away.

Megong strained his eyes as he studied the way ahead. "There seems to be no one," he said, without turning his head.

The boat hit bottom. The three men got out and dragged the light craft onto the sandy and muddy bank.

"Maybe they are hiding from us," Nuing suggested.

The other two men did not respond. Fear was never a good sign, because it meant that someone might be watching them now with the intention to kill them. Instinctively Nuing and Chaong fell back and Megong walked ahead of them.

Megong called out, "Hoi, is anyone here? May we speak with you?"

On hearing no friendly reply, Nuing and Chaong unsheathed their swords in as nonchalant a manner as they could muster. Megong continued to walk ahead, now with his hands held open in front of him, showing that he came in peace. "Hoi!" he called again.

Nuing touched Chaong's elbow and pointed to a form lying half covered in the sand. They approached it, and saw the skeletal arm of a person. Bits of muscle and flesh still clung to it.

Chaong said, "A wild animal must have chewed on it."

They looked about them and noticed a leg bone and another arm some yards away. Those too had been stripped of flesh. The wind changed direction for a brief moment, and brought to them the scent of death. Megong unsheathed his sword and they dashed back to their boat.

The others, who had been watching them with mounting anxiety, quickly readied their paddles, so that when Megong signalled for them to go farther upriver they were able to react instantly. They went up for another two miles, until they found a *nipah* forest that was dense enough to hide them from any marauder.

After making sure that the new campsite was safe, Megong, Nuing, and Chaong again returned to the village. They approached the huts stealthily but found not a single living thing, not even an insect or a sand crab. The water in the jars were foul and the rice grains covered with mould. There was nothing worth scavenging in any of the homes, but they managed to find some tapioca roots and breadfruit in the gardens. After quickly collecting as much as they could, they returned to their boat and left the place.

"They took nothing," Chaong said from the stern. His eyes frowned at the banks by turn as he moved his paddle from side to side.

"They took the people," Nuing said as he too studied the foliage from his position in the middle of the boat.

Megong was silent as he contemplated what he would say to the people. Maybe the marauders only attacked along the coast. There was no sign of any other villages along the river, anyway, so this might be a good place for him and his followers as they would not need to beg for permission from anyone to live here. That night there was a special treat because while the three were away scouting the village, some men had collected sap from the flowering clusters of *nipah* palm growing by the bank. The liquid sap was boiled until it was thick and brown then the sweet caramel was used to sweeten the roasted breadfruit and tapioca. Some *nipah* fruits were also gathered and cut open to yield a sweet white flesh.

Though the land about them was good, *Akik* Bada was not easy in his mind, especially after the conversation of the group returned to the condition of the village by the coast.

"I think the people there must have been attacked by *lanuns*," said Megong.

"We should be safe from the pirates. We have nothing," said Nambi, his sister.

Nuing shook his head in disagreement. "That is not true. They can still take you and the children as slaves."

Akik Bada said, "Nuing is right. We have come so far, we can still go a little farther upriver. I know that everyone is tired, but if we stay here all the sweat of our labours will be destroyed."

"We must do as *Akik* Bada says," Megong said. "We will

find a tributary, away from the *nipah* palms to where the water is sweeter. We will be safer the farther away we are from the coast."

Afraid that he might be forced to reveal the most shameful nature of his own curse, Nuing kept his head bowed as he said in a low voice, "We can still be attacked by pirates. My father's longhouse was built in a tributary and was attacked before I was born"

Megong was quiet for a long time, looking at Nuing's bowed head, sensing there a despair that he could not understand. Then he said, "We will find a place that we can protect. Maybe we will build our house on a hill. Or we can build a thick fence around it, so that it will be easier to guard."

Everyone thought that the plan was good, so that only after an hour of discussion on their other options, they all agreed to leave the camp ground come first light. For the next few days during their journey, mosquitoes tormented them, and they had to stop frequently to look for bark that would be smoky when burned to act as fumigants. The children grew weaker by day because there was little food that was nourishing to the body and spirit. The nature spirit, the *antu tukik*, of the place also seemed reluctant to let them pass quickly, so that it seemed as though they were hardly making any progress at all. Above them black pelicans called, startling them and reminding them that they were not out of danger yet. The land seemed unexplored for the most part because they only saw two large house structures, built right above the water on tall black columns marked by the muddy tide.

Sensing that they would not be welcomed, they avoided these homes and pressed on farther upriver. On the third day, the river began to narrow, and they no longer see islands within its flow. They camped as best as they could within the *nipah* palm jungle, harvesting sugar, salt and fruit from it. The days continued to be long and hard, so that the women began to braid calf bracelets from strings of palm leaves for everyone. They hoped that the bracelets would help them keep their spirit strapped to their body and support the strength in their muscles. Megong's bracelets, the ones braided by his sister Nambi, were especially fine and his tireless activities around the camp attested to the potency of his sister's skill.

After about a week of travelling, they sighted a large longhouse built a little way up the bank. Standing alone on the landing place was a burly man shading his eyes against the morning sun as he peered towards them. Megong told his sister, Nambi, to climb into the other boat with Gunggu while Nuing climbed into his, then Megong and Nuing paddled towards the landing place, while the others sat and waited in their crafts.

"Greetings, Friend," Megong called out. "May we pass this way?"

"There is no one but savages upriver. Why would you wish to go there?" the old man asked. Nuing stared speechless at the row of sharp canine teeth necklace around his neck. Gripped in his hand was a circle of stone, bone, and skin. The old man suddenly shook it with a laugh, and Nuing was startled out of his bemusement.

"My name is Juit. I am a shaman," the old man said as he squatted down on the platform. Then with a wave, indicating that they should come closer he said, "*Niki*, come up to my home. You are welcome here, Curse-bearers."

Megong frowned hard, for he did not recall telling the old man who they were. Yet the old man's strange behaviour of sniggering and snapping his head to and fro like a restless macaque persuaded Megong that a slave spirit must have told him of their coming. Why else would he be waiting at the landing place?

Nuing brought the boat alongside the platform, and they saw that the old man was taller than either one of them and so thin he seemed emaciated. Megong climbed onto the platform while Nuing remained within the craft.

Megong asked, "How do you know about us?"

"Ahh," the old man said with a raised finger. "I know many things. The little prawns scratch on the underside of my platform to tell me of your coming. The black starlings came to land on my shoulders, shrieking into my ears and staring down the Limut River with their red eyes. Telling me, telling me what the pelicans told them." He laughed, as though he had just told a wonderful joke. Then he jumped to a stand, startling Megong into taking a step back, and began to dance in circles. All the while he called out like an animal; shrieking, roaring, barking, hooting and hissing by turn.

Just as suddenly he stopped and stared down into Megong's uplifted face. His cackling madness now sombre, he said, "Yes, I know you, Megong son of Rangga. The gods curse you, the land curses you, and your people curse you." He pointed a finger into Megong's face, "You are cursed, from the day you were conceived. You should be dead." Then he laughed. "You should be dead!" he shouted to the river.

Megong swayed on his feet, as though in a trance. Then, like one who had only woken up from a fever, he said in a tired voice, "Yes, I should be dead. But I am afraid."

Juit cupped Megong's face with his hands, and studied it with as much gentleness as his madness could muster. In a soft voice he said, "No...No, you are not meant to be dead." He threw back his arms and shouted, "You are a warrior. A great man, and soon your name will be known by every man, woman, and child." He brought his face close and said, "And they shall tremble when they hear your name mentioned."

Megong's pale face flushed red and his shoulders squared. Half-doubting and half-wishing that everything Juit had said would come true, Megong asked, "How do you know this, Shaman? Who has told you these things?"

Nuing added, "Maybe you talk to demons."

Juit turned his piercing gaze to Nuing, who turned his face away after a few moments, for the old man's eyes were like nothing he had ever seen before. Where the white of his eyes should be was a golden yellow and the dark brown of his iris was shot with radiating grey lines. The old man hissed, turning his face sideways as though to listen. "You, you are hidden from me. Why are you hidden from me?"

He stepped back and looked Nuing up and down then he stepped from side to side as though he was playing with a child hiding behind a pillar. Then he squatted and purred, "I see you are a true warrior, unlike everyone else here. The python spirit that protects you is strong, and he could not be persuaded to reveal anything about you. You were once cursed, but no more. Why are you with these people?"

"My people think that I am cursed," Nuing said.

Juit chuckled then threw his head back to laugh aloud. "They are fools, they are blind. One day they will need you, and your guardian. But you will not be there. You are here."

His laughter sent chills down Nuing's back. He could feel the hair on his nape bristling, and he readied himself to pounce on the shaman, like a trapped animal that had no other recourse.

Fearful that the shaman would take offence on his companion's coldness, Megong explained, "Nuing is the son of a great warrior. His presence has been a blessing to us." Then he stared down at his hands, and asked a little shamefacedly, "You said that I will be a great man too. When will this happen?"

The shaman took a deep breath then he said, "Anytime you are ready to be one."

Megong's startled face turned to look at Juit. "But I am ready. I have always been ready."

"You are not invincible yet."

"I have done many meditations. I have been to every rock outcropping I could find. I have meditated in their shadows and offered sacrifices to the goddess Kumang that she may give me a charm blessed by her husband, the warrior guardian Keling. I have been ready for so long, but I have never received any dream that blesses me."

"If you are not afraid to suffer, I can make you invincible. No sword will cut your skin, no spear will pierce you and no one will ever again be able to make you submit. You shall be the greatest leader that has ever lived, and you shall be called *Mali Lebu*, Unbeatable, for no one will be able to overpower you." Then he raised a finger in front of Megong's eyes, as though in warning. "But, will you suffer through the pain."

Megong's breath came in short burst and his face began to sweat with excitement. Nuing touched his forearm and startled him into the present. "We must go," Nuing said. "It will be dark soon. We must make camp."

Juit turned Megong's shoulder and drew his head towards him then whispered in his ears, "He is afraid that you will become better than him."

Megong said nothing in return, but his face was angry as he climbed back into the boat. Turning his eyes away from Nuing, he glared his hatred for his companion at the sky and the trees ahead so that by the time they returned to the group, Nambi was surprised to see him frowning. She assumed that it was because the occupant of the house had been unfriendly to them so she did not ask him anything as she returned into their boat, and Nuing climbed back into his. They paddled upriver for another two miles until they came upon a small clearing and moored their boats there. Every individual began to go about their duties, and that night they were lucky because they found enough food for everyone to eat. Even the nets they cast from the bank had returned full of arm-sized catfish and snakeheads.

The people began to relax. This was good land and they expected to prosper in it, so that when Megong told them about what *Manang* Juit had said about the people in the interior, they were dismayed.

"Do not worry," said Megong, "I will protect you. The shaman has prophesied that I will be a great warrior."

"Through great suffering," Nuing reminded him.

"I am not afraid of a little pain," Megong said with a scowl on his face. "I will go to him tomorrow and get the charm of invincibility. Then you will all see what a great warrior I have become."

A few men in the group cheered. Gunggu turned to Nuing with a smile and was surprised to see his friend frowning. But after listening to Megong's excited speech for some time and seeing Nambi's face light up with pride, Nuing too began to wish that Megong would receive the charm of invincibility and his suspicion began to ebb away. By the time the people prepared for bed he was beginning to wish that *Manang* Juit had offered him the charm instead of Megong.

The morning after was foggy and cold with dew. Megong was too nervous to eat anything his sister had prepared for him. After telling everyone that he would soon return, he got into his boat and paddled downriver. The fog quickly covered him from their view, making it seemed as though he had disappeared into another realm out of their sight.

For the people, the day was spent gathering and hunting for food. Some distance from where they camped, Nuing and Gunggu found wild sago, figs, and jackfruits in an abandoned farm. The rundown hut in the middle of the weed-overrun field appeared to have been made from durable wood, indicating that the previous occupants had planned to live there for many years. In front of it were rows upon rows of tall tapioca plants. Carefully Nuing approached the house, holding the machete in front of him. He climbed the steps and peered inside. Part of the roof had fallen in because the *atap* covering of layered palm leaves had rotted away. The creeping vines and moss covered wall, however, had not been there long enough to cover the tell-tale marks of violence on the walls and floor. A chill shot through Nuing's frame, because he could see the scars of knives and clubs under the splashes of dried blood. He must warn everyone in the camp, and double the sentries for the night.

When night fell, Megong had still not returned. Nuing went to stand next to Nambi who had her face turned downriver. She was straining her eyes beyond the gathering dark, watching out for her brother's return. Nuing said, "I don't think he will return tonight. It is too late. Maybe he will spend the night with the shaman."

"Yes, you are right. I should not be worried about him. He has a proper roof over his head for the night. The *manang*'s magic will protect him and he will sleep better than us." She turned and walked back to the campfire.

Nuing had offered himself for the first watch, and now he took over her vigil of looking down the river. He wondered where Megong was, he wondered if the shaman had sent him away on an errand that would take days or weeks. The land around him began to take on a blinding darkness, so that when he looked up, the sky seemed to be filled with pin-points of light. He searched for the seven sisters of the Pleiades and the three of Orion's Belt, but could not find them. He wondered if his parents had started harvesting their rice crop. A shimmer of silver turned the dark sky a greyish blue. He looked up at the waxing moon. It would be full in another day or two he reckoned. He must remind everyone to look for more food than necessary in the morning so they could take a whole rest day to honour the full moon.

Above him a nightjar called *julok, julok*. As he listened, he began to imagine the moon coming down from the sky in the form of a man. Then he was surprised to see an actual man standing on the surface of the river. He watched as though paralyzed as the glowing man approached him. Once the man had reached his side, Nuing saw that he was a head taller and his shoulders so broad that it was as wide as a door. His face was so fierce, Nuing thought that he was about to be struck dead by the stranger.

The other man, however, only stared at Nuing for some moments then jumped onto a branch and looked down to say, "Why are you still here, son of Bujang Maias?"

"Who are you?" Nuing asked, his voice trembling.

"I am your namesake, Bungai Nuing. You may call me

Sempurai."

Nuing began to tremble. This friend and cousin of Keling's was well-known to him. Unlike Keling, who was heroic, righteous and fair of face, Sempurai was famous for his terrible temper. When enraged, he would turn into a demon-monster and run *amok*, destroying everything in his path. Nuing studied his face carefully, and was relieved to see that it was calm. Tentatively he asked, "What do you mean when you asked why I am still here?"

"Your friend Megong is dead."

Nuing's face paled and he blurted, "That is impossible. He is to become a great warrior."

"He placed his life in the hands of a trickster, so he is dead."

Nuing turned his face downriver, and saw nothing but a chasm of blackness. "How could he have died? The shaman was so confident that he could make him strong, make him invincible."

"Juit claims to know things that are beyond his right to learn. He claims to be a student of Selampandai, the divine blacksmith, but the centipede has never heard of him."

"He is only a frail old man. How could he have overcome Megong, a strong younger man?"

Sempurai peered ahead of him, as though spying into the home of *Manang* Juit through a hole of light in the wall of black night. After a long while, he finally said, "Juit told your friend that in order to make him as strong as iron, his flesh must be tempered like iron. So he burned your friend, who allowed it, and he beat your friend, who endured the suffering to the last of his breath. Believing, believing that he would be formed into someone strong, someone invincible."

Nuing fell on his knees, and he began to feel dizzy. As the horror of what had happened to Megong sank into his psyche, his body sweated and shook like it was fighting a fever then he vomited.

Sempurai leaned down from his perch and said, "You must leave."

"I cannot leave without proof."

"Then you will die." After gazing at Nuing and his immediate vicinity, Sempurai said, "Listen to your guardian spirit. Listen to the snake. It is telling you to run for your life. It is telling you to escape while you can."

"Help me. Help me become like you."

Sempurai threw back his head and laughed. "You are the son of Bujang Maias. You will never become like me. Your spirit sees too much, feels too much. There is no wall between you and the world. You were born as nothing, and you will become nothing."

"Help me. You are a great demi-god of the invisible world. In the name of your friend and brother-cousin Keling, help me. Give me a charm to overcome my cowardice. Give me a charm to overcome my curse."

Sempurai leaned down and gazed dispassionately into Nuing's face then he said, "Let me tell you a little secret: There is no charm in the world that can cure cowardice. Courage is not a lack of fear; courage is the act of fighting in spite of being fearful. The gods are not cursing you, Boy, they are testing you. Know the difference." Then he faded into the night.

Chapter 10

Early at dawn, while the silver of the moon was still in the far horizon, Nuing and Gunggu got into their boat and paddled to the shaman's longhouse without telling anyone, for they were afraid that the animals would tell Juit that they were on their way. By the time they reached the empty landing place, the sky had warmed to a reddish tint.

They moored the boat behind the bathing platform, where they deemed it could not be seen from the house, and carefully climbed the mud encrusted notched log to the dry bank. Nuing unsheathed his *ilang* as quietly as he could because he did not want to startle any animal or insect nearby. Gunggu likewise pulled out his machete. In front of them was a large ficus tree, with wide outspreading boughs and leaves so thick that the shadow beneath the tree seemed like night. Behind it, seeming to be at one with the tree, was a large longhouse. The wide path leading to the house was barren and trampled down to a hard clay surface. Nuing felt his toes curl beneath him as he stepped onto it. Any grass or vine that by some miracle continued to grow within the path was dry and shrivelled. Nuing's face began to sweat profusely when he finally saw the full size of the gigantic long building before them. He started to regret that he had not persuaded more men to join him. The pillar of that house, however, was low and its surroundings seemed unguarded. Though they were stealthy, the ground they traversed was open and anyone who looked out would have noticed them, yet not a single sentry had called to them and demanded who they were. Nuing's breath came shallow and fast, and his hands and feet grew colder by the moment but he forced himself to keep moving forward.

They finally reached the side and found a sloping bamboo ladder which seemed strangely small against the thick pillars holding up the verandah and the large open doorway leading into the gallery. Nuing turned to Gunggu and indicated with a hand over his mouth that they were to remain quiet. He did not want his friend to call out a greeting and warn Juit that they were outside the house.

Nuing climbed the ladder first, keeping his back low. On entering the open doorway, he waved Gunggu up. While waiting for his friend to reach his side, Nuing looked down the long wide common gallery. He saw that the *tempuan*, the path along the walls of the family rooms, were as wide as the whole gallery of his father's longhouse and next to this the *panggau*, the platform upon which bachelors slept and guests were entertained, was as wide as the whole length of his home from the interior room to the sunning verandah. The roof was lifted up to a height of five men and the smallest doorway was at least twice his height. Then his eyes fell on two large brass gongs that were hung from the rafters with the centre boss pressed against each other.

Gunggu tapped his shoulder to urge him forward. With light steps, bent back and sword held ready they approached the gongs. The buzz of flies grew louder as they neared the instruments, and the smell of two-day old blood that had pooled on the floor reached them. Nuing then noticed a bloody rope hanging in between the gongs and looked up. It was empty. Next to this contraption was a smouldering hearth. The stench of charred flesh and ripe blood filled their lungs and shrivelled their spirits. It soon dawned on Nuing that the blood must belong to Megong because the signs of suffering he saw about him were like the tortures described by Sempurai.

Gunggu pointed to the closest door which was slightly ajar. After taking a few swallows of the vile air, Nuing stepped towards it, his hands gripping and ungripping the sweat-covered hilt of his sword. Instead of entering the doorway, however, Nuing pressed himself against the *tiang pemun*, the ritual pillar holding up the door and peered through a gap between them. He saw a large mass in the dim room and, as his eyes got used to the lack of light, he stepped back with terror. Inside was not the tall, undernourished Juit that he had expected. It was a giant, a demon huntsman, with hair so thick that they were like porcupine quills.

Nuing took a deep, silent breath then kicked the unlatched door slightly, and it opened wider. The monster inside turned his head and grunted. "Is that you, *Bunsu* Ribut?" he said. "You should stop coming here to spy on me, Wind-spirit."

As the monster spoke, a foul smell came out of his mouth, filling both Nuing's and Gunggu's mouth and lungs with a rotting stench that they could taste, making them gag and struggle to hold down their nausea.

Sensing that something was not quite right, the monster stood up and opened the door wider. The two men held their ground before him, wielding their swords as they looked up at him with scowling faces. The *antu gerasi* smiled. He licked his lips and said, "I will make a good feast of you."

Nuing stared at the necklace of bone and stones around the monster's neck, and recognized that it was Juit's. Could the shaman have been attacked by this demon, he wondered. Then he saw a still bloody finger bone on the circle the monster was gripping in one hand and realized with a start that Juit himself was the demon.

"You lied," Nuing shouted. "You are no shaman. You are a demon huntsman."

Juit laughed. "That is not true. I am a *manang*, though not of your kind."

"Why are you doing this?" Gunggu asked.

"I need to eat."

"You lied to Megong. You told him that you would make him invincible. You lied," Nuing shouted.

Juit cackled. "You humans are so gullible. You would give anything for a charm, for strength."

"I didn't believe you," Nuing said.

"Yes," Juit said thoughtfully. "I had hoped that you could be persuaded too, but like I said, you seem to have a strong guardian spirit." He licked his lips. "If I eat you, I will eat it too." Then he turned to Gunggu and sniffed. "But you are strange. You smell not alive." His eyes narrowed. "What magic is this?"

Nuing imagined hearing a quiver of fear in Juit's voice and that thought gave him courage. He stepped forward with the sword hanging ready by his side. He gripped it so hard, he felt as though the hilt was burning into his palm.

Juit snarled and threw himself forward, swinging his arm out and smashing Gunggu to the side. Nuing jumped away before the other arm could reach him and slashed down, cutting off a hand. He could taste the smell of blood pouring out of the monster's arm, and his tongue trailed out of his mouth, dripping saliva like a dog anticipating a meal. Gunggu snapped his terror filled gaze from one to the other then turned and crawled away, pressing one arm against his bruised abdomen.

Juit roared and lunged once more. Nuing slashed out and cut a deep wound into the monster's thigh. Juit stepped back, his expression confused. He said, "What metal is this? No iron made by human hand can cut through my skin."

Nuing gnashed his teeth. "This is my father's sword. He used it to kill Taring Ai and I will use it to kill you." He let out a terrible shout and charged straight for Juit's belly. He sliced deep into the flesh. Juit grabbed him by the neck and threw him against the wall.

A torrent of blood poured out of Juit's open wound and he pressed his good hand against it to hold back the flow. Then he roared, mouth wide, showing layers upon layers of razor sharp teeth. Nuing arc his sword upward and cut off half of Juit's jaw. Juit swung his arm out and reached for Nuing's throat and just as he got it in his grasp but before he could tighten his fingers, Nuing chopped the monster's arm off with a fell shout.

Juit let out a howl of rage and pain. He dashed forward with his head lowered like a battering ram. Nuing pierced the sword into his crown, killing Juit instantly, before he was smashed against the column by the momentum of Juit's charge.

Gunggu, who had been watching as though spellbound by their violence, got to his feet and ran to his friend. He dragged on the shoulder of the dead monster and pulled him aside. Nuing was all covered in blood and unconscious. Gunggu cradled him and wiped his face with the tail of his loincloth.

Nuing woke and asked, "Is he dead?"

"Yes, he is, my friend. You have killed him."

Nuing struggled to sit up. Then he reached for his sword

which was embedded to the hilt in Juit's head, and pulled it free. Pieces of brain gushed out with blood. Nuing scooped some of the pale brain matter with his finger and stuffed the mess in his mouth, swallowing it with a shiver. He said, "Your spirit shall never overcome me, for I am not afraid of you. You are nothing but food to me."

With Gunggu's help, he got to his feet. Then carefully aiming his sword against the monster's neck, he cut into it. He had to chop down three times before he could cut through the whole neck. He then went towards the monster's room and pushed the door wide to let the light in. A stench of brine and preserved ripening meat assailed their nostrils.

Both men stepped into the room gingerly. On a shallow trough in the middle of the room was a partially eaten human covered in the jelling ooze of his own blood. Nuing turned his gaze towards the part where the man's face should be but found it smashed beyond recognition.

Gunggu said, "It is Megong."

"We cannot tell."

"The bracelet around his calf, it is the same one that Nambi made for him."

Nuing looked and saw that one bracelet still remained on the body, and he was forced to agree with Gunggu that it cannot be anyone else but Megong.

"What should we do?" Gunggu asked.

Nuing went to one of the preserve jars and opened its lid. He stepped back with a start, for inside barely covered by the fermenting brine were the tip of three human fingers. He closed the lid again, squeezed his eyes shut for a moment then opened them to stare at the line of bark cloth hung up on the wall in front of which the jars were lined. Deciding not to say anything to Gunggu about the hand, he said, "Let us explore the house first. Maybe it will show us what Juit is doing here."

Quietly, like thieves they went into the next room. Here too was the smell of preserved meat coming from jars upon jars lined along the wall, and in the middle of this room too was a trough large enough to fit a man. They went into the room after it and the next one after that, and found the same things in each and every one of them, the only difference being the quantity of jars and the patterns of barkcloth hanging on the wall.

On leaving the fifth room and as they were making their way back to Juit's, Nuing said, "There is no one in this longhouse."

"Maybe humans used to live here and Juit tricked them like he tricked Megong," Gunggu suggested.

Nuing stopped and turned to stare at Gunggu's pale face. His gaze then turned to the nearest door and to the one next to it then back to the first again. A realization dawned on him, as quickly as the blood that rushed back into his face. "None of the *bileks* has a *dapur*. There is no fire hearth in any of the rooms. We humans do not eat our food raw." And he ran. He slammed open Juit's door so hard, it swung on its hinges. He went to the trough, chopped off Megong's head and wrapped it in a cloth he tore from the wall. Then he pulled down another cloth, went outside to the gallery and wrapped Juit's head in it.

Gunggu stood at the doorway, one foot still inside the room and said, "We cannot leave the rest of Megong. They will eat him."

Nuing passed him Megong's head. "But they shall not have his soul."

With each carrying a head between them, Nuing and Gunggu

ran as fast as they could back to the boat. The sky was dark and a storm seemed to be forming in the horizon downriver. They paddled hard against the tide. A spear of light struck the water to their side, soon followed by the roar of thunder that sounded like drums. They paddled till their arms and shoulders throbbed for relief then they paddled harder.

By the time the reached the camp, both men were panting so hard they could not choke a single word out to explain their condition. Even so, the others sensed their panic and instantly called for everyone to return from their wanderings in the vicinity.

When *Akik* Bada knelt in front of a sitting Nuing, the younger man grabbed his arm and, between heavy pants, asked, "How do you stop demon huntsmen?"

"What do you mean?"

One of the sentries, Chaong, opened the larger bundle the friends had brought back and stepped back with a shout. While everyone still stared at the monstrous head in silence, Nambi screamed, "Where is my brother?"

Neither man answered her so Nambi's hands went to the smaller bundle, but Nuing grabbed them away from the cloth and held it close to his chest. "No," he said. "Your brother was a handsome man, and you must remember him that way."

She began to weep. "I must see him."

"He was tricked and eaten by a cruel monster. He would be ashamed to show himself to you now."

Nambi's weeping rose to a wail. Nuing released her hand then turned back his attention to *Akik* Bada. "Please, there must be something we can do. Do you hear that thunderstorm? That is the sound of their drums. If their rooms were any indication, Juit was the smallest monster among them."

Bada's grandfather fell back on his haunches, thinking hard. Everyone around him watched his muttering mouth and closed eyes in silence. "Telichu," he said, opening his eyes. "Telichu, the great grandson of Bejie turned into a demon huntsman while he was out hunting with his brother Telichai."

"How was he killed?" Nuing asked.

"He was not," *Akik* Bada replied, but his eyes shone with hope. "But before he changed, he taught his sister's son how to keep monsters away."

"I think I know the story," Gunggu said. "His nephew was *Manang* Jarai."

"Yes," *Akik* Bada said, his voice trembling with excitement. "Telichu taught *Manang* Jarai to burn the bark of the *selukai* to keep monsters away."

The moment he said that, the sentries ran off to tree after tree until groups of two or three of them each found a custard apple tree and began to strip off as much of the bark as they could. The fragrant grey and brown bark was familiar, even to the youngest of the men, for it was often used to fumigate mosquitoes. The thunder of the drums soon came so close that the ground began to shake, and the men hurried back to camp with whatever bark they managed to retrieve.

On reaching camp, everyone young and old immediately set on beating the bark to soften it. Muja, the sentry standing closest to the river suddenly let out a scream and everyone saw him being dragged by one ankle towards a cloud of darkness gathering at the river bank. Then they saw him being lifted by a giant hand and swung like a sling shot.

Akik Bada grabbed a fistful of bark and burned one end in the fire. When it began to smoke, he waved it over his head and around the body of people who had all by now huddled tight together. There was a loud snap, as though a branch had been broken, and Muja's shouts of terror ceased.

The sudden silence made a few children sob, but they were each hushed by the adult holding them. Imitating *Akik* Bada, Nuing also grabbed a fistful of bark and burned it. Then he went to stand next to the old man, peering into the stormy darkness riverward.

The ground shook and a giant, who was so tall that he hid the waning moon from their sight, came to stand just within the circle of their campfire light. With a growl he said, "You killed my brother."

Nuing swallowed then in a quivering voice that was loud to hide his fear, he said, "He promised a charm to our leader. But he lied then he killed and ate Megong."

The giant grunted. "That has always been the way of my brother. He lures his prey with promises." The giant growled and gnashed his teeth then he leaned down and said, "He was my brother, and I am duty bound to take revenge on his behalf."

Sensing that even the little courage remaining in Nuing was fading fast, *Akik* Bada said, "The young man took revenge for our leader's death. Blood must be paid with blood."

The giant squinted his large eyes and looked from one man to the other. His gaze settled on Nuing and he asked, "I am Sempekang. What is your name?"

Before Nuing could reply, *Akik* Bada pulled him back and said, "He has no name."

The giant leaned his face closer, "Why is he without a name?"

"Because he has no father and no mother."

Nuing stared with confusion at *Akik* Bada but made no effort to argue with him.

The demon huntsman said, "Then I curse you, Nameless. I curse you and all your followers. You will suffer like Padang and his people. As the Pleiades cursed Padang for killing a visiting star-man, so I curse you for killing my brother."

A sudden rage coursed through Nuing's veins, returning to him a courage that was lost at the sight of the army of giants. "I am not afraid of you," he said. "I have killed your brother single-handedly, and if I must, I shall kill you too." He had been hated and reviled all his life, so that Nuing had grown to feel that death and torture was nothing compared to the contempt he had been forced to endure all his life. His senses now heightened by his rage, Nuing instantly realized that the other demons were no longer standing behind Juit's brother. He went to the fire, picked up a burning stick and held it high as he turned his face to the jungle. That was when he saw them, standing around the camp like a wall.

On realizing what was happening, the other members of the group each picked up a bundle of selukai bark to burn, but Gunggu called out, "No, we will run out of bark before daylight."

Sempekang laughed. "Do you think that we will fade like mist under the light of the sun?"

Nuing looked about the camp, his mind quickly going through the limited options available to him. He was even considering giving himself up so the others could continue their journey unharmed, but *Akik* Bada suddenly said, "We have your brother's soul hostage."

Growls and snarls issued from the dark periphery of the camp in response to his words. *Akik* Bada swallowed then said, "If you kill us, we will make Juit's life in the netherworld miserable."

"I will never allow him a moment's rest," Nuing added. "I shall make him clear my fields and weed them. I shall make him hunt for food day and night to feed a great village. He is my slave and I can do anything I wish with him."

The giant roared in rage. "I shall destroy you."

Akik Bada said, "Or you can leave us alone and take back your brother's head."

The giant took a step back and inhaled deep as he considered their offer. He snorted then said, "Very well. I shall leave your group alone for five years if you return my brother's head now. But after that season, if your longhouse is not protected and hedged all about with the spirits of men from across the sea, my people and I shall make sport of you and your descendants forever."

At a nod from *Akik* Bada, Nuing lifted Juit's head which was still wrapped in bark cloth, and placed it at the old man's feet. They stepped back and the giant leaned down to pick it up. Then, after a grunt to the other giants hidden in darkness, he turned his back on them and moved down the river.

The darkness around them suddenly felt less dense and the air smelled less foul. Even so, the people all huddled close to the firelight and continued to burn the fumigant bark until the morning sun appeared in the horizon.

***

As soon as a discussion started in the morning, many in the group insisted that they must continue their journey upriver. Returning to the coast was not an option because it meant that they would have to paddle past the landing place of the demon huntsmen.

Nuing said, "But their leader Sempekang has promised not to

harm us in the next five years."

Akik Bada said, "They are demons, not men. We do not know if they would hold onto their promise. Maybe a few would be tempted to hurt us as we pass."

"*Akik* Bada is right," said Gunggu. "Demons are tricky and debase. They have no respect for the customary laws, and no fear of the gods."

"But this is their river," said Nuing. "They will find us and easily defeat us with the help of the spirits living here."

Akik Bada looked about him thoughtfully, at the river, the trees, until finally his gaze fell on his grandson. He said, "We will find a tributary at the other side then travel down it as far as we can. From there we will walk until we find another stream, which will eventually take us to a large river."

Having all agreed to do as *Akik* Bada suggested, they next proceeded to bury Megong's head at the base of a large dipterocarp tree, in the crook between its buttress roots. The ceremony was simple and done quickly, and no markers were left behind to indicate that it was a grave. Then they crossed the river to the other side and made their way upstream.

Fear propelled them and they all spoke as little as possible when they camped that night. Even the children were silent. *Akik* Bada listened to every call they heard along the way and in the camp, trying to find an omen of either good or evil, but heard neither. It was almost as though the gods had become silent about their fate. On the third day, when they found a tributary, a sigh of relief rose from the people.

The trees were so thick on either side of the banks that after about half a day they found themselves in a dim, eerie tunnel formed from overhanging branches criss-crossed by creepers.

Above them the waxy leaves shimmered, waving the reflected rays of the sun about with every gust of wind. But below, where they were, rootlets hung down from branches, like the shaggy beards of a Malay trader. Here the insects buzzed about them, getting into their ears, their nose and eyes. As the day grew late, mosquitoes added to the torment. That night when they camped, it rained before they could set up proper shelters. They had to sleep in the wet, not just for that night, but for the days after that. One after another, the people began to weaken. Children had to be carried to the boats and those past forty harvestings all complained of aches in their joints. Four days after they left the main Limut River, they were woken by the wails of little Jubang's mother. The baby girl had died during the night, her fever having overwhelmed her.

Their progress after that was slow, for after Jubang, they lost three more children and two elderly adults. *Akik* Bada was beside himself with grief, because one of the adults was his wife and one of the children, his younger grandson. A week later, the stream widened and two days after that, they came upon a river so wide that they thought it was the sea at first. The mouth of the Batang Rajang was filled with numerous islands. Through this maze they travelled, frequently losing their way in backwaters.

The mosquitoes continued to torment them, and the only way they could get relief was to burn wet palm leaves. They had run out of tobacco days before and no where along the banks nor in any of the islands could they find fumigant barks.

Even Nuing suffered under the onslaught of a fever, turning his eyes and skin yellow and making him vomit everything he ate or drank. Soon his body became so weak that he shivered with cold in the heat of day and burn with fever in the cool of night.

Though the strength of the group had been reduced, the people continued to move forward without waiting for the ill to become well again. After her brother's death, Nambi had abandoned their boat and rode with *Akik* Bada's family, but when Nuing caught the fever, she moved to his boat to help Gunggu with the paddling when Nuing slept or to hold Nuing down when he was overtaken with delirium.

When Nuing finally regained his senses, he was surprised to see the thinning mangrove forest about them. He ate some wild fern and water spinach leaves that the women had collected from the forest floor about a half mile inland from their current camp site. That evening he learned that one of the men, Chaong, and a young girl, Tinchin, had also died of the same fever that had weakened him.

Nuing coughed and swallowed back the spittle which still tasted of blood. "The curse of the *antu gerasi* has followed us. We shall all be dead before the end of the fifth year."

Akik Bada looked up to the trees as he tried to recall every word that the huntsman had uttered. Then he said, "He foresaw the house we will build."

Gunggu said, "You are right. I heard him say it too."

"That is why the omen animals have been silent about our fate," *Akik* Bada said, his face suddenly flushed with new hope. "They have nothing else to add to what he had said."

Nuing grimaced. "They should at the very least have told us about the sickness that had taken so many of us."

Nambi said, "We are all cursed. Sickness and death will follow us wherever we go. They have become our keepers. It is useless to hope."

Seeing how forlorn she looked, a sudden need to make her

smile again filled Nuing and warmed his cold fingers and toes. He said, "The *gerasi* promised that we will be protected if we can get spirits to guard our home."

"Spirits of men from the sea. We could barely keep our boats upright when the waves crashed in. How are we to get heads from the men who live there?" Nambi's eyes began to fill with tears.

"I will go. I will find a way," Nuing promised, the belief in his chest overcoming the reason in his head.

Nambi turned her face away, not wanting him to see the disbelief in her eyes. The despair she now felt in her being was weakening her and blinding her to anything that was good or nourishing. She had gone with the other women that morning, but had returned almost empty-handed, for her eyes had gone blind and her ears gone deaf with grief. Nothing received her attention anymore because the thoughts of death and the feelings of despair were too loud to ignore.

"There is a way," Gunggu said. "My father had talked about men who went into ships, and these ships can withstand the waves."

Akik Bada watched the young woman's face and felt an urgency to end Nambi's preoccupation with death as it was taboo and would weaken every member of the group. He said, "The demon has told us that we will build a house, so let us find land to build a house upon."

"The water here is bitter," Gunggu said. "We must find a place where the water is sweeter."

"On a hill," Nuing added. "High up so we can see all around us."

"I want a place with many fruit trees," young Bada said, prompting a laugh from the adults.

"Yes, a fig tree, full of fruits," Gunggu urged him on. "So we will know that the spirits of that land is friendly and welcoming."

Their hearts revived, the people began to joke among themselves and talked of things that they would plant on their new land. The men talked of hunting, the women of planting. All went to sleep that night in good spirit, even Nambi, and when morning came they all claimed to have dreamed of good omens.

Chapter 11

Tawang was the first to see the mouth of the tributary. He stood up on the lead boat and waited for the group to reach him. "Should we go in?" he asked.

Nuing nodded. Then after instructing *Akik* Bada to guide the people to a safe bank, he took three men with him to explore the tributary. It was not a long river and it only took them half a day to reach its end. There were also no signs of anyone else living there, for the jungle on either side of the banks looked as though it had never been cleared. Nuing threw his net in the water and caught about half a dozen fish, one of which was a catfish as large as his thigh. The water here was also sweet, and they could see the pinnated fronds of rattan reaching out towards the stream, and the long thin leaves of bamboos waving against a backdrop of blue sky.

They pulled up the boat onto the clay bank, treading alluvial mud for a yard before stepping on the humus floor of the cool jungle. Just yards away, they found a *kapok* tree that was giving off a sour milky smell. The straight bole tree was almost leafless, and the ground around it covered with brown fruit bursting with white or yellowish cotton.

Tawang said, "The women will be pleased to see this."

"I am pleased to see it," said Nuing with a grin, as he imagined lying on a mattress and resting his head on a pillow filled with *kapok* cotton.

Gunggu laughed and Nuing responded in kind, feeling suddenly lightheaded and free. This place felt like home, for it was welcoming and safe. Then they continued to explore the surroundings, and found edible fern and mushrooms. Shorea trees with tall buttresses and peeling barks of the many colours of the forest filtered sunlight from great heights. They also found the tracks of wild pigs and other smaller animals around the base of the trees. There was plenty of food to feed everyone and an abundance of materials to shelter and protect them, hence it was with joy that they raced back to camp.

A feast awaited them on their return, for the women had found wild jackfruit, figs, and fragrant *sabong* leaves which they had plucked from a gnetum tree. After their meal, during which time the men described the land they saw, the women gathered in a circle and took out the carefully packed sacred rice seeds that had been handed down from mother to daughter since time immemorial. They took out the bundles of grain from multi-coloured tube like baskets then unwrapped them with great care. These were so precious that covers were made for the baskets they were housed in. Then they took out their maize, gourd and cucumber seeds. Each seed was scrutinized by firelight to make sure that no rot had taken hold of their essence. Though some of the vegetable seeds were lost, everyone was relieved to find that the sacred rice seeds were still in good condition.

Before they slept that night, *Akik* Bada prepared some food to offer to the spirits of the land. He woke before dawn and, together with Nuing, took out a small boat and entered the tributary. Those who remained in camp would not say a word about the land to each other, as they waited half-hopeful and half-despairing. They prayed that the omens *Akik* Bada finds would be good, yet on the other hand they also prepared to leave the place at a moments notice in case the omens were bad.

And it was in this restless state of mind that Nambi went into the jungle alone, without a knife. The other women had assumed that she had gone to settle her private toilet, but when she had not returned by the time they were ready to start eating the day meal, they grew worried. Tawang offered to look for her, and while he was yet tying a machete to his waist, she returned with an armload of tapioca roots and a fistful of long tapioca stems.

When asked she explained, "I was looking for firewood when I saw a wild pig. I chased after it and it led me to these."

The women grinned from ear to ear and the men decided not to hunt the pig, believing that it was a spirit who had received them with a welcome gift. They considered this such a good omen that they waited the rest of the day with hopeful thoughts in their minds. Nuing and *Akik* Bada returned just as the dusk had turned to its most golden hue. The two men's smiling faces and the pair of augury sticks which were little more than thin branches were greeted with great joy.

"The white-rumped shama had appeared to you," Gunggu exclaimed.

"Yes," *Akik* Bada said, as he climbed out of the boat with the two sticks in his hand. "Nendak appeared twice to our right and once to our left while we were standing on an incline just yards from the river. It is the perfect place, for we face riverward when we look east."

Another hoot of joy greeted his words, and though the children did not understand the significance of the adult's discussion, they were also glad. Early the next day, the flotilla made their way into the tributary, making a grand noise to silence all bad omens. They finally reached an area that was less than a mile from the mouth of the tributary. Here the land sloped and, as revealed by the mud covered grass and bushes, the tideline only went up to about a yard above the current waterline.

"Why not go in to the very end, Grandfather," Bada asked.

Akik Bada replied, "Because it is taboo to build the next house downriver to this one. We build our first house here, so that if we want to continue to stay at this river, we can build our longhouse upriver to this one. Also, if anyone comes into this river, they will see our house immediately and will know that all the land upriver now belongs to us."

The men unsheathed their machete then walked up the lazy slope, hacking away at the vegetation until they came to a clearing where a large tree had been uprooted by a storm.

"This is the place," *Akik* Bada said. "Nendak had led us here." He lowered his basket to the ground, and laid it to its side carefully for the two augury sticks were inside it.

The men began to hack away at the fallen tree, cutting it into chunks to use for firewood. While the men thus busied themselves, the women cleared underbrush far from any large tree and planted the cut tapioca stems that Nambi had found.

They worked for days, taking turn looking for food and firewood. After they had cut a log for a pillar, the base of the tree was marked so that they would not plant the pillar upside down when they raise it for the house. To *Akik* Bada's sadness, their group was now only eight *bilek* strong. After some discussion, everyone agreed that Nuing should be the chief because he was a headhunter and he had killed Juit, the *antu gerasi*. So in that way, he became the keeper of the source pillar for the longhouse.

On the night before they were to raise the first pillar, and after everyone had gone to sleep, Nuing crept into Nambi's shelter and shook her toe to wake her. He then told her that he would like to take her as his wife.

"But I have nothing to help you with," Nambi said shyly.

"I too have nothing except for my strength."

"You are wise and a chief. You can choose any woman you wish. I am not as skilled or as nimble as the other women. I do not even have the *taya* cotton seeds in my basket."

"You are the only woman I am willing to die for."

"My brother had died for our sake, yet I wish that he still lives."

"If that is your wish then I will live for you."

Nambi laughed aloud then quickly covered her mouth. They both held their breath and listened, but nobody stirred. It was then that Nuing noticed that nobody was snoring too. Everyone lay on their side like stone, without the usual sleep murmurs. He suddenly felt shy and slid away from her shelter to return to his own. Gunggu too, he sensed was only pretending to be asleep. Blood rushed to his head, making his ears feel hot. He wondered how he was to hide his shame from the others when he realized that Nambi had not given him an answer.

The following day, Nuing did his best to avoid Nambi, yet whenever he felt she was not looking, he would steal a look. She caught his gaze a number of times; blushed, smiled, and turned her gaze away.

***

In the day before they had dug the last hole for the pillars of the house, so early that morning they bathed the source pillar with water. This piece of timber would be to their longhouse rooms as the trunk of the tree to its branches. Each family then contributed a pinch of rice seeds which were popped in a hot brass pot. After they oiled the base of the trunk with animal fat, *Akik* Bada sprinkled it with the pop rice as he chanted a prayer. Then a wild fowl was sacrifice and its blood smeared on the base of the same pillar.

Akik Bada next sang invocations to the gods of the Earth, Pulang Gana and his father-in-law Raja Samarugah. He begged Pulang Gana to bless their padi fields and kitchen hearth, and he asked that Raja Samarugah bless them with abundance from the jungle and the river.

Soon after his prayers ended, Garan who was standing next to him said, "We don't have a pig. Our sacrifice is incomplete."

Akik Bada would not look up as he collected the pieces of pop rice which had fallen on the ground onto a piece of large leaf. He also placed the head of the fowl and some of its feathers in the centre of the leaf. "I know what you wish to suggest," he said, "but I will not allow it."

"It will keep our house strong," Garan persisted.

Akik Bada looked up. "Which one of us is it that you wish to sacrifice? Which one of us here do you consider should die so our house will stand strong?"

Garan walked away, his face bowed with shame. He had watched over every child and was as heart broken as the parents when they died of fever or exhaustion. He knew all the adults because each had found food for him and many had nursed him when he had the fever. If only there was another longhouse or village nearby, maybe they could lay in ambush for a member to bring back to the site.

"How long will the house last then?" Nambi asked, for she had heard their conversation.

"It will last as well as the materials we have collected."

Nambi studied the pile of sturdy wood pillars and bamboo planks but her heart was not encouraged by *Akik* Bada's words. She watched him place the leaf and all its contents into the hole meant for the source pillar. She stood aside when the men raised the pillar and slid it into the hole, holding it in position as others filled the narrow gap with soil to fix it in place. Then more pillars were raised from the central one, radiating downriver. When the last pillar to that side was put up, the work continued upriver, radiating out from the centre. Other than the pillars that were erected to hold up the house and roof, the kitchen hearth of each room also had its own separate pillars. The last log upriver was put up an hour before the sun set in the horizon. They ate and rested.

The following day they put up the cross-beams to hold up the floors and the roofs, making sure to place the joint coming from the source pillar atop the one after it. It took them more than a month to build the house, fixing indoor floors, walls, doors, and roofs by turn. As the floors were being installed, joists were also added to the hearth pillars in each room. Racks and shelves were built over and beside it for keeping firewood and for smoking meat and fish. In the meantime the jungle and river provided them with all the food they needed. It was almost as though the spirits had tested them with death and sickness during their journey, so that they could be rewarded with health and abundance on reaching this land.

Slowly the bitter memories in their heart gave way to hope

and on the day when the last thatch roof was put up, the people built a bonfire in front of the house and had a great celebration. Early the next morning, those who had brought the earth from their homeland mixed it with the earth from the new land. These they used to fill their hearth-box which was then carried into the house and fixed onto the hearth pillars. Nuing, being the chief, made the first fire on his hearth and the other members of his longhouse took their fire from his kitchen and carried the flame back to their own rooms. After that the people started to move their meagre belongings into the house making sure to go in either from the upriver or downriver entryway depending on which side their family room was because it was taboo for them to move their belongings across the *bilek* of the chief, which was in the middle of the longhouse.

Two days before they moved into the house, Nambi had accepted Nuing's proposal. The following morning the people rejoiced when they saw Nambi use Nuing's machete, the sign of their agreement to be together. So the *bilek* that was prepared for her was taken by Gunggu, and while she waited for the wedding day, she stayed with *Akik* Bada's family.

On the day of the wedding, young men struck the shells of giant tortoises to make a grand noise that would drown out the call of bad omens. *Nipah* palm wine was served to the groom as he walked the length of the house three times before making his way to *Akik* Bada's veranda, where a shelter had been erected. There he was plied with more drinks and teased with love poetries and riddles. *Akik* Bada then demanded that he recited his family genealogy but since Nuing's father, Bujang Maias was too young to recall the name of his human grandparents and the ancestor preceding them, Nuing was forced to beg for exemption. He also could not recite the ancestral names preceding *Tok* Anjak because the orang utans do not recall or name those who had passed on.

"Well then," said *Akik* Bada, "since *Tok* Anjak had adopted your father, it means that your father's spirit has been replanted among the spirit of the orang utan's family. Nambi has confirmed that none of her ancestors had been adopted by an ape, so we can safely assume that your marriage to her is not taboo."

He turned to look at another elderly man, who nodded his assent in return. Everyone was glad, for many had worried about how the problem of Nuing's broken lineage was to be resolved. *Akik* Bada then led the groom back into the common gallery.

When Nuing stepped into *Akik* Bada's gallery, he was all smiles and ruddy cheeked, having blushed till his ears burned. He sat on a simple mat indicated to him. One day, he promised himself, his bride would have an opportunity to sit on a brass gong, and everyone who looked upon her would know that she was wife to a great man. But for the time being, he would sit next to her on a simple mat.

When the shy bride came out, like him she was led around the house three times to signify that their marriage would be long. Her hair was tied in a bun held down with a porcupine quill and she was dressed in her best: a faded skirt and a many patterned cloth which was slung over one shoulder. She seemed contented enough with her lot when she finally took her place by his side, but Nuing was not. While he waited for her, his gaze fell along the bare undecorated walls. He had built a weaving loom for his sister Lanai before, and he promised in his heart to build his bride one that would surpass the loom his father had built for his mother. He would also clear as much ground as his strength would allow, so she could plant the *taya* cotton for her threads. He turned his face to *Akik* Bada gratefully, for it was the old man had given Nambi his wife's cotton seeds. His granddaughter Lemba was too young to weave and his wife had passed away, so he asked Nambi to care for the seeds for her sake.

A betel nut was brought out and cut in perfect halves. The people rejoiced for it meant that Nuing's love for Nambi was equal to her love for him. Then it was brought into the *bilek* from whence Nambi had come out from.

An elderly woman soon came out of the *bilek*, carrying a basket inside of which the betel nut had been placed. The basket was wrapped in a woman's skirt and the woman who carried it on her back began crying like a little baby. The people laughed, for they saw that the 'child' was a girl which meant that the rice seed of Nambi's family would continue to have a guardian. She kept crying, and a few women called out consoling words meant for a babe. She placed the basket in the middle of the gallery, in front of the bride and groom. *Akik* Bada came forward to sit in front of the basket and began to sing a lullaby to it. After the lullaby ended, he sang another song to wake the 'baby'.

The food served was no different from what they had eaten in the days passed, but it was served in larger quantities and everyone had their fill and some more. It was a good day, and the people were glad when they observed Nuing return to his *bilek* with his bride.

That night, Nuing resolved to become the hardest working man he could physically be. On the first morning after his wedding night, he took his boat out early and together with the other men they searched for farmland along the river on the opposite side. After settling on a side that sloped gently into the river, the group moored their boats and then separated. Some men chose the land close to the river, others like Nuing and Gunggu went farther inland where they found fertile soil. For days they worked, Gunggu returning in the evening with the others, while Nuing remained to work under the light of the moon. He only rested on days of the full moon and new moon. Sometimes Nambi would be with him, helping him clear the underbrush. Though the work was hard, they were filled with hope.

By the time the seven stars of Pleiades started appearing in the horizon to the east in the evening, Nuing's farmland was more than twice that of the second largest piece of land. His people praised him and *Akik* Bada declared that he must be a true descendant of a great pioneer, one such as Busok. Then began the seven day *miring* ceremony when the people made offerings of meat, fruits and wine made of *nipah* palm together with a very small amount of pop rice to Pulang Gana, the god of rice, and Raja Samarugah, the god of land. During that time, a rattan vine was stretched across the mouth of the tributary river, to show that the longhouse was in taboo and should not be visited by outsiders.

Some weeks later, after the sticks and leaves in the cleared fields have dried, and the bamboo shoot, the *midin* fern and *taun* mushrooms began to appear in the surrounding jungle, the people started burning their land. While they waited for the Pleiades to show them the right time to sow their rice seeds, the women planted maize, gourd, cucumber, beans and cotton seeds along the boundary of their land. Many also planted the tapioca plant which was now growing in great abundance about their longhouse. The men started building a temporary hut in their farm, to rest in during the day, and to spend the night in for when the rice ripened.

When the seven stars finally rose to the centre of the sky in the pre-dawn morning, the people all got into their boats and went to the farm. Nambi, like most of the other women, had slung upon her shoulder a multi-cylindered basket which was woven with painted bamboo strips. She had three types of rice seeds, and at the edge of the field she dropped the fastest growing seeds first into the holes that Nuing dibbled. After they had crossed the field from one side to the other in a zig-zag pattern and finished the seeds of the first rice, Nambi began to plant vegetable seeds on the ground, to separate this *padi* from the next one that she would plant. By now, a light shower had begun, drenching the dry ground with moisture. For days they planted in this way, making sure to put a footbridge even over the most shallow drain or stream, so that the spirit of the rice would not be hindered from following them. On the last day, Nambi planted the source *padi*, the sacred rice of her family which had been handed down from her ancestor.

After the seeds had all been laid in the ground, Nuing started building traps around his field. He sharpened pieces of sturdy bamboo and hardened the tip over a fire. The crude arrow was place on a guide lying a few inches off the ground, and held back with another piece of bamboo that had been bent back to act like a spring. He semi-cleared the area in front of the trap and lined the path leading to the trap in such a manner that an animal would be compelled to follow it. Then he planted a bamboo stick with a leaf stuck into it as a warning to any passers-by, so they would know that there was a trap in that area. In places around the field where he planted a *teresang* offering pole, he would place three jackfruit seeds as its base, as per his father's promise to the macaque monkey who had led him to the demon boar Taring Ai.

In this manner he caught some small animals without much

exertion. These were brought back and shared with the rest of the longhouse. His peaceful days did not last long because a little more than a month after he planted the last seed in his field he began to worry once more about the demon huntsman's oath to destroy them. On completing the first weeding ceremony, and while the land was still in its three-day taboo, Nuing placed a shallow basket of smoking and chewing materials prominently in the middle of his common gallery. That evening everyone came to sit in the chief's gallery and once they were settled, Nuing explained his reason for calling the meeting. "I think it is time for me to go to the coast, for a curse still hangs over our heads."

Akik Bada nodded. "There are not many men you can bring with you though. Because even if we have not met with a single other person since we came, it is unwise to leave the house unguarded."

"You are right. That is why I intend to go to the coast and learn if anyone is about to go out on an expedition. I will ask to join them."

Tawang asked, "Who will you bring with you?"

"We can spare no one. I intend to go alone."

"No, you cannot," Gunggu said. "I have left my longhouse to be with you. You shall not leave me here."

Garan, desperate to prove himself a hero to his lady love, said, "No one has ever heard of a chief who goes to war without his followers."

Akik Bada looked at the group of young serious faces from one to the other. Finally he said, "Gunggu is right. He must be with you. I feel that it is his fate to be with you. The rest of the young men, however, must stay because we have just planted our first *padi* crop. If this harvest fails, it will be the end of us all."

Tawang argued, "Ketupong and Beragai have promised us a good harvest. Surely the blessings of the gods will not fail us."

"That is true," *Akik* Bada said. "But neither the rufous piculet nor the scarlet-rumped trogon will help us harvest our rice. If we do not harvest all the panicles properly, in their proper order, the spirit of the *padi* will be angry, and we will not have a good harvest the next time."

A murmur rose among the women, *Akik* Bada was right. It was backbreaking work to harvest the crop. Nuing said, "We will have to help one another. Labour will be paid with labour in kind, or with rice."

Akik Bada nodded. "The *Tuai* is right. Few of us can harvest our fields alone. We need to divide and plan our labours. We will start with the *Tuai*'s field. Because it is the largest and the one that catches the most sun. His large grain *padi* will be the ones which will ripen first. I think we can complete the first part of his field under a day. After that, we will move to the other fields."

"How can I be sure that my field will not be neglected?" young Jering asked, for she too had cleared a small farm for herself even though she was alone. She worked hard day and night because it was the only way she could dull the pain for the loss of her baby.

"Your harvest will not be neglected, *Endu*, I promise it," *Akik* Bada said.

"I will help you," said Garan, who had his farm next to hers. She nodded without looking at him and turned her face to the side with a blush. He too kept his gaze away. He had often helped her in the field, without her asking him to. He dug out the deep roots, fell the large trees, while she on the other hand had cleared the underbrush for him. After he burned both fields, she planted some vegetables on his field too. Then she agreed to plant his rice seeds, which made him glad for she was a woman who had brought a healthy daughter into the world.

Gunggu said, "Well, the durian has fruited, and the smell is very fragrant." His comments on the blooming love between Garan and Jering prompted a laugh from everyone. The two lovers turned their hot faces away and pretended not to understand what the comment meant.

When the conversation returned to Nuing's expedition, the mood was far more serious. The able-bodied men were disappointed that they had to stay but they also understood that they must remain for the rice harvest.

"I promise you," Nuing said to them. "This will not be my last headhunting expedition. Once we know the land about here better and we are more secure, I will lead you in other expeditions."

"If we survive the demons, you mean," Tawang said, dampening everyone's mood for a moment.

"Yes, we must fight the demons first. That is why I must go to the coast, to get heads of men from across the sea."

"It is a pity we do not have a pig," said Garan. "We need its liver for divination."

Akik Bada said, "There are other means. We can do a small *Keduran* ceremony, to persuade the spirits to appear to our two men in a dream." Having said that, the old man got up and immediately prepared food for an offering. He got some meat, vegetables and boiled tapioca, distributed each item evenly into five separate leaf-packets and then placed each of the folded packets into a roughly made small bamboo basket. He chanted a long prayer over the offerings, asking that the gods and spirits guide the two men who were about to begin their journey. That night, one *kelingkang* is hung over Nuing's sleeping place and the other over Gunggu's.

Both men went to bed in high spirits and, on waking the following morning, announced that they had good dreams. A third packet was placed at the bottom of the stairs. After Nuing and Gunggu had each received one of the last remaining packages, they stepped over the third packet at the bottom of the ladder to show that they had begun their journey. Without looking back, they walked down to the bathing platform, got into their boat and paddled downriver. Nuing could feel Nambi's eyes on him, so he squared his shoulders resolving to return to her whole and heroic.

On the first night, they made camp by the riverbank and before they slept, they hung the packets over their sleeping places. Again the dream omens were good the following morning, and they were made glad by it. On the evening of the fourth day, they reached the coast. There they decided to travel north following the shoreline. After paddling along for two days, they came to a small stream that fed clear fresh water into the sea.

That night over the campfire Gunggu asked, "You do not wish to continue northward?"

"I have been thinking," Nuing said, "if we want to get on a pirate ship that hunts for heads then we cannot stop at any of the villages. We must find these *lanuns* in remote places."

"But remote places are many, how do we know which remote place to pick?"

"This is a good place, because there are fresh water and fruit trees."

"It is a good place for us too." The matter thus resolved they started building a sturdier shelter for the night, for they reasoned that they might have to wait for weeks.

Chapter 12

They only had to wait for four days. On spying the ominous black sails coming towards shore, they knew instantly that it was a pirate ship. The *kora-kora*, with outriggers jutting out to either side of the hull, looked like a carrion bird in flight. Nuing stood tall and erect at the shoreline as it neared, his stomach knotted so tight, he could barely breathe. While the ship was yet twenty yards from the sands, the sails were furled. Then he saw five men climbed down to the outrigger to one side and slipped into the water to swim ashore. Nuing gripped the handle of his sword, but did not unsheathe it. Gunggu came up to stand next to him. He too put his hand on his sheathed machete.

The strangers who came ashore all wore black calf-length trousers and had a piece of red cloth wrapped around their head like a circlet. Four men stopped where the water lapped the sand and, like the two Iban men, readied their sword, but one man approached them with both hands held forward, showing empty palms.

"Who are you, Friend?" said the man.

"We were here first," Nuing said, "so it is you who must tell us who you are before we do."

The man smiled and bowed his head. "Of course, my mistake. Forgive me my rudeness. My name is Fakir. I am the navigator of the ship you see out there. We would like to rest here, because the water is fresh and the fruits are sweet."

Nuing crossed his arms over his chest, releasing his hold over the sword hilt. "I am Nuing," he said. "My friend and I are on a *bejalai*. We wish to find a ship to continue our journey."

Fakir nodded his head knowingly. Of course he was familiar with their need to travel, their need to prove to a sweetheart back home that they were adventurous and fearless men. "I have friends on my ship who are like you. They too have joined us in search of fame and fortune. Have either of you ever been on a ship before?"

"No, we have not. But we are not afraid," Nuing said, the frown on his face deepening.

Fakir turned his face to the four men standing at the edge of the sand bank and nodded. One of the men turned and waved both hands wide over his head. About half a dozen men climbed down to the outrigger and began to row towards shore. The low draft ship drew close, and when the keel scrapped against sand, the men paddling on the outriggers to either side, jumped into the water and began to push the craft to shore, onto the sand.

Nuing looked up to the bow, and saw standing there about eight Iban men, all burned dark by the sea and sun. He was glad to see that they were not wearing their war-cap or carrying their shield. A rope was thrown down the side and the men slid down it by turn. As they drew near, both Nuing and Gunggu could see that they were all great travellers, for their thighs and arms were inked with the tattoo of a scorpion, each designed differently to show the region they had been to. Every man also had a design of a crab or a prawn to show that they were protected by these animals from drowning in the sea. Yet the ones that the two friends envied the most were those with rosettes tattooed onto their shoulders and lines drawn on their back of their hands to show that they were men of great courage and heroism.

Neither Nuing nor Gunggu had any tattoos on their body to show their skill or prowess. They felt naked as these other men looked them up and down. They felt like cowards, like young boys who cowered in the hiding places when they sensed danger. Shame overwhelmed them, and they each resolved on their own to not talk about their adventures, or from whence they had come because they were ashamed and fearful that their sires great deeds should be judged by their lack of adventure.

"Little boys," said the man who stood foremost. "Should you not be returning to your mother's breast, *Buat*?"

The others laughed. Nuing's face burned red because the man had called him Boy, instead of the more equal *Unggal*, or Friend. Next to him, Gunggu began to fidget and Nuing, sensing that he was about to give an equally rude retort, quickly made up his mind to abase himself before the stranger and said, "Yes, we are still young in the ways of men. And we are grateful to find others more experienced than us on the ship. We hope that you will teach us and guide us."

The laughter and scorn among the Iban men began to mellow, and the first man again said, "Who are you, Boy? Who has given you a tongue that is sage and wise?"

"My name is Nuing and this is my friend Gunggu. Neither of us has a father or grandfather to guide us. I wish to join this ship because I have promised a trophy for my new bride."

The man turned to look at Gunggu. "And you, Boy, what do you want?"

Listening to Nuing speak had calmed Gunggu's temper, so he too replied in a humble voice, "I too wish to get a trophy, to impress the girls at my longhouse."

"Good," the man said and nodded to Fakir, who grinned back. "I am Rabai. And these other men are my friends. We met during our travellings, and we have been together for more than two years." Though Rabai openly approved of them with his words, his eyes looked them up and down with suspicion. He saw that Nuing was tall and his eyes grey, and he also noted the strange tones of Gunggu's skin. They spoke and dressed like Iban men he thought, but they did not look Iban.

Fakir returned to the boat and Rabai followed him. Once they were out of earshot, Fakir asked, "What do you think of them?"

"It is hard to say. They do not behave in the usual manner of young hot-headed men. They are humble and deferential, almost as though they have grown up in the presence of gods."

"You think they are not of this world?"

"I do not know. Even if they were slaves, they would have told us their sire's name."

"Maybe they are keeping it secret out of shame."

Rabai scoffed. Then in a more serious tone he added. "They are not like any Iban I have ever seen. That one Nuing has fair skin and is tall, like a Kenyah from the highlands, but his eyes are grey, like a thunder cloud. Gunggu's arm looks dead but he moves it like a normal arm."

Fakir placed a hand on Rabai's shoulder. "They are just normal men, my friend. They will bleed, you'll see."

Rabai turned his frowning gaze back up the beach, to where Nuing was helping the newcomers pile more firewood into a small campfire that was already there. Damp leaves and bark was added to create smoke. Over this, four Iban pirates placed a horizontal stick held up at either end by a thick branch. Then they hung up three fresh heads along its length. In the meantime, Gunggu showed the other three men where they could find ripened fruits. When he returned with these *lanuns*, he too watched with awe and envy the three heads being smoked over the fire.

Two of the Iban men, Lusong and Bangki, regaled them with stories of their adventures. "Yesterday we went to a fishing village," Bangki said, one finger playing with the sand. "We heard that it was a big place, with at least thirty families. Traders often stop there for food and water, so they were rich. But when we got there, we only found these three."

Nuing noticed the white hair and wrinkled skin of the heads for the first time. He wondered if all three were sick or dying when the pirates found them but he did not ask the question, for that would be a rude challenge to the man's courage. A life was a life after all, regardless of its age.

"I think many are hiding," Lusong commented, "because the village was empty when we reached it."

"Maybe they were all out fishing," Nuing suggested.

"No, there were at least twelve boats on the shore. What manner of fisherman goes out fishing without his boat? Anyway, even if they did go out, there would still be women and children left in the village," said Lusong.

Bangki added, "Panta also said that he saw a lot of people running on the beach." He turned his face to Lusong, "That was why he wanted to go deeper into the surrounding jungle to look for them."

"Yes," Lusong said, "It is a pity Syed Ahmed would not let us. Rabai is not happy because each time after the *lanuns* got what they wanted they rushed us back to the ship. What is the point of us going with them if we cannot get heads?"

Gunggu turned to Nuing and said, "Maybe we should wait for another ship."

"You needn't have to," Rabai said from behind, prompting the men to turn their faces and look up. Then he sat down on the sand next to Nuing and said, "I have told Fakir that we are unhappy. He said that the north easterly wind has started bringing merchants from Sina."

"The land of the flying serpent," Nuing said.

"You have heard of it?" Rabai asked.

"Just stories from an *Orang Laut* who used to trade at our longhouse," Nuing said. "The Malay merchant had never been to Sina, though he claimed to sell goods from there."

"Your longhouse must be rich," Bangki said. "A merchant would not trade with you unless you can buy their brass and silver at the very least."

Gunggu turned with a smile to Nuing. When he noted that his friend was not making any attempt at all to give more information on the riches of Bujang Maias's longhouse, he too remained quiet on the subject. Rabai studied their poor and threadbare loincloth then his gaze stopped on the ivory carved sheath of Nuing's sword. Again he wondered about them.

Partly out of curiosity and partly due to the need to end the awkward silence, Nuing asked, "What is a Sina ship like?"

Pointing to the single-sail *kora-kora*, Rabai replied, "It is far bigger than the one we are on now."

"They also have fire-spitting guns," Bangki added.

"We have a pair too," Lusong interjected, "and they spit more iron and fire than any other I have seen."

Tiong who had been quietly listening by the side since he

heard the word Sina mentioned said, "My father told me they also shoot arrows of fire."

"Like children," Lusong said with a sneer. "A true man would use a blowpipe."

Rabai was the only man who did not laugh. He frowned and said, "I have seen their arrowheads. The iron is so sharp and thick, you could use them for a spearhead."

After some moments of thoughtful silence, Nuing asked, "But arrows are often lost. Do they collect them back?"

"No, they don't," Rabai said. "I own a few of the arrowheads. They cut so deep, they can shatter bone. I have one of their bows, from a man I killed. The string is so tight and has to be stretched so far back, that no man of average strength could make an arrow fly from it."

"How far can one fly?" Gunggu asked, about the arrow.

"At least for the length of 12 doors. When I shot one across my verandah, I killed a chicken 12 rooms away from where I was standing. *Apai* Mang asked that I compensate him with the arrowhead but I gave him my favourite fighting-cock instead."

After a good laugh with the other men, Panta added, "I have seen a small bow, but it is very bulky and the string almost impossible to pull."

"Fakir has one too," Rabai said. "He showed me that it can shoot an arrow farther than the large bow I have. You have to put it down on the ground and use both hands to hook the string to a trigger."

"Like our animal traps?" Nuing asked.

"Yes, very much like it."

"What about swords? Do they have swords?" Gunggu asked.

"Yes, they do," Rabai said. "Some of their swords are very

strange because you can cut with the back of the sword too."

The other men nodded their heads seriously as their minds digested the information. One remarked that it must be useful to have a sword that could kill no matter which way you swung it, another wondered if it could pierce like a spearhead, so thus they discussed weaponry until the sun set in the horizon. Then they built another fire and started to cook their meal over it. The conversation continued until after dinner when Fakir the navigator and Syed Ahmed the owner of the ship joined them.

"Where did you get your fire-spitting gun?" Nuing asked. His mind set on obtaining one to protect his longhouse from the demon huntsman who had promised to look for him and his people.

Fakir laughed then frowned when he noticed the serious look on Nuing's face. Syed Ahmed sipped some more of the spiced-scented boiled water and said, "I got mine from a Sina ship. I overtook the ship and killed everyone in it." He did not tell them that the sailors barely put up a fight because the ship had been caught in a terrible storm and most were debilitated by disease that made the men weak and incapable of holding down food or water.

"How many heads did you get?" Nuing asked.

Syed Ahmed chuckled. "Our God and women do not need heads, so we only look for gold, silver, brass and jars to please them. We all need food though, so the food will be shared among us."

"It seems wasteful to just leave the heads," Nuing said.

"The heads go to us," Rabai said, "But lately we seem to collect more jars than heads."

Fakir grinned. "Don't worry, rain have started along the

coast. The Sina traders will be sailing down this way soon. None of their heads will be able to escape from you because there is very little place to hide in a ship."

Gunggu and Nuing shared a look. Each could tell that the other was not happy with the prospect of fighting in a ship. They wondered if it was possible to stand on their feet as the ship rocked on the surfs. Yet neither voiced their feelings because they did not want to show just how inexperienced they were compared to the other men.

The pirate ship was beached for a week and during that time, the bottom of the ship was cleaned of wormwood and barnacles. Both Nuing and Gunggu were also taught how to sit on the outriggers and how to row from there. It took them some time to overcome their fear of climbing out to the outspreading rig, but they were too proud to admit their fears so that soon they too were as agile as the least of the pirates.

For days they watched the surfs and the grey skies. They also smelled the wind and tasted it in the sprays that hit their faces in the morning. Then one day a dark spot began to grow beyond the horizon. The men ran to their ship and began to push it off the sand. Then Fakir and Syed Ahmed, together with all the headhunters and some of the pirates climbed into the ship. Others sat on the outrigging of the *kora-kora* and started to paddle.

The lone junk-boat was of medium size. Fakir saw the flaps of the main lugsail being lowered. He ordered his men to ready the two cannon guns. Syed Ahmed noticed a plume of grey smoke rising from the main deck, and realized that the merchant had lit the fire source of their cannons and arrows. He ordered that the rowers give the ship a wide berth and bring the *kora-kora* upwind. As the pirates passed, the cannons on the merchant ship fired. The rowers to the port side were splashed and one fell off his seat. The man grabbed onto the outrigging that passed him by and dragged himself up onto it. After passing the oncoming boat, the pirate ship turned and cut into the merchant's wake.

Fakir looked up to the row of flags strung down from the topmast to the bow of his ship. Each was pointing forward. He smiled, for the wind was now on their side. Even if the merchant ship was to shoot fire-arrows at them, the wind would blow these missiles short, or even back into the ship itself. A frown returned to his face when he saw the Chinese lugsail being raised again.

Syed Ahmed ordered that their sail too be unfurled. The *korakora* sped forward. It was low draft and soon caught up with the heavier merchant ship. Fiery arrows shoot towards them but only a few touched the deck. These were immediately put out by one pirate or another. Nuing's face began to flush. He gripped the sword in his hand so tightly that the knuckles showed white. Gunggu stood right behind him, ready to spring forward, and to his left and right were the other Iban warriors. The pirates stood behind them.

The bow of the pirate ship crashed into the stern of the merchant's. The Chinese sailors gave out a terrible roar as they rallied themselves to face the pirates. The headhunters scrambled into the Chinese ship racing against each other for heads. With each kill they shouted to indicate to the others that the head belonged to them.

When Nuing cut down his second man, he felt a sharp pain in his shoulder. He broke the small arrow, leaving the head inside his flesh. When he again looked up he saw Rabai, arms raised to strike down a sailor, suddenly pierced by a long arrow through his chest. He turned his gaze farther up and saw the line of archers hanging onto the spars, shooting down at them. Nuing felt another sting, this time in his shin. This arrow, however, had only grazed him. He looked back to their ship and saw that the pirates had not come aboard to help them. Rage suddenly took hold of him, for they called themselves comrades but now they were proven useless. Nuing swung his sword against an advancing sailor and at the same time tried to find cover under the torn lugsails. Smoke had begun to cover the deck because a barrel of pith had spilled and was now spreading fire like a slow lava flow. Nuing looked about for Gunggu and, on finding him, hurried to his side. By now the arrows had stopped flying because the thick smoke made it hard for the archers to tell friend from foe.

Panta ordered a retreat because there were too many Sina sailors to fight off. Nuing returned to the stern and found the three men he had killed. He cut off their heads with one blow each. Gunggu cut off one. Just as they were about to climb back into the *kora-kora*, a Chinese man lunged at them. Gunggu cut him down with a yell and took off his head.

They managed to get back on the ship just as it was pulling away. One headhunter, Tiong was left behind in the merchant ship. Nuing's blood chilled when he heard the man shout for help, and he stared as though mesmerised when a group of Chinese men started to beat him with clubs and fists. If both he and Gunggu were but only a pace slower, they would have been left in the merchant ship too. Nuing could hear Fakir urging the rowers on as he watched Tiong being cut down by half a dozen men.

Nuing was not the only one staring with horrified silence at the violence unfolding before him, for other than Fakir's voice giving out orders to press their retreat, everyone on the *kora-kora* was silent. All eyes were on Tiong's and Rabai's body as they were strung up then set on fire. Gunggu called out and pointed, and they could see that a triangle sail had been raised and the ship was starting tacking manoeuvres to move upwind. The merchant ship was giving chase.

Syed Ahmed yelled at Fakir, "Take us to the nearest shallow river!"

Fakir redirected his order and turned the rudder shoreward. He knew which river to take them to, and he prayed that the tide was high enough to allow them through the sandbar but low enough to stop the heavier merchant ship.

Nuing turned to Panta and said, "Rabai said that these merchants are an easy target. Yet he is killed on that ship."

Panta stared wide-eye at the other ship then his brow furrowed with confusion. "This has never happened before. Always they would surrender and usually we have to argue with Syed Ahmed because he would not let us kill the prisoners. He always let those who surrender go free."

Nuing gave Gunggu a look. Then he wrapped the long braided hair of the heads he had taken tighter around his hand. What if the other Ibans guessed that they were curse-bearers? Would they be able to escape? Would they have time to escape? Both men looked about them at the desperate activities of the other men. Then they looked to the shoreline just yards ahead.

The ship hit a sandbar and for a breathless moment, Fakir was silent. Then he ran to the side, looked down and ordered the rowers to get off their seats and see if they could push the *kora-kora* over the sandbar into the river. More men jumped into the river to help them.

Nuing and Gunggu put down their sword and trophies then went into the water. The sandbar was soft, and Nuing found that if he dug in his foot deep enough, he could collapse part of the sandbar. He shouted and told everyone to dig with their feet. Soon enough water started to collect under the boat, and it began to glide over the sand.

A canon on the Chinese ship boomed, smashing into the stern of the *kora-kora*. Fakir screamed in pain. More cannons blew, hitting the water and part of the ship. The men kept pushing and Nuing could feel his wounded shoulder growing stiff. A sudden dizziness almost overwhelmed him. He splashed water on his face. He must go on. He could not stop because Nambi was relying on him. He must bring back the heads for her, for his people. He must protect them from the demon huntsmen.

After what felt like an eternity, his feet began to tread water. Following Gunggu's example, he climbed up the outrigging and made his way back into the boat. Two gaping holes were now on the open deck and a large portion of the stern was gone. A man hovered over Fakir who was now covered in blood and burning flesh. Even from where he stood, Nuing could see that the white of Fakir's eyes were showing, but he was still alive because he was trembling violently.

A single cheer went up, and a handful of weaker ones trailed after it when the pirates saw that the merchant ship was now turning away from them and returning to the deeper parts of the sea. Nuing went to the bow and was relieved to find that the five heads were still where he had left them. He took Gunggu aside and they squatted down next to the heads.

Nuing said, "We must leave these people."

"They will suspect us."

"They don't suspect who we are yet. But they will be asking questions soon. If they learn that we are cursed…"

Gunggu wiped his eyes to indicate that Panta was coming towards them.

Nuing turned and looked up. He cocked his head towards Fakir. "That looks serious."

Panta squatted down next to him. "Kamal says that he will not survive through the night." He fidgeted with the tail end of his loincloth. "This is the first time that anything like this has ever happened. We have never lost this many people before."

Ujan joined them. He used a rag to cover a gash on his face. "This is the first time I've charge a ship with so many soldiers."

"There are usually not these many?" Gunggu asked, like a man suddenly given an opportunity to save himself.

"No," Syed Ahmed said, his tall shadow casting over them. He turned to Panta. "Did your gods say nothing to you?"

"The omens were normal this morning. None of my men had reported a bad dream. You two did not see any bad omen did you?"

Both Nuing and Gunggu shook their heads.

The drifting boat scratched against a bank and came to a sudden halt. Syed Ahmed barely swayed where he stood. "We will camp here tonight."

The men got off the boat and waded to shore. Fakir, still alive, was lowered with a rope. Gunggu helped Nuing pry out the arrow head from his shoulder, which thankfully was not embedded deep in his flesh. It was deep enough, however, to cause profuse bleeding. Just a few yards from the bank was a cluster of banana trees. Panta looked for a few ripe fruit and mashed the skin. Then he and Gunggu smeared this onto Nuing's shoulder, holding it in place with a leaf strapped down with a raffia string.

Gunggu then joined Panta and two other Ibans to search for

firewood. Not long after Gunggu returned with an armload of wood. Nuing started a fire and, after he got the fire to blaze, one of the pirates came to him and asked for a flame. Nuing gave him a burning stick, allowing the pirates to start their own fire.

Without taking his eyes off them, Nuing asked Bangki, "Are they always like this?"

"I have not seen them build a fire," Bangki replied.

"That is not what I mean. Do they ever do things on their own?"

"They let us ride their ship and allow us to take the heads."

"But they did not fight with us today," Nuing said, with more ferocity than the remark need cause for because he was trying to lay the blame of the day's failure on the pirates.

"They do, but only towards the end. They want to give us the opportunity to take as many heads as possible."

The rationale behind Bangki's explanation was sound to Nuing but he still needed to find a way to prove to himself that it was not his curse that had killed Rabai and Tiong. He noticed Syed Ahmed watching him, so he turned his face away. By now the foraging Ibans had returned with more firewood and a deer. Nuing immediately set himself to the task of preparing the meat.

The Ibans who were not involved with the cooking, built a third fire that was some distance from the campsite and started to smoke the heads they got. Keeping the flames low, they kept adding bark, twigs or leaves that smoked so much the heads were often hidden from view.

When dinner was ready, two men stayed behind to tend to the smoke. Syed Ahmed then invited Panta to join his group of pirates for a meal. This was Rabai's place before, so Panta was anxious to appear worthy.

After Panta had taken his seat next to the pirate leader, Syed Ahmed asked, "What do you know of those two men?"

"They are pioneers, looking for heads to give their brides, I think."

"Strange. Warriors on expedition usually travel in a group."

"Not so strange if they come from a small community."

"But don't you usually band up with other adventurers from another village?"

Panta was silent for a long while as he pondered over the question. Syed Ahmed was right. Every warrior knows that there is strength in numbers, and young men were always looking for opportunities to prove themselves.

Using the knowledge that he had learned through his long association with the headhunters, Syed Ahmed said, "Maybe they are here to break a curse. It could be possible that no one wants to join them because they are under a curse." He waited for Panta to reply, but when the other man remained silent, he continued, "We have never had such bad luck before. The presence of you and your men is a great blessing to my enterprise. None of my attacks have failed since you joined us."

"You are right. Something is wrong with those two." Panta turned to eye Nuing and Gunggu suspiciously.

Syed Ahmed started to roll a cigarette. "I hope you will get rid of them. I cannot ask any of my own people to do it because one of you might feel compel to take revenge."

Panta nodded with a deep frown on his forehead. Then he got up and returned to his men.

Syed Ahmed watched him take two of them aside for a conference. Kamal came to sit next to him and reported, "Fakir is gone. Should we bury him tomorrow?"

"No, it must be today, before the sun sets." He turned his gaze back to the Ibans.

"Are you expecting trouble?" Kamal asked.

"I was, but I think the problem is now settled."

Kamal nodded and moved away, to make burial preparations for Fakir. The Ibans watched with curiosity as Kamal washed Fakir's body and wrapped it in a piece of cloth. Then they stood some distance away as the pirates buried him in an unmarked grave in the jungle.

It was Nuing and Gunggu's turn to watch the smoking fire next. Gunggu smacked away a sand fly from his shoulder. He looked about him restlessly.

"You feel it too?" Nuing asked.

Gunggu looked towards the other fire, and the men watching them turned their eyes away. "I think they are watching us. Maybe they don't trust us. We will just have to earn it from them."

Nuing nodded then returned to tending to the smoke. He stared into the flames, wondering when their troubles would end. Then he saw a black paw stretched out of the fire and scratched the sand, making a hole that was fast filling with water.

Nuing panicked, for if the water got into the fire it would ruin the smoke. He leaned forward and reached out to cover the hole, but instead he fell in. Nuing jumped to his feet and found himself in a dim clearing surrounded by a wall of darkness. It felt vaguely familiar, and when he saw the fire, he suddenly remembered that he was back in the spirit world.

Then he saw him, *Bunsu* Jugam, coming out of a fog that surrounded the clearing like a fence. The human form of the sunbear spirit approached the fire and sat down. Nuing took a seat next to him.

"You will die tonight," *Bunsu* Jugam said.

"How do I stop it from happening?"

Bunsu Jugam stared into the fire for a long while. Then he said, "You can make Gunggu die in your place."

Nuing jumped to a stand. "Impossible. I would sooner die in his place."

"That may be so, but Gunggu does not have much longer to live. He only ate one fruit when he was in the home of the greater coucal spirit."

"I will not kill him."

"You don't have to kill him. You only need to let him die in your place."

"Friends do not do that to each other."

Bunsu Jugam growled under his breath. "It is the way of men." He looked back into the mist behind him, and cocked his head to listen. "Do you hear that? It is the call of a dead man. He is still looking for his warriors. Can you hear him?"

Nuing listened hard and heard a faint voice in the breeze. His eyes widened with recognition then his face frowned with grief. He could hear *Tuai* Aso calling for Jantan, for Kuti and for himself.

"You let him die," *Bunsu* Jugam said. Nuing sat back down and made no effort to respond to the accusation. "When his men cited bad dreams you did not pull out of the expedition. Instead you made him go into a fight with a small number of men. Every expedition leader knows that you cannot take down a Kantu longhouse with less than sixty men."

Nuing could feel despair oozed out of him like sweat. The faint voice in the distance echoed inside him, over and over until it felt as thick as the smoke enveloping him. A hand shook his shoulder and he looked up with a start.

Gunggu's face stared down at him. "Are you well? You should go and rest. I can watch the fire on my own."

"No. You go and sleep first. You can take the next watch."

"But Bangki and Lemetak will be doing the next watch."

"I know," Nuing said, his voice barely above a whisper, "but we must make sure that at least one of us is awake the whole time." He looks towards the other Ibans, and sure enough two of them were awake and watchful. Panta smiled when he caught their eyes.

"Very well," Gunggu said. "I will lie here next to you."

Nuing sat a little away from the fire, so he could get a wider view of their surrounding. It was a quiet but tense night for everyone. None of the men bother to smoke their cigarettes to keep the mosquitoes and sand flies away because they needed the annoying insects to keep them awake.

Nuing was to see the dawn break through the horizon. Though he had lain down after waking Gunggu and had pretended to sleep when the next two men took over, he could find no rest. Before breakfast, Gunggu went into the jungle under the pretence of collecting firewood but he returned with an armload of palm leaves.

"Is it not too soon to take those?" Panta asked and pointed to the fronds.

From behind him Nuing replied, "We have been away from home for a long time. We hope to return in time to help with the harvesting."

Panta shrugged. "I hope you find your folks well."

Gunggu squatted down in front of the fire, and after Panta walked away, Nuing also did likewise, but on the opposite side of the fire so they could both watch each other's back. Gunggu wrapped the first warm head. None of the Ibans came to them to offer advice or help. This again was confirmation to Nuing that his dream was right. He could feel them watching him, waiting for the right moment to strike. Since neither Gunggu nor he was from the same community as Panta and his men, there would be no taboo to hold back the pirate Ibans from killing them. Nuing was now wrapping the fifth and last head. Still no one had come to talk to them.

They put the heads into their basket, three in Nuing's and two in Gunggu's then they went and joined the Iban group at the campfire proper. Their smiles, Nuing saw, were a little too friendly. He was hungry, but he did not dare eat the food they put in front of him and Gunggu because it was taboo to eat the food prepared by your enemies.

"We will be leaving after this," Gunggu said.

"That is a pity," Bangki said. "We are short of men now."

Nuing nodded but made no effort to reply. From the corner of his eye, he watched Panta walked to his weapons and pulled out his sword. Nuing began to tense as he calculated how fast he could reach his basket if Panta and his men were to suddenly attack them.

Nuing smacked Gunggu's shoulder loudly and got to his feet. "Come. We must start our journey now before the day gets too late."

Just before Gunggu could get to his feet, there was a sudden shout behind him. Panta's claim of his head, however, was thwarted by Nuing who blocked his arm. Gunggu got to his feet and together with Nuing took a few steps back.

Nuing said, "We don't want any trouble. Let us be on our

way."

Panta's mouth foamed as he said, "My friends are dead because of you. We don't even have their bodies to bury."

"That is a terrible accusation," Nuing said, with more conviction than he felt, "What proof do you have?"

Bangki replied, "Nothing like this has ever happened before. Our raids had always been successful. Some among the pirates may have been killed before, but nobody from our house has ever been killed."

Gunggu said, "Maybe your pirate friend has miscalculated this time."

"That is impossible," Syed Ahmed retorted. He had been listening to their argument from the side. "I am a *Tuai Kayau*. I have led many Iban warriors to war, and I have always won."

Panta's men began to close rank behind their leader as he advanced. Nuing and Gunggu moved back, towards their pack and weapons.

The men suddenly charged with a loud shout. Nuing ran the last few steps, pull out his *ilang* and turned to face the onslaught. Gunggu, he saw, had received a cut across his shoulder that was now bleeding down his back. Nuing gave out a terrible shout and attacked. He met each stroke they threw at him and drove them back because he was more desperate than them. He used quick jabs, so that when they swung their sword, his blade would cut into their flesh. He felt rather than saw Gunggu fighting with mounting desperation next to him. The Ibans pulled back, surprised that Nuing and Gunggu had managed to fight off their combined attacks.

Seeing their hesitation, Syed Ahmed signalled to his Malay pirates. They each picked up a spear or sword and approached the foray. Nuing jerked his head back and Gunggu retreated with him. They slung their baskets over a shoulder, all the while keeping their eyes on the advancing men. Then they turned and ran.

The friends dived into thick foliage and it immediately closed behind them. Though they could now not see their pursuers, they could hear them closing in. To one side of the undergrowth they were traversing was a wall of tall, thick fern and behind it a dense curtain of liana vines. Nuing dragged Gunggu through it then they both dropped down to the ground and crept to the side, hunkering low under the gaping root of a fig tree. The voices crashed past them and soon began to fade to a safe distance. Nuing touched Gunggu's arm. They listened then Nuing pointed to a direction. They sneak forward furtively, making sure not to disturb the foliage. Suddenly there was a shout some distance behind them. Lemetak had found their tracks.

Gunggu grabbed Nuing's arm. "You must go, without me."

"We will go together," Nuing whispered back vehemently.

"You have a better chance than me. You know how to travel in the canopy, like your father."

"Then you will come with me too."

"I cannot climb like you. I will fall and break my neck sooner than I will die by their sword."

Nuing began to weep. "You are my friend. I cannot ask you to do this."

"You are not asking me. I am telling you." The voices drew closer. Gunggu unstrap his basket and slung it over Nuing's shoulder. "I have died once. This time I will cross the bridge and not look back." He pushed Nuing towards a tree under a layer of thick creeping vines. Then after making sure that Nuing had climbed to a height where he could no longer be seen from below, he ran to his left. Gunggu could sense that their pursuers were close because they were now silent. But the moment he started running, he could hear them give chase with whoops and yells. The hilt of his sword felt slippery from sweat, and he gripped it harder. He began to weep with fear and started to look about for a tall tree to climb. But then he remembered why he must keep running, away from the trees, from the canopy which was his friend's only safe escape route. A terrible shout cut into his spirit and he felt a force fall on his back, and the ground came up to meet him. A deafening roar of water filled his ears and he struggled for breath. He felt a sharp pain and a loud snap then there was silence.

Chapter 13

Nuing tried to peer through the leaves and vines cocooning him but his gaze could not penetrate through their many layered veil. He almost released his hold on the branch when he heard a shout of victory, soon followed by Gunggu's cry. There was no mistake what that shout meant. Gunggu was lost to him forever, and instead of tending his own farm in the afterworld, his soul would now be enslaved to the man who killed him. A tightness in his chest choked Nuing and he struggled to breath. Then he began to tremble violently as he struggled to contain his grief.

Below him Panta shouted, "We have your friend's head. He is my slave now. Come out if you want it back."

"He is a coward!" Bangki called, "That is why he left his friend." There was laughter.

Nuing clawed the branch so hard his fingers bled. One part of him wanted to shout back a challenge but another part reminded him of his duty to his people. He must bring back the five heads else the *antu gerasi* would kill everyone in the longhouse. He would be a coward for their sake. Then he corrected himself, as he suddenly realized that he would do anything to see Nambi happy. For her, he would bore this curse and pain willingly.

The voices below him started to fade as the men moved away. Nuing listened hard to his surroundings. When he could again hear the call of birds and insects, he climbed higher up the tree. Higher and higher he went, until he was forced to crawl out of the vines onto a branch because the roots were becoming ever tighter around the trunk. Nuing could now see the river from where he was, so he decided to move away from it. His progress was slow because he was burdened by the two baskets and his grief. When it became too dark to move between the branches, Nuing built a nest the way his father had taught him. He was exhausted and he lay on his back the whole time but he could not sleep. The worst part was that he dared not sing a lamentation to his friend because he was afraid of being heard. All he could do was sob silently.

Up in the canopy he travelled southbound for days until he felt that he was beyond the reach of the pirates. Then he climbed down and continued his journey on the ground. On reaching the expansive Rajang River two weeks later his senses heightened. The pirate ship would have no problem sailing down this place, he realized, for the river was so wide the line of trees to the other side was only a thin line in the distance, and the river so deep that even a man with the strongest lungs cannot dive down to touch its bottom. After he built a simple raft from bamboos, he waited for nightfall because he could not be sure that Gunggu had never told the pirates where they were from. When darkness finally fell and the tide started moving inland, Nuing slid the raft into the water then lay down flat on it, making himself almost level with the water surface. The cold water laps his face and moistened the smoked heads, but he did not care. The raft moved inland, carrying him steadily along with the tide.

Shivering from the wet and cold, Nuing drifted in and out of sleep. Dawn eventually came to light the horizon after the seemingly endless night. Nuing looked back, and, on seeing that there was no boat behind him, sat up stiffly. He was soaked to the bone and trembling so violently his teeth chattered and his joints felt twisted but he was alive. With a piece of halved bamboo he began to paddle to shore. The tide was changing and moving back to the sea, so he decided to go to shore first to get his strength back. On reaching land, he pulled the raft out of the water. For a long moment he stared at the placid ochre river, numbly wondering what he should do next. Gunggu had always been the practical one, not him. Then as though driven by a need outside of his own will, Nuing went into the jungle to forage. He found a bunch of ripe *jambu bol* and ate his fill. The acidic taste of the ball-shaped red fruit was refreshing and revived his spirit. He searched about him some more and came across a tapioca plant. He pulled out the tuber roots, cleaned the soil off it and started to eat it raw. It tasted bitter and sweet at the same time. After swallowing a few mouthfuls, he began to feel sick and he vomited.

Nuing tried to stand up but his surroundings began to spin in a dizzying manner. He lay down on his side and began to pant to try to control the nausea. Slowly he drifted off to sleep. From the red bushes behind him came a loud snort. Nuing jumped up on all fours and crept into the bush. He sees a wild pig, a female, digging roots, eating some, then replanting the rest.

The female senses him and asked, "Do you like the roots I planted?"

"It is nice, but it makes me ill."

"That is because you are a human. You cannot eat the white powder that grows naturally in the tubers. It is poison to you."

"Am I going to die?"

The pig turned to look at him. Though her snout was covered

with dirt, Nuing could see that she was very beautiful.

"Will you marry me?" she asked.

Nuing was taken aback, but he dared not laugh aloud at the ridiculous idea because it was taboo to laugh at an animal. Kindly he said, "I am sorry, but I am already married to another."

The pig snorted in contempt. "That woman is barren. She cannot bear you children. The *padi* she plants will not grow well."

"But it is her brother, not her who is cursed."

The pig came to stand in front of him. "My name is Gema. I am *Bunsu* Babi, the youngest of the seven children of the pig king. My gift is in planting roots. Everything I plant grows abundantly." She watched his face change from shock to wonder. "If you marry me, you will have many children."

"But my father tells me that it is taboo for a man to marry an animal."

Gema snorted angrily. "I can be a human if I want to. I can also change you into a pig if I want to."

Nuing edged back slowly. He didn't want to anger a spirit, especially one who could appear in his dream. Gema seemed to sense his reluctance.

"Very well then, I don't want you too. I curse your union with that woman. Nothing good will ever come of it." She turned her back on him and walked away.

Nuing woke with a start. The light about him had grown dim. Though he was feeling weak, he was afraid to spend another moment at that place. The tide had also turned again, so after cutting a long sturdy stick, he pushed the raft back into the river. This time he stood and poled himself upstream, making sure to stay as close as he could to the bank. Late into the night, on the back of the swift tide, he reaches the tributary leading back to his house. After rafting down it a short way, he camped on the bank. He felt safe enough to build a fire here, so for the first time in days, he had a warm meal.

The next day, while the mist still hung heavy over the water, Nuing cut some palm fronds and wrapped them around his forearm and calves. He also made a circle for his head and stuck bunches of them into the two baskets. Again he wept for his friend then got back on the raft.

When he was within sight of the bathing platform, he gave out a victory shout. His call was returned by the two men washing their hoes and knives. Then more and more people came out to welcome him home. Many noticed that he was alone, but since Gunggu had not been close to anyone else other than Nuing, no one wept for or wondered about his absence because all their attention was on the returning hero. Nuing slung a basket on each of his shoulders and climbed ashore. On reaching the main ladder leading into the house, he found Nambi waiting for him with an empty winnowing tray. He took all five of the heads out and arranged them on her tray.

That afternoon, they had a feast to welcome the heads into their home. After feeding and singing to the new spirits, Nuing and two old men took the trophies into the jungle and cleaned out the brain matter in a stream that no one in their longhouse ever used. When they returned with the skulls, they saw that holding baskets had been woven to hold each individual head. Again the feast of the *Enchaboh Arong* continued. Sometimes Nuing would forget that his friend was dead and he would turn to talk to Gunggu, but each time he would see someone else sitting there. Nobody noticed his grief, however, because they were rejoicing and were filled with new hope. The festival lasted for three days and a pig was sacrificed and eaten for each of those days.

Though the people were exhausted on the morning of the fourth day, many woke early to go to their fields. Nuing also went, and when he reached his field he was surprised because, though the rice was growing, the panicles on each stalk were few and some were nothing more than empty shells. He could sense Nambi's forlornness so strongly that he was embarrassed for her.

As he cut the rice panicles with a small blade and dropped them into the medium sized *sintong* basket slung down the side across one shoulder, he said, "It will be better next year, you'll see. I have the heads now. We will be prosperous farmers."

Nambi turned to look at him with a smile. "Yes, you are right. Today the harvest may be poor, but next time it will be better."

There was so little rice growing in their expansive farm, that they were done just before dusk. Nambi knew in her heart that the rice they had collected would not even last the two of them to the end of the next harvest. She was almost afraid to tell him that the tapioca plants in their backyard were also not doing well. A sudden shame overwhelmed her, for she suddenly realized that she had brought no peace, no prosperity, and no children into his life. He was an accomplished headhunter, while she on the other hand had accomplished nothing.

Before going on the expedition, Nuing had woven a large *lanji* basket to carry back the rice from his field because he had expected a rich harvest. Hence he was ashamed that he had to make only two trips, and the second trip did not even fill the four-post basket to the brim. Within the longhouse, a suspended threshing mat had already been built in his part of the gallery. Since he was the chief, his rice panicles were poured onto the mat first. Two men climbed up, clinging to crossbeams placed over the loosely woven mat and started to thresh the padi by rubbing their feet against the panicles so the grains would come loose and drop through the weave onto another mat placed on the floor below.

The people around him were rejoicing and praising him for their rich harvest, but not once did anyone mention or ask about his harvest, for it was obvious to everyone that his larger field had produced far less than their smaller ones. Though Nuing was now home and safe among friends, his chest and his belly trembled with an excitement or an anxiety that he could not explain. Each time he walked out of the longhouse or worked in his farm, he would look out for trouble. The omens were good, but he could not shake off the feeling of approaching calamity. After a month of suffering thus, he expressed his wish to meditate in the jungle.

"But you have only just returned from your expedition," Nambi said, "why must you do a *nampok* now?"

"Something is not right. I feel it in my being but I cannot explain it."

Tawang, one of the sentries said, "Let me go with you. You need someone to guard you."

Nuing thought over the offer for a moment, but then shook his head. "I don't think it is necessary. I know how to live in the trees. I will be safe."

Akik Bada let out a long breath. "Well if that is what the spirits wishes for you to do, you will have to obey."

For the next two days, Nuing collected eggs, tobacco and caught a live fowl to prepare for the offering. Early on the morning after Nambi had popped some rice and put aside some wine for his meditation, he took the boat upriver. The whole day he paddled along the tributary looking out for a sign to show him where to do his meditation. But he saw and heard nothing. He went as far as he could, until he reached a point of the river where he could go no farther by boat.

He pulled the boat to the bank, turned it over and covered it with leaves and branches before making his way into the jungle. The world here was silent too. Warily, Nuing made his way about the bush, looking up, down and around, searching for that one thing that would have a spirit who might help him. Then he found it, the single thick root of a strangling fig that hung down from the edge of a rock outcropping. He gripped the natural rope and began to climb. As he approached the top, the roots from above became thicker, and soon he could feel the tiny hairs brushing against his face and shoulders, as though they were feeling him. It was getting harder and harder to breath. His palms sweated and he had to grip harder as he climbed, for he was suddenly overwhelm with the terror of falling. He fought the fear with all his might and he would not allow himself to consider climbing back down. By the time he reached the top, he was out of breath from both anxiety and exertion. The fig tree towered above him, like a man of sinews and muscles looking heavenward.

Nuing knelt in front of the tree to catch his breath. After taking a drink of water from a gourd bottle tied to his waist, he unrolled a large leaf and laid it flat on the ground. He pulled out five individually packed food from his basket and started opening them by turn, arranging them in a row in front of him. He unsheathed his machete, bit down on the iron to strengthen his spirit then touch the back of the knife once to each shoulder. Cradling the rooster with both hands, he waved it over the food then with a small knife he made a cut in the cockscomb of the rooster, making it bleed a little. He dab some of the blood on his finger as a form of protection. After he tethered the rooster to a jutting root, he poured a cup of rice wine onto the ground. He took out strips of bamboo and began to weave a rough flat and square basket. He tied the four corners with twine to make a handle before putting in the wide leaf on its flat surface. Then with the blood smeared hand, he picked a little food from each of the packs and arranged them on the leaf starting from the middle with a little pop-rice and glutinous rice. Then he added on top of these, a hard-boiled egg still in its shell, sliced betel nut, a betel vine leaf daubed with a bit of limechalk and shredded tobacco leaf.

He hung the offering up on one of the branches above his head. Then he ate and drank the remainder of the food and wine. The day stretched on. Nuing dozed off but woke with a start when he felt a chill climb up his spine then down the side of one arm. Warily he looked down, and instantly became stiff when he saw a large dark cobra making its way over him to the fig tree. The demi-gods of either Gelong or Panggau Libau often took on the forms of cobras so he wondered which one of them had come that day to respond to his request. The widely spaced dusty gold rings along the whole length of the snake disappeared into the canopy of leaves.

Once Nuing gained back his courage, he looked up. He saw a man staring down at him and realised with a start that he knew the warrior. It was Sempurai, the spirit that had told him about Megong's death and Juit's treachery.

Sempurai asked, "What knowledge is it that you seek?"

Nuing said, "I am a successful headhunter, and a chief of my people. Yet nothing my wife and I do prosper. Is there some curse that is still upon us?"

"You have rejected the pig princess. She is not happy with

you, so she puts a curse of barrenness on your wife."

"But I do not wish to leave my wife. Is there no way to free Nambi from her curse?"

"When you leave this place, you shall go to the bamboo forest yonder," Sempurai said as he pointed to a ridge bristling with bamboo leaves. "There you will find a baby girl who has been abandoned by her family. She is one of a twin."

Nuing frowned. "But will she not add more curses into our lives?"

"No, she will not, because she is the elder child. Her younger sister is far comelier, so her mother asked that the other be kept and she be abandoned."

Nuing looked up hopefully. "She will break Nambi's curse?"

"Yes, but you must remember to do the rite of adoption as soon as you can, else her spirit will die in the sun. Name her Ratai, so she will never forget that you found her among the dry bamboos."

"I understand," Nuing said, his body tense with urgency.

"But *Bunsu* Babi can still put a new curse on your wife."

Nuing fell back on his haunches once more, as another heavy burden of dejection pinned him down. "What must I do to stop this?"

"The pig princess is arrogant. You are not the first man she has cursed. After you completed the ceremony of Ratai's adoption, you must sleep seven miles from the longhouse for three nights. A pack of dogs will be watching you. But you need not worry about them."

"They will help me stop Gema?"

"They will want to kill her."

Nuing's face shot up with wide-eyed shock, but the branch

was now empty so that the newly formed question on his mouth faded into the air. The day was growing late, he saw, and the urgency he felt began to return doublefold. Leaving the offerings where they were, he returned his tools and the live rooster into the basket and climbed down the roots as fast as he could.

He scrambled over logs, slid down slopes and cut his way through the thick vegetation with as much speed as he could. A jungle after all was no place for a newborn child. He was also worried that an insect or a bird had heard what Sempurai told him and was even now telling the pig princess about the baby that would break her curse on Nambi. The thought that Gema would harm the baby if she reached her before him, heightened his sense of urgency. By the time he reached the edge of the bamboo forest, he was struggling to get back his breath. The weak cries of a baby reached his ears and a new burst of energy filled his limbs. He dashed forward, looking left, right and ahead as he searched for what he expected to be a small bundle on the ground. Soon he found her, lying at the base of a cluster of bamboo.

She was naked and a sorry sight, for she was covered with ants and parts of her flesh swollen with their stings. Nuing brushed the insects off, ignoring their fiery bites of protest. Then he wrapped the baby in a fresh loincloth that his wife had put in the basket for him and cradled her in his arms.

She whimpered piteously. He uncorked his drinking gourd and poured water into her mouth. She coughed and the water spewed out of her mouth and nostrils. Nuing panicked and turned her so he could pat her back. She needed to drink, he knew, but he did not know how to feed her without choking her. Then he recalled the days when he had sucked at the edge of his father's loincloth. He wetted the edge of the cloth wrapped around his new baby then put it to her mouth. She suckled.

Nuing stood up with a big smile on his face, as though she was his own child. Then he realised that she was, because she was given to him by the spirits. He began to make his way out of the forest, towards the river. On the way back, he sang her a lullaby, telling her about the forest she was in, about himself who was to be her father, and about her new mother. Then he sang to her about the things he would do for her as her father, and about the cloths that her new mother would weave for her. He sang about the baskets of fish he would bring home, and the loads of meat he would find for her. He sang also about the rice her new mother would plant for her, and the fruits and fern she would pick for little Ratai. He sang and sang, filling his own heart with an overflowing joy. Sometimes his song would stop because he had to laugh, other times because he had to cry.

When he finally reached the boat, the day had grown dark, so he lit a torch, planted it at the bow then placed the sleeping baby in the boat. As he paddled back to the longhouse, he sang quietly of his happiness, so he would not wake the now sleeping baby.

One of the sentries, Libau called out when he was yards away from the bathing platform.

Libau, "Who goes?"

"It is I, Nuing."

Libau's voice soften as he says, "We did not expect you to return so soon."

"I had a reason to rush back," Nuing said as he moored flush to the side of the bathing platform. Libau held the boat steady for him and watched with surprise as Nuing gently put a newborn baby at his feet.

"What is this, *Tuai*?"

"A baby I found in the bamboo forest. Sempurai told me that she will break the curse on Nambi."

After making sure that the baby was safe in Libau's arms, Nuing paddled to the end of a row of boats and moored his craft. He slung on his basket, picked up the paddle and stepped deftly over the other boats to make his way to the bathing place. Then he took the sleeping baby back in his arms and both he and Libau made their way back to the longhouse.

* * *

Nambi fed Ratai the liquids of rice gruel, carefully making sure that the food will not spill over her cheeks because it still festered from ant bites. The baby had started to breathe easier that morning and her fever hot face had also cooled. Nambi tenderly brushed away a wisp of hair.

Nuing came to sit next to her. "Everything is ready," he said with a smile. It had taken them three days to prepare the items needed for the ceremony of Ratai's adoption.

Nambi got up with the baby and stepped outside into the common gallery where a group of people were already waiting. A circle of seven leaf plates filled with single food items had been arranged on the floor. *Akik* Bada sat facing them holding a hen in his arms, with one hand gripping its legs and the other cradling its chest. To one end of the rows was a tray filled with tobacco and betel vine leaves. Next to it was a jar of wine.

Akik Bada began the ceremony by blessing the food offerings. He called out a long prayer asking for blessings and peace on the family and the new child as he circled the hen over the offerings. He called on the gods to come and keep Ratai healthy, to help her in times of trouble and to bless all her work. Then he sliced the throat of the hen, and collected the blood in a bamboo cup. He dabbed a bit of blood on his finger and on the finger of the other men involved with the offering.

He walked over to Nambi and smeared Ratai's forehead with the blood. Then he smeared blood on Nambi's and Nuing's forehead to preserve them from any troublesome spirits as well as to make sure that the adoption would be auspicious.

While he was busy blessing the family, one of the sentries Garan wove a simple square offering basket. He was done by the time *Akik* Bada returned to the circle of plates. A wide leaf was placed in the offering basket then *Akik* Bada picked a piece of food from each leaf-plate to put in the offering basket. He poured some rice wine down the side of a pillar. Garan hung up the basket on the same pillar then returned to his seat.

Akik Bada turned to Nuing and asked, "Do you have the knife to cut her *ayu* ties to her natal family?"

Nuing passed him a wrapped bundle of a knife and a small empty jar. *Akik* Bada unwrapped the cloth, folded it, and placed it in front him. He put the knife in front of Nambi and said, "Take this knife on behalf of Ratai, so that she can cut her spiritual ties with her natal family."

Then he picked up the jar and put it next to the knife. "Accept this jar too, for it shall protect her from danger."

Lastly, he gave her the cloth. "This will shade her spirit as it is replanted in your family's cluster. May she grow healthily and abundantly on your side of the mountain."

And thus was Ratai welcomed into her new family. The remaining food and the cooked hen were then shared among the people of the longhouse.

Chapter 14

"Must you go so soon?" Nambi asked. They had only completed the adoption ceremony the day before.

"I have to," Nuing said. "I must kill that demon before she puts a new curse on us."

Nambi held Ratai tighter to her breast. "I don't understand. Why would she want to hurt us? Was it not the pigs who gave us the tapioca plant?"

"Maybe she wants some form of payment," Nuing said, keeping his eyes fixed on the *kerupit* basket he was filling. The travelling basket would be light because he had only packed two meals. There was very little food in their room as it was, and he did not want to take too much away from his young family. He felt like a failure because he could sense that the other men were beginning to pity him for his wife's bad harvest and for the lazy calls of Ketupong the rufous piculet which put a curse on his hunting or fishing plan. A sudden sense of despair swept over him and he wondered if it would not be better for everyone if he were just to die, or to never return again.

Ratai began to fret. Nambi looked down with an anxious frown then smiled to calm the baby as she rocked and cooed to her. Nuing reached out and Ratai grasped a finger. The swelling on her face and arms had begun to recede but the ones on her belly and chest were turning into painful boils.

Nuing said, "I must go, for her sake."

"Did Sempurai give you a protective charm?" Nambi looked up then down again at the baby.

"No. But he promised to give me something better – hunting companions."

Nuing stood up and tied the raffia rope strung through the sheath of a machete to his waist. No one in the longhouse had milk to share with Ratai, so Nuing was grateful when Tawang gave them some honey he had harvested from the day before. Nambi was now boiling it in a clay pot with some water and a pinch of rice grain to make a sweet liquid for the baby to drink.

Nambi followed him up to the door of their family room then watched as he crossed the gallery and stepped out onto the veranda. She wished she could walk with him for a while, but she was a mother now and she did not want to take the newborn baby outside. Though she had not given birth to Ratai, she was still expected to go through the period of confinement for the baby's sake. So instead of going down to the fields, she would remain in their room, making sure to stay warm and to spend time with the baby for the next five weeks.

***

The day was overcast and the world around him seemed greyer than Nuing ever recalled. It was almost as though he was suddenly colour blind. As he got into his dugout boat, he tried to focus on the basket and paddle laid in front of him. He tried to think of Nambi or Ratai but though he could remember the sound of their names, he could not see their faces in his mind. Nuing splashed some water on his face. Dawn had only broken through the horizon about an hour ago yet the water felt lukewarm and not at all refreshing.

Nuing unmoored the boat and started to paddle downstream. Just before reaching the mouth of the tributary he crossed to the other side. On feeling the bottom of the boat scrap against the sticky clay mud, he got out and dragged the boat out of the water, away from the tideline. He took out his supplies then hid the dugout under leaves and branches. Steadily northward he trekked, heading to the campsite where Nambi first found the tapioca plant. Since he also met the pig princess while camping along the Rajang River, he assumed that he could hunt her down in that same area. After some hours of walking in the grey jungle canopied by tall trees, he started to get the sense of being watched. The feeling was so strong, the hair on his nape stood on end and his legs felt like they were walking through a cold fog.

A wild dog howled.

Nuing stopped in his track, his eyes wildly searching the sparse ground about him. He spotted a golden medium sized dog in between the gap of two tall trees and watched spellbound as the animal approached him slowly. Another dog howled, and another, until the area seemed to be saturated in their cries. Nuing took a deep breath to control his terror then continued moving farther into the jungle. He could see them circling him and hear the heavy pant as they ran past. The day grew late. Nuing continued to walk ahead while collecting firewood at the same time. He tried his best to ignore the dogs, keeping his eyes focused on the way in front of him. When his arms could carry no more branches or twigs, he stopped and built a fire.

The howls about him continued. The pack, he sensed, was still moving in circles but coming closer by the moment. The calls suddenly stopped, but now he could smell them. Putting all his trust on Sempurai's promise that the animals would not harm him, Nuing stayed his ground within the circle of light. His stomach was knotted so tightly with terror that he could neither eat nor drink. Every now and then he would doze off but the sudden touch of an insect wing, or a snap from his crackling fire would wake him with a start.

When morning came, Nuing saw that he was surrounded by five wild dogs in various shades of brown and yellow. He watched them and soon noticed that four of the dogs seemed to defer to the largest in the pack, the golden dog he first saw. Nuing took out a packet of food, opened it and placed it in front of the alpha male. The dog sniffed the food but did not eat. Nuing peeled a hard boiled egg and put it atop the rice. The dog licked the egg and took a tentative bite. Then it came towards the smouldering fire. The other dogs left their positions and began to each take a mouthful of food from the pack. Then like their leader, they too approached the fire.

Warm sunlight started to radiate down in patches, clearing away the chill and dim of the night. The alpha male stood up and sniffed the air. Then it let out a howl, driving the other dogs to a barking frenzy. Nuing picked up his spear and slung on his travelling basket.

The pack began to run and Nuing chased after them, all the while keeping his eyes on the alpha male. After about two miles, the leader again let out a howl, and the other dogs bay a reply. Imitating them, Nuing too shouted loud and long. The ground began to clear and they picked up speed. Nuing could now see the animal that they had been chasing. It was a sambur deer which was starting to stumble from exhaustion. The lead dog let out another bark and the dogs howled after him.

The deer stepped into a sinkhole and tumbled forward, spraining its foreleg. The pack was still yards behind when it managed to pull itself out. It started to stumble forward on three good legs when Nuing threw his spear, hitting it in the back of the throat. The deer let out a cry as it fell onto the ground and the dogs pounced on it. Nuing grasped the shaft end of the spear and drove the spearhead deeper. The deer struggled, but by now had no more strength left to lift itself up. The dogs, feeling its life ebbing away, began to calm. The alpha dog looked up at Nuing, as though waiting for him to complete the hunt.

Nuing unsheathed his machete and started to gut the deer. The smell of warm blood drove the dogs back into a frenzy of barks. He cut away his share of the hindleg, leaving the head and organs for the leader of the pack.

While the dogs ate, Nuing built a small fire then singed the skin of the hind leg over it. He scrapped the skin clean with his machete then cut it into chunks. These he cooked over the fire. When his meal was finally ready, the satiated dogs came to lie down next to the warm blaze and watched him eat. One young dog approached Nuing, but the alpha male growled and it instantly moved away a few paces then lie down on its back, showing its soft belly.

Nuing watched their interactions carefully, for his father had told him that animals living in packs have their own leaders, and like humans, they too have their own set of rules. So he watched how the other dogs behaved before the alpha male and he treated the lead dog with as much respect as the others did.

For the rest of the day, Nuing kept the fire going, all the while wondering how he was going to get the dogs to kill the pig princess for him. That night Nuing slept early, hoping to get a dream, a guide to advice him but nothing came to his aide. Even the omen animals would not give him their divination during the day. On the morning of the third day, Nuing grew restless, and that feeling was tempered by a sense of helplessness. He wished that the wild dogs would hunt again, but he knew that they do not eat daily. Some men even claimed that they eat only once a week.

The jungle in the afternoon heat seemed to stretch interminably, a day he both wished and feared to end. The dogs too appeared restless, almost as though their feelings were entwined with his. Even if they did not speak the same speech, their natures began to merge and mix, so that by the time when the sun was halfway down the western horizon, the alpha male came up to Nuing and stared into his face. That was when Nuing realized that this dog too might have come in search of him because of a message from Sempurai.

Nuing got up and made his way farther west. After about an hour the tall trees gave way to saplings, bamboos and ferns, and the land grew brighter. Nuing searched for and found a row of tapioca leaves. He came up to it, and sure enough, he found fresh snuffling marks at the base of some of the plants. Nuing grabbed a handful of soil, and offered it to the alpha male for a sniff.

The dog growled and barked. Then it howled and started to chase the shadow of a scent. Nuing ran after the pack with excitement mounting. He was going to be free of the demon princess, and as the thought began to grow inside him, the joy of the chase rushed over him. They ran with great speed, jumping over or crawling under any obstacle in their way. Soon, Nuing could hear a great mass running in front of them, and as the land began to slope upward, he caught sight of her: Gema, the youngest pig princess. They were gaining on her.

The pack crashed out of the thick undergrowth and into the shoulder of a grassy knoll. Some of the dogs ran straight up, others ran to the side at an upward incline. By the time they reached the summit, *Bunsu* Babi was surrounded. She turned from side to side with a ferocious growl. Then she saw Nuing and stopped to face him. She rose on her hind legs and the upper portion of her body became human. Her soft pale human skin and long silky hair made her appear fragile and utterly defenceless.

"I am sorry," he said between pants, "but you leave me no choice."

She looked at him. "You still have time to change your mind."

"I cannot. My life is with," he struggled to remember the name. "... Nambi and our new baby."

"I give you one last chance," the princess said, "for I still care for you."

Nuing turned his face away. The dogs attacked. Their growls and barks were of a ferocity that chilled Nuing's blood. This was no way for a princess to die, he thought and he turned to look at the fight, to see if there was a way to stop it, to see if he could persuade the princess to leave him alone.

The dogs were snapping at her heels, biting her hind, drawing blood. *Bunsu* Babi swung one arm out and as she did, claws as long as knives grew out of her fingers and she sunk it into the back of one dog. Then she swung the other arm and sank the sharp nails of this hand too into the side of a second dog. She lifted the animals over her head and threw them down as she hollered a call that was deep and fell. As she called out, her dark human teeth grew longer by the moment and became as black and as sharp as a hunter's spearhead. She grabbed the alpha dog, thrust his head into her now monstrous-sized mouth and bit it off. Nuing stood transfixed. He could not move a muscle, either because of terror or because of an enchantment he could not tell.

The fragile woman he saw moments ago was now a demon. The dogs' cries of the hunt had turned into yelps of pain and death. One by one, she tore into them and flung their carcasses down the knoll. When there was no more left, she turned her gaze towards Nuing, walked up to him and towered over him. She looked down, dripping blood and saliva onto his sweat and tear stained face. He still could not move a muscle.

Slowly, she changed back into the woman she was before, making her blood-stained mouth appear strange on her pale feminine face. Soon Nuing sensed other presences around him, but he could not turn his face to look, so enchanted was he by her.

"Should we kill him too, Princess?" a man's voice said.

"No, he shall be my slave," said Gema.

Nuing felt himself being held back by a pair of arms to either side of him as the princess walked away. He longed to follow her, but he could not. Then as the line of half-pig, half-man warriors begun their march, he was dragged after them.

They walked into a land of mist and Nuing could make out nothing about him. He could only tell if he was going up or down, and the type of ground that was beneath him. A terrible heaviness began to overwhelm him, like a sleep that could not be fought off. His heart pounded and his mouth panted, but try as he might he could not keep his senses awake. Just before he fell into a deep sleep, he felt himself being lifted off the ground and onto the back of one of the warriors.

***

When Nuing finally woke, he found himself in a hut, and he saw other men sitting or lying about him. In the centre of the hut was a firehearth with food cooking and black smoke rising to the thatch roof of the hut.

The other men turned to stare as Nuing pushed himself up from the bare floor. An elderly man helped him sit up. The man stared at Nuing's legs and Nuing likewise stared at his, and saw that he had the legs of a deer. Nuing looked about him and saw that the other men were all as strange as the old man though their hoofs and claws appeared to be of other animals. Beyond the latticed wall he could hear the brazen call of pigs, as well as music and laughter. Nuing tried to stand up, but sat back down in a daze.

"Do not try to get up yet," the elderly man said.

"Who are you?" Nuing asked, "Where is this place?"

"I am Bantak," said the deer-man. He pointed to a man who looks like a monkey with a long tail and said, "That is Pikah." To the monkey-man he said, "Come here, Pikah."

Pikah turned his pink face away and ignored the request.

"I am Rimbun," said a man with sharp curved beak. "I was a warrior hawk from the house of heaven. I was caught when I went out hunting in the world of men."

"I was caught while trying to protect my family from those pigs," said a bulky dark man.

"That is Tanduk," Bantak explained, "He is a rhinoceros." He pointed to a small shivering man who was crouching in a corner. "That one there is Kunchit. He is a dove."

"Greetings," said Kunchit. "If you are hungry, there is food."

"How long have I been asleep?" asked Nuing.

Tanduk snorted, "You arrived before night fell."

"Why am I here?"

Pikah turned his bright face to eye Nuing. He said, "Because the pigs need a new slave, maybe."

"A slave?"

"Not just any slave," Kunchit said.

Bantak stared at the dove-man while the others turned their face aside. Nuing asked, "What do you mean?"

Kunchit said, "I heard the pigs say that you are the personal slave of the youngest princess, *Bunsu* Babi."

"Her father would never allow that," Tanduk said, shaking his large grey head.

Nuing stared at his trembling hands. He crushed them in frustration as a wave of helplessness swept over him. The deer-man touched Nuing's shoulder and, with his other hand, indicated to the food. All the men approached the hearth. Kunchit passed a thin stick to Nuing and showed him how to prick a piece of meat with it. Nuing ate. Then he noticed that though they had tapioca and meat in plenty, there was not a single grain of rice. After they had eaten their fill, his companions lay on the floor and were soon asleep.

The peace of sleep, however, would not come to Nuing. His mind groped about him restlessly. He felt that he must be someplace else, but he could not remember where. He tried to think of faces or names, but all that he could remember was the face of the princess and her name. Yet behind that memory is the heaviness of a great loss, and it frustrated him not to recall what that great loss was. He began to cry silently, though he could not remember why he was crying. The fire diminished, shadows grew on the wall, and the noise from outside faded into silence. Nuing peeked through a hole in the lattice wall, and saw that the land about the hut was pitch dark. There was nothing he could see, there was no where he could run.

***

The hut, Nuing saw the following morning, was built at the edge of the front veranda, and was guarded at all four corners with thin sticks carved in pig-man form. The morning had dawned clear, the sky golden all about, and the longhouse stretched far to either side, seemingly endless and winding like a great river.

Beyond the veranda, the land of the pig-people stretched before him, diminishing into the far horizon. Every which way he turned, Nuing saw a great endlessness and in that space the tall trees and tidy clumps of bushes lined in rows seemed to all point to one place in the distance. He could not tell the manner of grass that grew here because a blanket of mist lay over the ground hiding it from his view. Though he was standing outside in the open verandah, the air about him was thick with the scent of unwashed bodies and cooking food.

After their quick cold meal, the slaves were lined in a row in front of the hut. A large pig-man with heavy tusk and rotund belly looked them up and down. He twisted Nuing's face from side to side and slapped his chest and shoulders then he pointed him to the closest ladder with a squeal. A diminutive elderly man, a human, came out of the longhouse and approached them. He wore an unadorned short barkcloth, and though he was covered in tattoos, he was naked of ornaments. His long well-trimmed hair was tied at his nape and hung down over a bent back, but his eyes were war-like as he focused them on Nuing. On noticing the elderly man, the pig-man stopped Nuing from going down the ladder. The man pointed to Nuing.

The pig-man grabbed Nuing's shoulder and dragged him out of the line. Then with a shake of his head, he indicated to the ladder once more. The other slaves climbed down it, while Nuing followed the old man back into the longhouse.

Once through the door, Nuing saw that the gallery was long and undulating, and that the floor and walls were covered in clay and muck. The columns indicating the gallery boundary of each family were also scratched and frayed in many places. Heads of many shapes, and in various state of decay hung on the walls of many of the rooms. The doors, he saw, were all made of bark and heavy with hanging spears and knives.

Nuing was jolted out of his thoughts when a pig-child crashed into him. The pig-children who had been chasing each other, now squealed in affected terror and ran back the way they came. *Bunsu* Babi, with a basket slung on one shoulder and a knife in one hand, stepped out of her family room and looked him up and down sternly. Nuing lowered his face. He sensed her moving away and, like the old man, he followed her behind silently.

They crossed the veranda and climbed down a tall ladder to the ground. Though he could not see because of the layer of mist, Nuing sensed that the ground was of sticky clay. They walked on the plain for about a mile, until they came upon a cluster of tapioca bushes. The princess began to dig and Nuing helped the other man collect the roots, lying them on a pile to the side. They worked until late in the day.

Then a woman came and brought them food. The princess ate from a tray laden with boiled tapioca, meat and sweets. Nuing and the other slave ate boiled tapiocas drenched in palm sugar. After the meal, Nuing and the old man continued working while the princess napped under the shady bough of a tree. More slaves came by and collected the roots they had put to the side in large baskets. Nuing did not recognize any of them.

Once the sun had sunk low in the horizon, they returned to the longhouse. Not a single word was exchanged between him and the princess during the course of the day. That night, Nuing learned from Bantak the deer-man that the other human was Puing, and that he was cursed by the king of the pigs to never talk, else he would be killed.

"Why is that?" Nuing asked.

The others only shrugged or shook their heads. "We only learn of his name from one of the guards," Tanduk explained. "But none of them know why he is not allowed to speak."

Nuing pondered over this news the whole night, and for many days after that as the same routine was repeated over and over. Like Puing, the princess too seemed to have been struck dumb, by a warning maybe. Nuing could not tell, for neither one would speak to him.

But one day, after his meal and as Princess Gema lay down on her usual mat under the tree, she called to him. He went to her with face bowed. She waved a fan woven of grass in front of her flushed face as she watched him for some moments.

Then she said, "Do you enjoy being a slave?"

"No, Princess, I do not," Nuing replied with great reverence. "If you so wishes, I can be free."

"Whether you become free or not is up to you."

Nuing's head shot up with hope. "What must I do?"

"Marry me. Take me as your wife."

Nuing's bright face darkened. He bowed his head once more to hide his despair. His mind felt slow and foolish as he tried to think of a polite reason not to accept her proposal. He sensed that there was one, but he could not remember it.

"If you agree to marry me, I will set you free and make you a prince." After a long silence, *Bunsu* Babi added, "I am the youngest of seven daughters. I am the most powerful and the most loved among my sisters. If you marry me, you can have anything you wish." She turned her face sideways and said, "I will even steal my father's spear for you, if you wish."

Nuing frowned as he wondered why she would offer to do such a thing for him. Seeing his hesitation, she said, "The spear will help you kill your enemy."

What enemy, he wondered. "But I cannot..." he wrinkled his brow hard, trying to remember, trying to recall the reason until he finally said, "I cannot marry you."

Bunsu Babi slammed the ground with a fist, sending the mist away for a brief moment with her rage, long enough to reveal that the ground beneath them was covered with layers upon layers of motionless red and green worms. Nuing's toes curled tight, and if he could he would have levitated himself off the ground, off of them, yet now he could only stand stiffly over them. The princess waved him away. His heart was inexplicably heavy when he returned to his work.

For the next few weeks, he was again treated with silence, but each day before the new moon and full moon, the princess would ask him to marry her, and each time he would refuse because beautiful though she was, his heart, he eventually decided, belonged not to her. On the night of every full moon, Nuing would carve a notch on the floor where he slept, and with each one he added, his heart grew wearier and he became quieter, so that by the sixth full moon, he stopped talking totally, unless it was to reject the *Bunsu* Babi's proposal.

Months after months of the same routine, then on the 25th month, *Bunsu* Babi's grandfather passed away. He had been ill for a long while, and had been kept alive with the fruits and the nectar of *nipah* palm. On the night that he died, there was a great lamentation and the house shook with grievous wails and songs.

In the hut, a different mood prevailed. Tanduk, the largest and bravest of them, watched the door like a caged animal. Kunchit could not be persuaded to come out of his corner. Nuing watched their behaviour and guessed rightly that one among them would be picked to paddle the spirit boat for the dead old chief.

The door opened, and a guard called them outside. They filed out as slowly as they dared and stood in their usual row, though shrunken and bowed with dread. The guard grunted. A large pig-man, with two guards to either side, came out to the veranda and looked up and down the row of slaves. He pointed to Nuing. The guard looked up with surprise then bowed to show he understood.

"No!" *Bunsu* Babi called out.

Her father walked up to her, grabbed her by one arm and whispered vehemently, "You have embarrassed yourself enough. I will not tolerate his insolence any longer. He insults me when he insults you."

"No, Father, please," the princess said with tears streaming down her face.

"He shall join your grandfather. And after the funeral, you will marry a warrior who will treat you with honour and respect."

He let her go, and she fell on her knees like a toddler who had not yet learn to stand on her own. The face she turned to Nuing was dejected and broken of all pride. With her eyes she pleaded with him, but Nuing only shook his head. Death, he realized, would not free him because it meant that his spirit would become the slave of the old king, but he felt a sudden sense of relief of being free from Gema and her love. He did not struggle when he was taken away by the guard, and led to the ground where he was tied by the neck to a pillar. There he stayed while the funeral rites continued in the house.

While the air was still cold with night, and the pre-dawn morning pitch dark, a hand touched his shoulder and woke him. Nuing stood up thinking that it was the guard. He felt the rope around his neck go taut and a cold blade touch his flesh for a moment as it slipped under the rope to cut him free. Then a callused hand gripped his arm tightly and led him away from the house.

Nuing wondered if he was being led to the grave site, but as the day began to lighten he noted that the man carrying a spear beside him was not a pig-man. "Puing!" Nuing said with surprise.

Puing dragged him away harder. "We must be quick. They will soon notice that you are gone."

"I don't understand."

"The princess asked me to help you escape."

A feeling of guilt overwhelmed Nuing. "Will she be punished for it?"

"No, she will not. I will be."

"But you will escape with me, would you not?"

Puing released his arm and began to run ahead. Nuing chased after him. The mist beneath their feet began to clear and Nuing saw the ground covered with snake-like creatures, writhing here and there.

"Do not look down," Puing said. "Do not look down, or you will die from your fear."

Nuing ran after him, every footfall seeming to shrink away each time it was about to hit ground. They ran until they came to a ravine. Here Puing gave him the spear.

"You must go down this ravine alone," Puing said.

"Come with me. They will kill you if they catch you."

"I cannot leave. If I do, my princess will be punished. I cannot let that happen."

"She does not care about you," Nuing said, "You have no reason to save her life."

"She may not care for me, but it is because of her that my children and grandchildren prosper. She brings edible roots to the barren land they live in, and she send pigs to them for meat. I need her to stay alive, else my family will die."

Nuing stared. Then he asked, "Is that why you are not allowed to speak?"

"No, that is not the reason. I know the secret of this spear, and the king made me swear to never tell anyone about it."

"What can it do?"

Puing shook his head. "Follow this ravine and you will find your way back to the world. Creatures will try to hurt you, but they will stay away when they see the spear. Once you reach the world, you must throw it back into the river."

"Why?" Nuing asked.

Again Puing shook his head. "I have promised not to say." Then after a quick look behind them, he urgently added, "You must go now, before it is too late. I will lead them away."

Nuing made his way down the foetid ravine which was covered with ankle-deep black mud. After about a hundred yards, he heard the call of pigs and he knew that they had found Puing's tracks. He stayed as close as possible to the side, hiding himself under the shadow of the overhanging rocks and leaves above him. Snakes poured down from the side of the ravine but they parted before him like a wave as he advanced holding the spear. He wondered what would happen if he were to strike one of the snakes with it, but his anxiety that he would be discovered got the upper hand so he did not risk striking any of the animals that got too close. Instead he pushed them aside with the spear. The trickle of water grew to a stream and soon the water of the stream reached his knees.

Since the sides were still too high and slippery to climb he decided to make his way downstream by swimming. By now the water was clear and sweet. After about an hour of swimming and floating with the tide, Nuing suddenly recognized the area as he looked about. The sheer wall of the ravine was gone and he was now in the middle of the tributary that passed in front of his longhouse. The faces of people and their names came back to him in waves. Then Nambi's face filled his mind, and his last memory of her holding Ratai in her arms overwhelmed his whole being.

Nuing turned to look behind him in terror, for he also remembered where he had just escaped from. But the ravine he expected to see was no longer there, and the torrents of snakes were no where to be seen. Then he looked at the spear he was still grasping and saw that it had turned into an ivory stick. Nuing swam to shore and rested. He felt old and weak. He looked down at his arm and saw that the skin was loose and wrinkled. He had to use the stick to get up, and to walk. He recalled Puing's words, that he must throw the stick back into the river. Yet he could barely stand without its support, let alone walk back to the longhouse, so he decided to throw it away after he reached home. Throughout the journey he stumbled every few steps, and his muscles ached and joints creaked, but his desperate need to see Nambi and Ratai again drove him beyond pain, beyond exhaustion.

Chapter 15

It was dusk on the second day when he finally reached the house. The land about had changed, the young jackfruit trees he had planted with the others had grown tall and a few were showing signs of producing their first fruits. The bushes of cotton and cucumber plants were now thick and blooming. When he reached the edge of the garden, a sentry called out to halt him.

Nuing called back and was surprised to hear the sound of his own voice, for it sounded ancient and strange.

"Who are you, old man?" Tawang asked, barely older than when Nuing last saw him.

Nuing wondered if he should tell his own name for a moment then decided that he should make full use of the disguise. "I am Ukir," he said. "I have been travelling for many days. May I stop by your house?"

Tawang said, "Where are your friends, Grandfather?"

"I am alone. I was fishing in my boat, but it was turned over by a large wave. I swam to shore and have been walking these two days."

Tawang looked worriedly to the dark sky beyond, and listened warily to the sound of distant drumming which sounded like thunder. Then he said, "Our house has no taboo, but we are expecting trouble in the next few days."

Nuing turned to where he looked and was surprised to realize that the five-year truce between him and the demon huntsman had ended. He was glad he had returned to his people in time, but was dismayed that he had aged beyond usefulness.

"I will stay," said Nuing. "And help where I may."

Tawang nodded and led him back to the house. Everything was as he remembered them. Then a young toddler ran out of his family room, wearing a flat circle of coconut shell to cover her front like an apron. He knew without asking that it was his Ratai. How he longed to stretch out his arms for her to run into them, but when he reached out to touch her face, she ran back towards the door of her room with a squeal.

Nambi came out. She was thinner and older, but still as lovely to his eyes as when he first saw her. She nodded to him and invited him to sit on her part of the gallery.

Akik Bada came out from his *bilek* next door and sat down next to him.

Then Nambi said, "Welcome, old man. I am *Indai* Ratai. Where are you from?"

Nuing's voice shook with emotion but he managed to answer, "I am Ukir. I live alone at the source of this river."

"*Indai* Ratai is the wife of our Chief," *Akik* Bada said, feeling the need to explain why a woman should be talking to a strange man. "He is away for the time being, so she is representing him."

"How long has the chief been away?" Nuing asked with curiosity, looking to Nambi as he did so.

"About two years," she replied, with a weary sadness in the timbre of her voice.

Nuing's heart ached but he could not tell her who he was. Not yet anyway, he thought, at least not until he had changed back to his former form.

Then Nambi returned to her family room to prepare a meal for the visitor, while Nuing and *Akik* Bada tried to exchange some news. Their conversation was irregular and seemingly absent-minded, for *Akik* Bada was distracted, his words kept drifting into silence as part of him listened to the distant thunder that seemed almost to grow louder with each beat.

Dinner was a simple thing, a meal of sago, fern shoots and a little fish. After the meal, more men joined them, but none noticed that Nuing was not talking or boasting about himself, which was the normal nature of travellers. Everyone was intermittently staring at the walls of the house, nobody was talking, but it would not have mattered because no one was listening. The approaching darkness heightened the anxieties of their mind gradually, taking firm root in it, like a drop of dye in a bowl of rice wine that spread vine-like and thin.

The cicadas outside the house sang a symphony that mimicked the sound of a throbbing heart. The sky above was speckled with pinpoints of light and the sentries kept watch on it intently, for they knew from experience that when the demon huntsmen arrived, they would come with a fog so thick, the light of the stars and moon would be shut out. They waited the whole night, and was relieved to see by dawn that the sky remained clear throughout. It meant that they were free for another day.

During breakfast that morning, Nuing asked, "How long have the demons been signalling that they are on their way here?"

Akik Bada said, "For about a month now. At least we still have another day without fighting."

Nuing looked about him and noticed the dark shadows under the eyes of all those who were sitting with him. He wondered about it, and after some thought realized that the demon huntsmen were wearing them down. The fighting men of the longhouse were being driven to exhaustion by constant anxiety and sleeplessness.

"They are trying to weaken you," he said.

"What do you mean?" Tawang asked.

"You are all anxious and afraid. You do not eat well. You do not go out hunting or fishing because of fear. By the time they arrive, you will all be too exhausted to fight them."

"But what can we do?" Nambi asked. Her face flushed with frustration. She turned it aside to hide the tears that were fast brimming in her eyes.

This was not a battle that they could fight without the help from a stronger source, Nuing realised. Was there no demon-god who would not wish to impress his sweetheart? Was there not a spirit who would want to adorn the pillars and wall of his house with the heads of demon huntsmen? If he were to invite them to his house, if he were to invite them to kill the demons, would they come?

Nuing grabbed the ivory stick and stood up. He tapped the bottom end against the floor and the sound reverberated throughout the house. A song, a *pengap*, began to fill his heart and he tapped a monotonous rhythm on the floor as he walked around a column across from his room's ritual post, singing to welcome the gods and spirits into their midst.

Without being told to do so, the people all returned to their rooms and came out with offerings of food, wine and tobacco. They arranged these around the same column that Nuing circled.

As he sang, Nuing named the gods and heroes one by one. He invited Sengalang Burong and his warriors, Keling and his men, as well as the brave god of rice Pulang Gana to come to the longhouse. He called on the princes of demons: *Raja* Remaung and *Raja* Sempurai. He named the hills, valleys, rivers and bridges that he had to pass as he made his journey into their land. On reaching each longhouse, he told the gods and demons about their troubles with the demon huntsmen and invited them to come. Then he told them the way to his longhouse, giving the names of hills, valleys and rivers in reverse. He told them to bring with them the charm of courage, the charm of invincibility and the charm of healing. The longer he sang and the more he tapped on the floor with the ivory stick, the braver the people became, the more invincible they felt.

His taps grew louder and the floor, which had been as pliable as the bamboo they were made from, was now as hard as rock and echoed like iron whenever he struck it. The air about them grew cool, then colder by the moment until the older folk and children were forced to cover themselves in blankets. The sentry-men's eyes grew sharp and the war frown on their faces grew fierce. Their breath began to steam, the floor began to mist and though the chill stung their skin and burned the tip of their fingers and toes, a deep fire heated their bellies, spreading warmth throughout their bodies. The warriors around him shouted and yelled. Then one after another, they ran into their rooms and soon returned having donned their war gears of hornbill and argus pheasant feather, or pelts of wildcat, bear or pangolin skin.

They stood in a circle around the pillar Nuing travelled around, urging him on as he made a journey up a spiritual spiralling path that went round and round and up and up the main pillar to the house in heaven. Nuing described every longhouse he visited and named all the spirits living within each. On the evening of the second day he reached the house of the warpath god, Sengalang Burong. Here he remained for hours as he sang their troubles to the eldest of the seven gods, the eldest grandchild of Raja Durong the lawgiver, to persuade the god and his household to return with him to his longhouse along a tributary of the Rajang River. His well chosen words and the music of his ivory stick eventually melted even the most stubborn resolve of the warpath god, so that he agreed to come down to the world to bless Nuing and his people with his divine presence.

For three days and two nights Nuing went round and round the pillar, detailing every step he took and every word he uttered to persuade the people of the invisible world to come into their visible one, so that by the time he ended the *pengap* in the afternoon of the third day, he collapsed in exhaustion.

Akik Bada was the only person brave enough to approach him and rolled him onto a mat. Then the people noticed a strange phenomenon. Certain parts of the mist on the floor swirled and emptied as though a solid mass had been put down upon it. Yet they could see nothing. Then there were more spots, some seemingly to indicate individuals, others a group. Tawang touched *Akik* Bada's shoulder and nodded to one of the swirls, to alert the old man to those presences.

Akik Bada turned his gaze to Nambi and said, "Offer our guests food and drink."

The young were told to go into the rooms, lest they say anything or behave in any manner that would offend a god. And glad were the children to go, all of them huddling together in one single room at the very end of the longhouse.

Platters of offering were placed before the empty swirls. Then women began to beat on gongs and drums, and *Akik* Bada started dancing to welcome the gods and spirits. After him, an elderly woman stood up to continue the entertainment. As dusk approached, the mist on the floor began to twist and turn together with the music. It was then that Nuing woke from his death-like sleep. He struggled to sit up.

The first spirit that Nuing saw was *Bunsu* Remaung, the sole survivor from the tiger tribe of Sarawak. His mother was pregnant with him when a hunter entered their longhouse and wiped *ipoh* poison on the walls. Every tiger who touched the wall was killed. *Bunsu* Remaung's mother managed to escape and gave birth to him, and since then he had lived in the invisible world, cursed to be alone. Nuing also recognized Sempurai who was sitting to one side by himself. He looked up to the dancer, and his breath caught in his throat, for before him was the perfect Iban man, the great warrior Keling whose courage, skill, and knowledge was the aspiration of every Iban man.

When he again looked about him, Nuing caught the fierce gaze of Sengalang Burong and quickly turned his eyes away. Next to the warpath god, but sitting by himself, was an old man as pale as the moon. A beautiful elderly woman separated from a group of women and went to sit next to the pale old man. Next Nuing turned his gaze to the group of women of various ages, the older sitting facing the crowd, the younger ones whispering and giggling behind them. He saw that they were all beautiful and perfect, yet one woman stood out even among the most beautiful. From the way she watched Keling danced, he suspected that she was Kumang because her gaze was that of a bold lover's.

Tawang touched Nuing's shoulder lightly. "Are you all right, Grandfather?"

"Yes, I am well." Nuing looked about him and noted the frightened eyes of the people.

Keling stopped dancing and returned to his seat next to

Sempurai but the music continued. Nuing raised a hand to signal the players to stop then he moved himself towards the guests with his hips, pushing forward the stick in front of him with his feet, until he was within a hearing distance whereby he need not raise his voice when he speaks with them. He crossed his legs and leaned his shoulders forward.

"Welcome to our humble home," said Nuing.

"Why have you invoked us?" asked Sengalang Burong harshly. Though the people could not hear his words, they heard a fierce screech as though through a blanket of water.

"Trouble is at our door," said Nuing, "and we do not know how to fight it."

"You killed his brother," Keling said, "Sempekang is within his rights to take revenge."

"Gunggu and I killed Manang Juit in self-defence."

Nambi stifled back a shout of surprise but said nothing, because she too like the others was afraid of speaking out of turn before the gods.

Pulang Gana, the old man who shone like the moon, said, "Then you must defend yourself once more."

Nuing looked down, to hide the frustration fast showing on his face. He gripped the ivory stick hidden under the mist hard then said, "Is there a charm you can give us, to protect us from the demon huntsmen?"

Sempurai said, "You already have the heads hanging from your pillar."

"But we need to be stronger," said Nuing.

Keling laughed. "There is no strength in your world that can help you fight an army of demons."

Nuing again squeezed the spear stick. It began to warm in his hands. A voice whispered *Cunning*. Nuing looked about him with a start, wondering who had said the word.

Sengalang Burong got up on one knee and began sniffing the air. He said, "There is a terrible stench in this house."

"It is the same stench that has brought us here," said Keling. "Where is he, the pig king?" He looked accusingly at Nuing, outwardly showing that he believed Nuing had hidden the boar to trap them.

"He is not here," said Nuing, gently laying down the stick, so it would not stir the mist. "I have just escaped from his kingdom. Maybe I still carry the stench of that place on me."

The demon tiger, dangerous and beautiful in a feline manner, crawled on all fours to him, and sniffed the back of his head. He said, "Yes, he still does smell a little like a pig." He growled and crawled back, keeping his eyes on Nuing's face. Then he roared and pounced.

Nuing instinctively raised the spear-stick with both hands to bar him from reaching his face. *Bunsu* Remaung pushed back on the stick and gave another roar. Then he released the stick as though burned. The stench of mud and filth from the pig kingdom fouled the air, turning the white mist grey. *Bunsu* Remaung again roared and sprang forward once more with heightened rage. He slapped the stick away from Nuing's hands and slammed into his chest. Nambi screamed. Though she could not see the spirit beings, she could hear the roar and see Nuing being thrown on his back.

Nuing's arms stretched up and he wrapped his hands around *Bunsu* Remaung's throat. The demon struck his face and cut open a gash that exposed the bone of his forehead. Nuing squeezed harder. *Bunsu* Remaung clawed his hands, Nuing clung on, squeezing ever harder, not daring to let go. Even if the tiger demon was to tear his arms out he willed with all his might that his hands would stay around his throat, to throttle out every last breath from him.

Pulang Gana stood up and stomped. The house and the air shook, and Nuing felt his bones rattled. "Stop this! Now!"

Nuing released his bleeding hands and *Bunsu* Remaung moved away from him. Pulang Gana's wife, Endu Endun Serentum Tanah Tumboh, left her husband's side and sat next to Nuing, who had remained lying on the floor, panting from the exertion of his struggles and the pain of his wounds.

Endun took out a roll of thread and a needle of bone from a woven pouch tied to her side. She threaded the needle then cut the string of cotton with a small knife. After carefully studying the wound on Nuing's face, she folded back the skin hanging over one eye and matched the tear carefully to its corresponding side. The whole time she did this she sang, lulling Nuing into a drunken daze. He could not tell if he was the one spinning or if it was the gallery. He kept his eyes focused on Endun because she was the only one remaining stationary. As she sewed, he could hear his skin and flesh pop each time the needle pierced them, but he felt no pain. After gently touching the completed stitch, she cut the thread free. Then she sat back and smiled, seemingly pleased with her handiwork. Next she looked at his hands. The flesh and skin hung down like ribbons. She turned to her husband Pulang Gana and shook her head.

The god of rice rose from his seat and came towards them. He made Nuing sit up then took both of his hands and placed them flat on his own knee. He picked one hand up and wrapped a strip of cloth tightly just below its wrist. He repeated this action on the other hand. With care he arranged the red flesh back into the hand then with an incantation he stemmed the flow of blood. Endun dampened a piece of cloth from her pouch with water from her drinking gourd. After she had cleaned the hands, Pulang Gana unhooked a small bamboo tube from his waist and poured out two dollops of clear rice glue on the back of one hand. Nuing flinched. Endun started singing again and Nuing felt himself being lulled into a hazy, dream-like state once more. After some moments, Pulang Gana began to lay back the strips of skin gently over the flesh. He repeated the process to fix the other hand.

Endun turned to the group of women and nodded her head to one. "Lulong, please bring me some *lemba* leaves."

The young woman addressed stood up and went outside to the veranda. She reaches out her hand and a pair of lance-shaped long leaves broke free from their clusters and flew into her open palm. She returned to the gallery and handed the leaves to Endun.

Endun then chewed a mouthful of *sirih* leaves. She expelled out the wad and spread it over the back of one of Nuing's hands before covering it with one of the *lemba* leaves. Lulong helped her hold the leave in place as Endun tied it down with a string. Endun then chewed another mouthful of *sirih* leaves and wrapped the other hand too. Throughout this time, the people saw what was being done to Nuing, but none could understand what was being said or see who was doing it.

Nuing looked down at his hands, his fingers stiff and splayed. He said, "Thank you, goddess, for your blessing and cure." He wanted to add *Now please give me a charm to fight the army of demons,* but his heart was too despairing and he did not feel that he could fight off another enraged spirit.

Lulong returned to Kumang's side and whispered into her

cousin's ear. Kumang in turn moved her gaze to Keling, who by now was sitting next to Sengalang Burong. "My husband," she said, "Can you not spare a charm for Nuing?"

Keling frowned. "That will bring trouble to us."

"His mother has woven the spirits of the sun bear for him. Surely there must be something you can do for him."

Keling shook his head then turned to *Bunsu* Remaung. "Can you give him nothing? The *antu gerasis* have been hunting your kind for many generations. Surely there is no love lost between you and them?"

"I would have," *Bunsu* Remaung said, "But the stench of pig is strong in him. I will never help someone who is allied to the pig king."

"I am not," Nuing said, "He kidnapped me and forced me to be his slave."

Bunsu Remaung snarled. "Yet he gave you his spear stick before he set you free."

"He did not," Nuing said. "He wanted to sacrifice me for his father's funeral. Another slave helped me escape and stole this stick for me."

Bunsu Remaung stared then he laughed. After he calmed down, he said, "You stole his most precious weapon."

"What can it do?" Nuing asked.

"It has been cursed to kill Sempekang, the chief of the demon huntsmen," Sempurai said.

Nuing who had up to that point avoided looking at Sempurai because of the raging anger in his belly now turned to the demi-god and said coolly, "Thank you for telling me." His eyes glared with rage and accusations as they turned to face the demi-god.

Sempurai slammed his fist on the floor, smashing it into splayed tendrils. He turned darker and larger. Keling threw himself at his cousin then turned his scowling face to Nuing, shouting, "Bow down and show respect! Apologize for your arrogance!"

Involuntarily Nuing fell on his face. A painful sense of betrayal stung his eyes, but his mouth managed to say, "Forgive me, Great Sempurai. My tongue has spoken without care."

A darker and larger Sempurai roared with rage. "I did not send you to kill *Bunsu* Babi. I sent you to get the spear-stick. It was you who chose to stay there for two years. You should have agreed to marry the princess then bring the spear back for your people." After a few roars he added, "I made you forget your family, so you will be more pleasant to her."

Nuing's head shot up. His face first turned to surprise then as the meaning of Sempurai's words sank in, to regret. He pressed his brow against the floor and with all his heart said, "Forgive me, I am a fool."

Sempurai's roars calmed to heavy panting then to silence. Nuing looked up once more and saw that the demi-god he was named after was drenched in sweat though now sitting quietly. Bungai Nuing, he thought to himself, was truly not a spirit to be taken lightly, for though charming and fine in his human form, when incensed would turn into a raging demon who would have laid his home to waste in moments.

In the ensuing silence, *Akik* Bada brought out a resin lamp, leaning it at an angle against a stick on a stone slab. More lights were brought out from the other rooms, for the darkness had started to cover the land and seemed to bring with it strange forms and movements. Tawang bravely placed a light before the largest group. Shadows of the goddesses were cast against the wall and everyone could see that they were tall and fine, and that crowns bristled from their heads, quivering with every movement they made.

The people's fear began to turn to one of wonder and soon one after another the women began to notice the shadow hands working or touching each other in a peculiar and fine manner. They began to surreptitiously imitate those same fingers and hand movements. The way a goddess held her spindle and how she twirled her cotton into thread. The way another goddess held her needle to sew, or how another wove find reeds into a basket. Their movements were elegant and fluid, making the women who imitated them feel more and more beautiful and feminine by the moment.

Nuing finally found the courage to raise himself up from the floor. He sat and turned his shame-glazed eyes to Sempurai. "I could have stayed in that land forever," admitted Nuing.

"I waited for you to return," said Sempurai. "When you did not, I looked for you. The snakes told me that you have become enthralled by the princess, like Puing."

"But I was not," said Nuing. "I was merely her slave." After some moments he added, "If her grandfather had not died, I would still be here." He looked down at the stick, recalling the promise he made to Puing, and feeling glad that he had broken it. He turned his gaze to Sempurai once more and asked, "Will I succeed in defending my home?"

"You have the spear," said Sempurai, "how you use it will depend on your courage."

Nuing turned to Sengalang Burong. "Please, Great Father, have mercy on our house. Our number is few, and they are many."

Sengalang Burong glared at him. "You are still a fool."

Nuing was taken aback by the response he had never expected.

He began to think and wonder what the god had meant.

Seeing his confusion, Pulang Gana said, "You have often misinterpreted any information that is given to you. You make your decisions quickly, always choosing the way of least effort. Bujang Maias, your father, was a wise man, so it is frustrating for us to deal with his foolish son."

Nuing's face flushed red, for being ashamed to be derided in front of the goddesses, and his ears flared when he heard them tittering on him being called foolish.

Bunsu Remaung said, "The spear is better than any gift I could have given you."

"You must understand," explained Keling, "we have no quarrel with the demon huntsmen. The retribution he promised to deliver onto you is within the boundary of the customary law. If we were to help you, it will start a war between us and them."

"Is there any other way then, to end this quarrel?" Nuing asked half-heartedly.

Sengalang Burong said, "You must kill him, so the cycle of revenge will end."

Akik Bada touched Nuing's shoulder to get his attention. "What are the gods saying?" he asked.

Nuing turned to look at him sideways, saying, "They cannot help us because the demon huntsmen are right to avenge *Manang* Juit's death."

The old man's face flushed and his eyes widened as he said, "Can we not pay them a *Pati Nyawa*? When one of Semelanjat's men accidentally killed Kanyong's, the two great chiefs negotiated a compensation in exchange for the life that was taken. Surely we can do the same. We only need one of the gods to help us speak with the demons."

Sengalang Burong said, "Juit's death was no accident. Sempekang has also woven baskets for each and every one of your heads. That is a sure sign that he would rather hang your heads at his pillar and make you all his spirit slaves."

Nuing shook his head and said to *Akik* Bada, "It is impossible to negotiate now."

The old man sat back and hunched over his crossed feet. He stared at his hands and cursed them for being old and weak. The storm outside grew louder and the house began to tremble from the gusts of wind and vibrations of the thunders.

Sengalang Burong looked up to the trembling rafters then turned his gaze down to Nuing. "They will be here in five days."

Bitterly Nuing said, "Why not tomorrow? Why not just come and end our torment."

"Because they want to exhaust you," replied Keling. "When your spirit is broken, not even the trophy heads can protect you."

Nuing's brow wrinkled as he turned his face to the side, thinking hard. Finally he said, "We must do something to keep our spirits strong."

"That is correct, son of Bujang Maias," Pulang Gana said.

In his excitement, Nuing raised himself a few inches from the floor, saying, "Then when the demons arrive, I can kill as many as I wish with the pig's spear."

"No," Sempurai said, "The spear will only kill one demon because the pig king had cursed it to kill him alone."

"Do you mean that there is nothing for us to do but to die?" said Nuing despondently.

"You have more than charms," said Keling, "You have men who would die to protect their family and land."

Nuing turned to look at the men of his house who now sat

together in a row before the gods. Their faces were like confused and frighten children, eyes frowning but mouth quivering, and shoulders stooped. "There is no fight left in them," said Nuing, and with those words his spirit too gave up hope.

Then with a shout Pulang Gana said, "You are weak. A strong man looks forward to death in battle. A strong man does not become immortal by growing old and dying in his bed. He becomes immortal by the strokes he struck in war."

"I have heard enough," said Sengalang Burong. Then he stood up and walked outside to the veranda. He ran across it, turned into a Brahminy Kite and flew away.

Pulang Gana turned back his gaze to Nuing, "I will speak to my father-in-law, and tell him to order the spirits of the land not to hinder your plans in any way. You may take anything you wish from the jungle to aid in your defence."

The mist in the gallery began to thin and the shadows of men and women turned to birds or cobras or wild cats. That was when the people saw them leave the longhouse with their own eyes. The air was suddenly thick with the perfume of the divine, and just as suddenly the sounds and smells disappeared. Nuing continued to stare down at the floor.

Akik Bada waited for some minutes. Then he cleared his throat and asked, "Did the gods promised that we will win?"

"No, because they cannot help us."

"*Tuai*," said Tawang, having realized that the old man before him was his chief. "What did they tell us about the coming battle?"

Nuing looked up and his wrinkles began to smoothen, his bent back to straighten, and his shrunken frame to fill with flesh. "They said that the demons will be here in five days." To the questions in their eyes he explained, "The huntsmen are trying to make us afraid, to break our spirit so that even the trophy heads would be unable to help us."

"That can only mean that the trophy heads you brought home are powerful," said *Akik* Bada with a hint of joy and hope in his voice.

"What do you mean?" asked Tawang.

"Don't you see?" the old man started to explain, "When a warrior plans to attack a longhouse, all he needs is a surprise. A battle cry in the dark of night is all he needs to quail the spirits of a longhouse and break their protection long enough to allow him to kill the people of the house. But the demons are trying to break our spirit long before they attack. That can only mean that the protective cover of the heads is very strong."

A murmur rose as the people discussed this new information. Garan asked, "What should we do then?"

"We keep our spirits up," said *Akik* Bada, "We don't let anything weaken our resolve."

"We have five days to build a physical defence," said Tawang with sudden understanding of the importance of the message.

"Yes," Nuing said, "We have time to collect the bark of the custard apple tree and spears from the *ibol* palm."

"I can help too," *Akik* Bada said, his eyes shining and mouth smiling, like a child looking forward to an active game.

"No," said Nuing, "I need you to talk with the trophy heads. Find out from them what needs to be done."

On hearing this suggestion, the women immediately offered to look for offering items to help *Akik* Bada with his meditation. Some men also offered to build a room at the end of the veranda in front of the chief's portion of the longhouse, so the trophy heads could be moved there and *Akik* Bada could have more quiet for his meditation. Duties were assigned and even the young children were not spared because they were told to make a ruckus about the house with shouts and gongs and drums in order to mask the sound of demon drumming coming down the river.

Before the morning dawned, the men were out of the house, going to various parts of the jungle to look for wood, bark and palm stalks. They all carried spears with them so they could also hunt and bring meat back to the house, in case the siege lasts for many days. They returned before nightfall, their backs bent under the load of materials.

The women too were not idle, because they collected leaves and bamboos that could be used to pack food or to ferment meat and fish. They looked for the *pantu*, *lalis*, and *bindang* palms, cutting away the soft core from the young stems. The house was so busy with activity that most times the people didn't even hear the sound of demon drumming anymore. Even the children were enjoying themselves and the atmosphere was like one for the preparation of a festival rather than a battle.

Nuing's spirit rose too, with the shouts and songs of the people. As his spirit settled in his body and abandoned any idea of flight, he felt strength fill every sinew and muscle anew. His stooped shoulders squared, the frown of worry on his brow turned to one of warrior rage and his voice grew deep with conviction as he gave instructions to his people.

An offering was given to the trophy heads before they were moved to a temporary room at the end of his veranda. Unlike the rest of the house, this sanctuary was quiet. Once *Akik* Bada was shut in the room, he studied the heads on the winnowing tray then fed each a piece of food from a pile of offering on a wide leaf platter. He told the spirits what he wished of them then he went into meditation, swinging from side to side as he hummed a tune under his breath. He was in this trance until nightfall, at which time he lay down to sleep, covering himself with a sacred blanket.

The drumming downriver grew louder, and louder until it felt as though the sound of his own heartbeat had begun to synchronise with it. The beat became so loud, *Akik* Bada could not hear himself think. Then he heard the sound of laughter and crude bantering outside the room. He became annoyed. Couldn't those fellows outside understand that he was trying to meditate? Have they no respect for his work? He pushed the blanket aside and stormed out of the room. On the ground below he saw five strange naked men who traipsed about and danced obscenely to the sound of drumming. They were laughing hysterically at each other, and they behaved in manners that could only be judged as mad. Though it was so dark that *Akik* Bada could barely see his own feet, he could see the five men because they glowed with a dim light, like lamplights behind a layer of leaves.

"Ooi, you fellows," shouted *Akik* Bada, "Be quiet. I am trying to sleep."

A shout of laughter came from one of the men, and another said, "But the music is good. We want to dance."

"Then don't dance here. Go somewhere else!"

Said a third man, "But this place is good. There is food and drink."

"Food and drink!" shouted the other four in unison. Then all five sang the line over and over as they danced in a circle. Suddenly they jumped twenty feet up onto the veranda, startling *Akik* Bada. They dashed against his meditation hut, and began to tear down the walls and door. *Akik* Bada was about to curse them for their sacrilegious behaviour but as the walls came down, he saw tall jars of wine in place of bamboo tubes and a hundred platters of rice, egg, meat, fish, palm and fern lying atop one another, instead of the single platter that had been presented to the heads.

He paused to think then wondered why it was so hard for him to think. He watched the five men dumbly as they gobbled up the food and fought over the wine. One man burped and this shook the very floor *Akik* Bada was standing on. Another man lit a cigarette as large as his own arm. When he inhaled, a scent of green and flowers filled the air. When he exhaled billows of smoke came out of his mouth, nose, ears and eyes. The smoke was soon so thick, *Akik* Bada felt enveloped in it.

When reason finally reached him in that world of dreams, *Akik* Bada realized that he was talking to the five trophy heads. He approached them until he was just within an arm's length from the closest head and sat down. He watched them eat and drink and smoke and fling half-eaten leaf plates about, scattering the leftover food. He listened as they cursed one another and laughed violently over everything. When there was a lull in their play, *Akik* Bada asked, "Will you help us protect our house?"

One man who was sitting with his back to the old man twisted his head around until he was looking full face at *Akik* Bada. He said, "Why should we? It is not our trouble."

Another, his mouth full of food, said, "It does not matter to us who lives or dies." He stuffed another fistful of eggs into his mouth.

The others heartily agreed with loud shouts and one man stood up to give a vulgar dance. Then suddenly the man farthest from *Akik* Bada yelled and pummelled the floor with his fist. His rage shredded the wooden timber and tore his flesh until his bones showed. There was sudden silence.

"If you help us fight," said *Akik* Bada, with a firm lilt in his voice, "we will offer you more food and drink. But only if we win." The five heads remained silent, keeping their eyes on the floor, on the food, or on each other; anywhere but in the old man's direction. *Akik* Bada continued, "If we lose, you will be abandoned and be cold and hungry. You will be forced to search for new masters but everyone will flee from you in terror."

One man stood up and he rose so high that *Akik* Bada felt as though he was looking up at the moon when he turned his face up to meet the man's eyes. The man said, "You will abandon us," and the certainty in his voice made his words sound like a prophecy.

"As long as you protect us from ill-fortune, we will continue to keep you. Our children and grandchildren, and their descendants will continue to keep you in food, drink and tobacco. You will never be cold because we will light a fire to warm you every night."

The man looked ahead, as though to a great distance. Then he said, "One day there will come a time when we are no longer necessary. Then we will be hungry and cold." He looked back down to the old man. "Listen then for this is what I have to say: if we are abandoned without fault on our part, we will curse our masters' fields and terrorize them with a hunger and thirst that can never be satisfied."

"I understand," said *Akik* Bada.

The man turned back to look at the house. "Tell your men to build crossbows on five points along the length of the veranda. Make sure that the bows are large enough to aim *ibol* spears."

"A giant bow? A child's toy?"

The man glowered down. "Yes, a bow. I have killed many men in my lifetime with a bow."

"But why a bow?"

"Because you cannot fight the demons at close quarters. They will crush you with a punch and send you flying with a swing of their arm."

"You can also use fire," said another trophy head. "Scatter the ground in front of your house with resin, pith, charwood and oil. When the demons climb up your bank from their boats, slow them with the spears then light the ground with fire. Even their oily grimy hair will catch fire quickly."

The heads laughed and resumed their revelry. *Akik* Bada bowed low, realizing that he had found the answer for his people. When he looked up again, he found himself lying under the sacred blanket. He rolled to his side and saw that the heads were still on the winnowing tray and that the walls of the hut were still intake. He stood up, and caught a whiff of the food and wine which had gone stale and mouldy. With a spring in his steps, he left the room.

Though it was dark, and the sun was still hours away, many men, including Nuing were already up and sharpening knives or adzes to take with them into the jungle. When *Akik* Bada told Nuing that he had met the spirits of the head, the other men immediately left their work and stood around to listen.

"Five bows," said Nuing. "You are sure?"

"Yes, there is no mistake," said *Akik* Bada.

"But where should we aim them?" asked Tawang.

"They said the demons will come from the river," replied *Akik* Bada.

"I have seen the bows from the Sina ship. They are not held upright in front of you, but on their side. This house is about twenty feet off the ground, we can build each low and still aim a kill shot at the demons," said Nuing.

"I have made many bows when I was a boy, but I have never seen one that is held on its side," said Tawang.

Nuing then took out a small knife and began to carve a rough diagram on the surface of a split bamboo. He showed that the cross-bow is different from the bow they were used to, in that it had a stock with a flight groove carved into it. He also explained about the hook and trigger.

"That is like our animal trap," said Garan. "We use springs and triggers too."

Tawang added, "There are some *meranti* and *kapur* trees growing less than a mile away. They will make good lathe limbs."

"We only have three days left," Nuing reminded him. "It is impossible to cut down a tree then carve it down to make five bows."

"The chief is right," said *Akik* Bada. "A bamboo and rattan may not last many years, but they will hold for many days."

After further discussion they finally decided to use bamboos reinforced with rattans for the lathe limbs. It should be springy enough for their immediate needs. The stock would be fixed to a bamboo mainstay with vines, rigid enough to hold it in place, but not so rigid that it could not be moved from side to side. They also needed to look for more *ibol* palm to make spears that would fit into their crossbows.

When the women heard about the crossbows, they offered to prepare the strings. After the men left, the women began to twirl together strips of long animal skin and gut. They then hung the damp strips to dry, stretching them as they did so. Since it would take too long to dry them naturally, Nambi decided to risk partially drying the strings over warm embers. The women took turn watching the fire, and when a string started to feel dry to the touch, it would be moved away from the ember and left to dry under the sun.

The men returned in the late afternoon with clay and bamboos of various length and diameters. The large diameter bamboos were cut to about three feet length before they were filled with clay. These heavy mainstays were then fixed at five points with ropes to the crossbeam holding up the floor from below. A groove was next cut into a long piece of wood to guide the spear. This stock was then lashed down to a mainstay, with a small piece of bamboo covering the groove, so the straps would not press down on the guide and block it. Next they halved a long piece of bamboo, filled the inside with three rattan canes, and wound strips of vine to hold the materials together. This was the lathe arm, which they lashed to the end of the stock. The strings were not ready, so the men set to carving out hooks and triggers for the crossbow. They used a simple design, where the hook is nothing more than a standing hard stick which is held upright by a plug beneath it. When this plug was pulled away from the side, the stick would drop forward and release the string.

The days passed quickly, and with each passing day the people's hope began to rise. This hope reached its peak when the strings were deemed ready to be tied to the crossbows. After ascertaining the length of the lathe, they tied either end of each string into rings and hooked these firmly into the ends of the bent bamboo and cane arms. They pulled the string back onto the hook, placed a spear on the stock, and released the string. The spear pierced through the branch of a jackfruit tree and broke it. They tested each of the next four crossbows and found every one of them to be as fearsome as Nuing had described. The people were jubilant and began to look forward to the fight, expecting it to be more of a challenge rather than a precursor of death and suffering.

Chapter 16

"When should we do this?" asked Tawang, as he leaned forward, trying his best to keep his voice just loud enough for the other four men to hear. It was dusk, and they were now standing at the bathing platform, and though they could see no other living thing around them, they could never be sure that no animal was listening.

Nuing turned to *Akik* Bada with the same question on his face. The old man said, "Legend has it that the demons only come out when it rains on a sunny day."

"Should we do it at night then?" asked Libau, one of the sentries.

Nuing shook his head. "Other demons will be active at that time. They will see us and tell the demon huntsmen."

"Then let us do it at dawn," suggested Tawang. "Whether they see us or not will not matter now because we only have another day left before they come. If they see us, they will break the traps. If they don't then we have the element of surprise."

Nuing nodded; Tawang was right. The spears were ready and they had collected plenty of bamboo to use as spring boards. Coils of fresh rattan now lay at the bathing platform before them. All the materials they needed for a trap to overturn the lead demon boat were ready.

"We are sure that they will come by boat?" asked Garan.

"Yes," said *Akik* Bada, "One of the trophy heads said they will climb our banks."

"Good," said Nuing, "We will start early tomorrow morning." After a pause he asked, "Who is on sentry duty tonight?"

"Your wife Nambi and a few other women have offered to take it up," said Libau, a young man who was a teenage boy when Nuing left the house two years before. "They want to make sure that we are all properly rested for tomorrow's work."

Nuing nodded. He did not expect any trouble from the demons that night, but if there was trouble, he knew that his wife would know how to deal with it. The men then returned to their individual gallery, and instead of sleeping in their room, they slept outside like bachelors. The house was silent, its occupants having fallen into watchful sleep. Outside the drums still rolled.

***

The scent of morning woke the men. They took their machete or adze and a personal paddle then stole out of the house like thieves. They heaped split bamboos and hastily made spears into two boats, and after piling into these, dragged the coils of floating rattan behind them. They travelled downriver for a hundred yards or so, about where the jungle on either side of the bank was densest and populated with springy saplings.

First they stretched out about half a dozen canes of rattan across the river. Then they strapped the rattans together before submerging them in the water, using rocks to hold them down. They went to one side of the bank, bowed a springy tree towards the surface of the river and held it in place with a rope fixed to a peg that had been driven into the bank. This peg in turn was held in place by a trigger. The free end of the rope held down by the peg was tied firmly to one end of the rattan bundle. They repeated this on the other side of the bank. Next they tied the ends of a sturdy cord to both the triggers holding the pegs in place. Nuing made sure that there was enough slack in the cord to allow it to lie just below the surface of the water regardless of how high or low the tide was.

Next they set up spring traps downriver to the two springy trees. The cords holding the springs in place would be released from their switches by the two trees when they spring back and lift the rattan trap from inside the river. Spears would then shoot out from the jungle to either side. Barely a word was spoken between the men as they worked because all the plans had been discussed and agreed upon the night before.

The immediacy of their need and the desperately short time of their mission made every man single minded. There was not a single petty discussion on how high a spear should point or how much tension should be applied to each springboard. Every man did the best he could to the best he had learned by experience and observation. No man judge another man's handiwork because they each realized that it would be akin to judging the value this man placed on his life as well as the life of everyone else in the community.

They worked, quietly, quickly, and desperately. Yet they thrived on their desperation because it provided the fuel they needed when exhaustion and hunger or thirst came close to overwhelming them. They pulled, cut, tied and sharpened until their fingers felt stiff and useless, and until their back, shoulders and arms felt like sharp blades were being driven into them. Still they worked, until dusk reached them.

Then they quickly got into their boats and paddled home. They could not tell if their own anxiety had amplified the sound, but the drumming seemed to be closer now. Except for one sentry, Libau, who was watching out for them, the landing place was empty when they reached it.

After mooring the boat, Nuing dipped himself into the river for a quick wash. He looked up to Libau who was eyeing the stream upriver intently. "Have the spikes been planted?" asked Nuing.

"Yes, *Tuai*," Libau replied without moving his eyes. "The older boys did a fine job. We had to replant some bushes in parts of the garden so we can hide the spikes under them."

"That is good. The demons will not see them," said Nuing encouragingly, though his mind suddenly realized that the demons would soon learn not to step on any low bush after they've stepped on one. Yet he dared not vocalise his grim thoughts, lest they put a curse on the work of the boys. Darkness began to creep up the river like a fog, towards them. The men quickly climbed back up onto the bathing platform and hurried back to the longhouse.

They passed the boat shelters, each instinctively looking under the thatch roofing to make sure that no sharp tool which could be used as a weapon had been left inside. Most of the shelters were still filled with partially carved dugout boats, many of which had not been touched in months because of the worry of oncoming battle. The children had done a fine job, Nuing admitted, because there was not a single tool left behind.

Garan, however, did not think that they had done enough when he looked up towards the longhouse beyond the garden in front of him. His brow frowned with worry and he said, "We still have time to build a wall tomorrow." The spikes were not as well hidden as he had expected, and the bushes were replanted in an unnatural way. It was obvious even to him that they were there to hide a trap.

Nuing shook his head. "No, nothing we build will be able to withstand them. And they are so tall, even if we were to build walls as tall as our house they could still jump over them."

Tawang said, "*Tuai* is right. Anyway, if we build a wall now, they might come from the side then the cross-bows will be useless."

"But the spikes will not stop them too," said Libau, unable to contain himself. He knew it was taboo to speak ill of the defence plan, but the sense of absolute doom inside him was too large to ignore.

Nuing stopped and pointed to a spike. "That one is tall and sharp. It will pierce through the feet of a demon and slow him down long enough for us to shoot a spear at him. It is good because it will allow us more time to fight them from a distance. Once they reach us, we will have very little hope to survive."

The rest of the walk back was silent, as the men pondered over Nuing's words. Moment by moment, the darkness in their heart began to brighten so that by the time they reached their gallery, hope had begun to show in their words and manners, like a young padi shoot on the first day it broke through the soil.

The air had been hot and oppressive since before dusk. Now it felt thick with rain, and sure enough, that night, a terrible thunderstorm raged about them. It frightened the community so bad that no one wanted to sleep in their own family room. Instead they lay or sat together in the gallery where they were startled constantly by the bright flash of blue light and the roar of thunder that shook them to their core. Wind blasted at the longhouse from every side, every so often penetrating the woven walls and blowing rain water onto the occupants.

Nuing was unsettled. He worried about the cross-bows outside. He worried that the ground would be too wet on the morrow for the charwoods and resins that they had tediously prepared. Then he became restless when he thought that the spears they had planted would be exposed or ruined. He got up and went to stand by a closed bark door leading to the veranda outside.

Above the din of thunderstorm, he heard a strange sound, and instantly his muscles tensed. He rested one side of his face against the door and listened. He heard laughter: Insane, shrill and demeaning. He pulled out the plug holding the door in place, cracked it open a little and looked out. The rain sprayed on his face, forcing him to squint.

It was dark outside, but he could see pinpoints of red light darting here and there, and being flung about by the wind. One of the red lights suddenly stopped mid-air then flew towards him. Nuing quickly shut the door and slammed the plug back. The door shook violently followed by a peel of laughter. Nuing stared hard and with terror. The thunderstorm suddenly stopped, and the laughter outside stopped.

Nuing struggled to calm his panting breath then returned to Nambi's side. Everyone had by now settled enough to fall asleep, except for two women on sentry duty. Nuing remained sitting, listening and staring at the door. Nothing else happened for the remainder of the night and when Nambi woke before the dawn, she found her husband still staring at the door.

***

Morning light revealed the ravages of the night before. Outside the ground was littered with leaves, twigs and sticks broken off trees in the vicinity. All of the tapioca plants had been blown on so hard that the stems were now lying almost vertical with the ground. A couple of cotton bushes had been uprooted, and many were stripped bare of leaves and bolls. So it was with amazement that Nuing looked up to the roof of the house and saw that not a single thatch had been dislodged. Nuing asked two sentries to clear a path to the river, so that no one would accidentally step on a spear on their way to the bathing platform. Then he sought *Akik* Bada and told him his experience of the night before.

"Did you count how many red lights there were?" asked the old man.

"I could not count them because they were moving fast and seemed to be everywhere at the same time."

"You said they were laughing like madmen," said *Akik* Bada then waited for Nuing to nod. "They must be the trophy heads. Maybe the thunderstorm last night came from them."

Nuing turned his eyes up to the rafters for a moment then back to the old man. "But why would they soak the ground with rain after they had told us to layer it with charwood and resin?"

"They did tell us to do it a day before battle. Let us wait until this afternoon before we judge their actions as traitorous."

Nuing was about to say something else then firmly shut his mouth. He had often been careless with his words, and now he feared that he was about to make another wrong assessment of the situation. Today might be the most important day of his life, because it meant either the death or survival of his longhouse. He could not allow himself to utter a single careless word to curse any plan made by the trophy heads; even if that plan seemed like a betrayal to him now.

The morning sun burned down hot and bright, so that soon the top layer of twigs and leaves were stiff and wrinkled with dryness. Then Nuing understood. The layer of leaves and twigs hid the spears totally, both providing a camouflage as well as tinder for the charwood and resin that they would be scattering that evening. Another change also came that afternoon. They had all become so used to the sound of the drums that when it stopped, it took a while for the sentries to notice. Everyone was ordered back into the longhouse, except for the men who were carefully making their way about the garden, spreading kindling like seeds.

Once the men returned to the house, only the sentries were allowed out on the veranda to keep a watch on their surroundings until it becomes too dark to see. They had collected enough food and water to last them two weeks, if need be, hence no one had any excuse to step down to the ground.

Throughout the day, the children were encouraged to make music with gongs and turtle shells to distract them from the oncoming darkness. Their play and laughter kept the adults' spirit up. After their meal, the women gathered and went to Nuing as a group. They offered to fight alongside the men. Nuing was reluctant, but Nambi insisted, "We are just as strong and as brave as the men. We will not cower before those demons."

"But you are the seed keepers. You cannot spill blood in battle," Nuing insisted.

Nambi said, "We are allowed to kill in self-defence."

Tawang said, "But they will see that you are women and they will attack you first."

"Then we shall be the ones to fight them first," said Jering, who was a shy frightened single mother when she first joined the group but was now a farmer, trap-maker, and cloth weaver. "This home was built by us, and this land discovered by us. I shall not allow a band of demons to take this blessing away from me and the children."

"Jering speaks for all of us," said Nambi, and so with that, Nuing allowed them to arm themselves. They changed their skirts for loin-cloths and put unadorned war-caps on their heads to symbolically take on the role of men.

The night was long and silent. Not a single omen animal or frog or cicada called. It was as if they too were waiting and listening. A sudden gust went up the river, whistling through the cracks and into the crevices of their house. With it, the wind brought a strange foul stench. Nuing signalled his warriors to make ready.

Every armed men and women took up a position near a door. They waited but nothing came. *Akik* Bada began to burn some *selukai* tree bark.

"Why are you doing this now?" Nuing asked.

"I think they have sent a scout or two ahead. I fear that if they come too close to the house, they will see all the preparations that we have made."

Nuing nodded to indicate that he agreed with *Akik* Bada's reasoning. He then took an armload of the smouldering bark from the old man and walked out the door. Tawang followed him out. They walked to the downriver side of the longhouse, lowered a bamboo ladder then climbed down. The smoke of the *selukai* enclosed them like a cloud. Nuing picked up a stick, thrust it upright into the ground and thrust a tied bundle of fumigant bark into it. Tawang went ahead and did the same. Thus they worked along the edge of the jungle that was only yards away from their garden, from the traps they had set for the giants.

Nuing suddenly sensed a looming blacker darkness in front of him, and he threw the last bundle of smouldering bark at it. The demon jumped back, breaking and cracking bushes and trees as he did so.

"Tell your chief that we are waiting for him," said Nuing. "Tell him we are not afraid."

A growl emerged out of the darkness. "I shall have a taste of your flesh before the sun sets tomorrow."

Nuing laughed, the sound modulated with a touch of insanity. "Then come. We have woven large trophy baskets for your heads."

A snort of contempt burst from the foliage then they heard the demon move away. Nuing looked about and saw five pin-point red lights. To them he said, "Help us, *Antu Pala*. Help us hide the traps we have set downriver."

A peel of contemptuous laughter responded to his request. Then the lights moved away and disappeared under the longhouse.

Tawang remained close to Nuing as they made their way back to the house. Though the trophy heads belonged to the house, and were in essence his comrades, these spirits were also known to play cruel tricks on their human master. They could frighten a man, shrivel his spirit and make his soul leave his body. Then he would die a slow and painful death. Tawang did not want to die slowly and painfully, so he followed Nuing as though he was his chief's own shadow. On their return to the gallery, they told everyone what the demon had revealed, that the fight was expected to end by the next sunset.

Chapter 17

Morning came bright and unusually quiet. It was so bright the green reflected off the leaves hurt the eyes of the sentries. Tawang was the first to feel a cool drop of rain on his shoulder. But it was so hot it almost instantly fizzed into nothing, so he thought that he had only imagined it. Soon, however, the sparse drops of a drizzle started to darken the grey wood floor of the veranda in front of him. Rain with no clouds was a sign that the *Antu Gerasis* were out on the hunt. He looked to the river then to the sides of the longhouse, staring hard into the shadows beyond the wall of jungle.

Far in the distance he heard the shrill yelps of the *pasun*, the merciless hunting dogs of the demon huntsmen. He had seen them once before when he was a boy and the memory shrivelled his spirit, making his muscles tightened so violently that he felt as though he was being squeezed by a large snake. The *pasuns*, he recalled, looked like badgers with sharp snarling teeth and black claws. A pack of at least a dozen chased him one time while he was on his way home from the field. He was alone and was so engrossed in collecting wild berries along the path that he had not noticed the rain. It was only on hearing the strange, unfamiliar barks that he realised he was in danger. He reached the house just in time, but he did not have a lucky escape because one of the *pasun*s managed to scratch him, and the wound from it almost killed him. He survived, but the call he now heard coming from downriver renewed the terror that he thought he had outgrown. He gripped a spear with his trembling hands in an effort to steady them.

Then he heard the sound of sticks and vines whipping through the air and a splash. The traps downriver had been set off. Instead of screams, however, there was laughter. Like Tawang, the other sentries were also confused then the confusion turned to fear because they had all hoped that the traps would wound and weaken the giant army.

Suddenly the air cracked with the sound of splintering wood and a tree that had been snapped mid-trunk flew through the air towards them. Tawang, like every other sentry who saw it, instinctively fell on one knee, curled his spine and covered the back of his head with his arms. The projectile landed with a loud crash, into the row of boat shelters close to the bathing platform.

Then from downriver came the sound of a great cheer followed by a whoop of victory. Tawang snarled before getting up again to stand resolutely next to the trigger plug which was now keeping the taut bow string in place. He poured curses and hate onto the spear he was holding then laid it on the guide-groove on the stock of the cross-bow. He crouched down and ran his eyes along the shaft of the bamboo spear until the point where it looked through a small gap in the centre of the lathe arm.

Tawang felt a presence next to him and looked up. Nuing's face was deep with warrior frown and its fierceness reassured Tawang of his chief's plan. The first trap had failed but the house was not without defence. The noise of their enemy grew louder by the moment and soon they saw the foul beasts riding on boats that were as wide as their gallery and as long as their longhouse.

And what beasts they were, for even if an Iban man had never seen one, a description of their foul form, hulking size, and raiment of animal skin adorned with rows of canine teeth would have struck terror into his heart. Tawang sat back on his haunches, trying to move away from the image as far as he physically could in that squatting position. Nuing placed a firm grip on his friend's shoulder and, with a shake, indicated without words that Tawang must remain by the cross-bow regardless of what would happen in the ensuing battle.

The first boat smashed into the row of smaller dugouts moored to the side of the bathing platform, cutting each in half by its sheer size and weight. Other boats cleaved into the bank before expelling ten to fifteen demons each onto it. The *antu gerasis* were so huge, Tawang saw, that their eyes appeared as large as Chinese plates and each strand of their hair seemed as thick as a porcupine quill. Their immense mouth stretched from side to side like a catfish's and Tawang could imagine himself being swallowed whole by one. Large ears stuck out of the thick manes of their lank hair, and their belly was so large and protruding, it looked as though they had each swallowed a man whole before coming to battle.

About their filthy bare feet were their vicious but small hunting dogs. The *pasuns* snarled and drooled then sniffed the air. One started to let out a sharp howl, which was quickly picked up by others in the pack. One giant picked up the tree which had been thrown against the boat shelters and cast it aside as though it was no more than a twig. Yet none of this show of strength and scourge shook Nuing's courage.

But as they began to move away from the mud of the river and reach the grassy slope, the fresh green plants and grass about them shrivelled to brown. An awful rankness hovered over them and it was only surpassed by the awful smell that came out of their breath when they let out a roar.

Nuing felt his hands and legs go numb and his courage shrivelling back into his scrotum until it was nothing more than a tiny knot. His eyes looked about wildly for a way to escape. There was still time for him to run. He could abandon the house, his family, and escaped alone into the jungle. No one would think him a lesser man for it, and most probably no one would survive to tell about his cowardice.

His breathing grew heavy and his heart pounded so hard, it masked the war shouts of the advancing demons. The world seemed to slow, forcing him to see and think with a single-mindedness that he had never experienced before. In those moments of clarity he saw Sempekang, the leader of the demon huntsmen. He was so large, he seemed to tower a head above the other giants.

A sudden calm returned to Nuing. He was still afraid, but at that moment he began to accept that he would always be afraid whenever he faced death, like his father Bujang Maias. As he watched the demons make an extravagant show of their advance, by roaring and smashing, he suddenly understood the source of his father's fear. The taking of one life would always come with revenge and retribution and, regardless of whoever won, the cycle would never end for as long as the descendants of both men survived. If he killed Sempekang that day, then other demons would avenge their leader's death. If Nuing himself were killed, his children would be duty bound to avenge his death. It was with great effort that Nuing pushed aside the thought, for he must return his wandering spirit to his people now.

Nuing sensed the building panic about him, and he lifted his hand to stay his warriors. It was too soon to shoot at their enemies because they were still out of range. They had also taken great pains to hide the existence of the cross-bows from the giants, so to show them now would mean that they would lose their element of surprise. The last giant to come up to land turned to the bathing platform and stomped on it, splintering the hardwood on his second try. He let out a great victorious shout, as though he had just killed a man.

Nuing held his breath, wishing yet dreading that the demons would move closer and step into their trap sooner. Sempekang advanced ahead of the group and stopped just yards away from the first line of hidden spears and spikes.

He looked at the longhouse before him and laughed. "Your trap failed. See, every single one of us is still here. Do you think us so foolish that we have never seen or heard of traps that Iban men set on warboats?" He spread his arms wide, looking about him as though to stress their dire situation. "Even *Bunsu* Ribut would not leave you in peace. See how the wind god scatters your fruits and herbs. See how he plucks your cotton tree from their roots."

The other demons laughed uproariously, some making faces by scowling, grimacing, and stretching their leather-like cheeks. The demon dogs were so keen on attacking that they trembled with anticipation. Sempekang stomped then charged forward and his demons chased after him. Their roars of courage, however, soon turned to raging pain. The *pasuns* stopped in their tracks and looked back to their masters, suddenly confused and wary.

Nuing swung down his hand and his warriors shot out the well-aimed spears. Shouts of pain and curses issued out of five demons. Troughs filled with fire and oil were carried out to the veranda and placed next to the cross-bows. The Ibans dipped rag and vine wrapped spears into the troughs to soak up the oil then to pick up the fire on its surface. These were placed in the guide groove of the cross-bow after the bowstring had been set taut on the trigger once more. More shots went out, each now aimed to the ground. Droplets of fiery oil fell among the demons as the spears flew past.

Many among the demon huntsmen were confused and wondered what manner of men could be throwing spears at them from that distance. No man had ever stood to face any one of them before, so that the death throes of their comrades now held some of them back. Then the fiery spears flew at them and they watched these fall to the ground. Their courage returned and they resumed their charge. The fire quickly spread about them and started to lick their feet. Some stomped on the ground to try to put the fire out, and sent sparks flying. The sparks landed on their hair and clothes of animal skin which were grimy with oil and dirt. The *pasuns* were also not spared, for many of the demon dogs were either burned by fire or crushed by the feet of their stampeding masters. The demons who were aflame gave out such terrible howls that the people inside the longhouse cringed tighter together and hunkered low on the floor as though expecting a physical onslaught just from the sound alone.

Warriors who were not manning the cross-bows ran to the edge of the veranda and began to hurl down clumps of smouldering bark. The licking flames rose into towering infernos as more demons caught fire, one after another. The heat rising from the ground also created its own storm, whirling and spiralling upwards with every new gust of wind. The demons could not approach the house for the smoke from the custard apple tree bark rose like an impenetrable wall before them, burning their eyes, their nostrils, and their skin more than the actual fire itself.

Sempekang took a deep breath and blew a clear path before him. Nuing placed the pig spear in an empty cross-bow guide and pulled back the bow string, fixing it into the hook and setting the trigger. He turned the cross-bow until he had Sempekang in his sights. Then he released the trigger. The spear stick flew towards its mark at lightning speed but was struck aside by an even quicker Sempekang. It fell to the ground, into the fire.

The shout of victory that was poised in Nuing's throat dropped back into his belly like a stone. He almost fell on his knees in despair. Yet when all hope seemed lost, a sudden image of Nambi and Ratai being torn from limb to limb, and being preserved in jars of fermenting meat suddenly made a roar rose in his chest. It was a roar that only a man who had no other defences left to him could make. He could not run. His spirit and his soul had no space, no world, no other life to flee to even at that moment when the worst of his fears was barrelling his way towards him.

Nuing pulled out the sword he had inherited from his father Bujang Maias, the *ilang* that was gifted by the warrior guardian Keling himself. He let out another fell shout as the bone-hilt of the sword burned and seemed suddenly to be fused to the bones of his hand and his arm.

Sempekang smashed into the veranda and heaved himself up onto it. Even in that tumult about him, Nuing could hear the pillars and wood groaned under the giant's weight. Nuing took a few steps forward then looked up defiantly. If Sempekang wished to kill everyone in his longhouse then the demon would have to kill him first.

"Small, insignificant man," shouted Sempekang.

"We are not insignificant," shouted Nuing in return, "We have killed two of your followers and maimed many others." Nuing pointed to one side, where some demons stood, moving their gaze from side to side like animals looking for escape. "See, they are afraid."

The terror that Sempekang had caused by his first utterances melted away in the heat of the other Iban fighters' returning hope. One man added a stone into the groove of his cross-bow guide, so he could aim the spear a little higher. The projectile he let loose struck a demon in the eye and sent him falling with a howl. Fire engulfed his oily mane and caused the most terrible death throes. Another demon rushed to this fellow's aid but was held back by the flames.

Sempekang grabbed Nuing by the waist and Nuing thrust the sword into the flesh between the demon's thumb and the index finger, cutting open a tear in it. Pain and surprise made Sempekang release him.

"What is this?" said the demon. "How is it possible that you could have cut me?"

Nuing made no reply. He was panting and quaking with relief for having been released. Sempekang's face scowled into a deep terrible rage. He fisted his wounded hand and smashed it into Nuing, throwing him hard against the cross-bow and twisting his backbone. Nuing struggled to get up, but his twisted body would not obey him. A terrible pain coursed up and down his back like lightning. He could do nothing but watch the giant approach.

Sempekang reached down with a grin on his face. Suddenly the grin frowned and the frown became wide-eyed with pain. The flesh in front of his heart stretched outward then a horn-like tip pierced through the skin, making the stretched skin suddenly pull back. Nuing saw that it was the tip of the pig spear. The spear continued to run its full length through Sempekang's heart before it flew out of his chest and drove itself into the floor next to Nuing. Sempekang swayed where he stood as though unsure whether to charge or retreat. Then he fell back, releasing his soul even before his heavy body touched the ground.

The shocked silence was soon followed by howls of rage. The sentries readied themselves to meet this new attack. They waited but none of the demons charged towards them. Then they noticed a strange thing; the remaining demons were beating on another demon, the one who had tried to save his burning friend. They were calling him 'murderer', 'coward', or 'traitor' and they were cursing his father and mother for having begotten him. They stomped on him until there was nothing left and they stomped some more until every single tissue of his body became infused with the ground turning it into hard rock.

Then the demons turned their eyes to the longhouse. A handful approached. Four giant took away the body of their leader, but one remained running his saucer-sized yellow eyes along the length of the veranda, looking at every single man and woman standing there until they finally stopped to glare at Nuing.

"Sempekang is dead. We have no more quarrel with you."

Nuing swallowed with difficulty and with equal difficulty asked, "How?"

The giant looked behind him, at the hard ground. "He threw the spear that killed Sempekang." He turned back to Nuing. "The accursed fellow will be forced to stay with humans and his soul shall have no taste of the afterlife until the Earth releases him."

The giant then turned away and returned to the river. Their dead and wounded were collected and placed in the boats.

Tawang came up to Nuing and tried to move him, but the chief cried out in pain and begged to be left where he was. So the men built a temporary shade over him to shield him from the waning heat and the oncoming dew.

***

After the house had fallen into a restless sleep, Tawang went outside and sat on the mat placed next to his chief. It pained him to see Nuing lying on the bare floor, but each time they tried to move him, he would let out such a terrible cry that it quailed the heart of even the stoutest man. So they had left him there. Nambi had spread the blanket of the sun bear over him, hoping that the essence and strength of a master weaver would revive his spirit.

"Did we lose anyone?" asked Nuing.

"No, *Tuai*. Many of us were bruised by the sticks and rocks the demons threw, but all will heal in the next week."

"That is," began Nuing then swallowed a breath before continuing, "good to know." He began to shiver, imperceptibly at first then violently.

"Are you cold? Let me bring more blankets."

"No," Nuing said between chattering teeth. "I will face this… as I have faced… everything else… I will not break." Then with vehemence, he said, "I am the son of Bujang Maias, the son of *Tok* Anjak. I will not break." The floor beneath him began to rattle.

Soon the whole house shook, waking its occupants, and the ground trembled, quivering the branches of every shrub and tree still standing in the vicinity. The sentries ran out to the veranda, their eyes squinting into the darkness, expecting the return of the demon huntsmen. The air was suddenly filled with the stench of mud and rotting vegetation. It was unfamiliar to the men, but one that Nuing had come to hate.

The voice of the pig king called out from the pitch dark ground below. "Is your home bound by taboo?"

The men started, for a night visitor was unheard of in their land. They looked to Nuing, and he said, "Invite the king up."

Tawang walked to the edge of the veranda with a lamp and said, "No, our home is free from taboo. Please come up." He turned and nodded to the men standing behind him. A bamboo ladder was brought forward and lowered to the ground. Then the men stood back, first watching the top of the bamboo bend and settle under the weight then eyeing the strange dark form of the pig king climbing up to their level. Two other pig men came up after him and flanked the king on either side.

Raja Babi nodded at the Ibans and Tawang led them to where Nuing lay. The king sat down on the mat and soon a sentry appeared with a basket of tobacco, betel nut and betel vine leaves. He also offered the king a gourd filled with rice wine. *Raja* Babi drank and smoked. Nuing took a sip of the wine and a puff off the cigarette Tawang had rolled for him.

The pig king said, "You have caused me much trouble, Nuing."

"I have only done what any man in my position would have done."

The king laughed. "Any normal man would have quietly waited to be offered as a sacrifice. After all, it is not a dishonourable thing to be a servant of a great warrior-pig in the afterlife."

"I am no servant. I am a free man."

Raja Babi pointed to the spear next to Nuing. "I see

Sempekang is dead."

"I am sorry I took your spear."

"I was sorry too, but now I realise that you have saved me the trouble of going after the demon myself."

"You have come to gloat at my suffering."

"No, I have come to take back the spear, so I could bury it with my father. The demon hunted him down, crushed his spirit, and made him suffer for many years. I placed a curse on the spear, so it would never rest until it has killed Sempekang. It has done its work, and as promised, it shall rest with my father."

The pig king stood up and pulled the spear out of the floor. Before he left he said, "I shall send my shaman to you in the morning and he shall heal your back. Tell your people that they are not allowed to spill blood tomorrow. Not a single bird, snake or even fish must they harm. The shaman will also take away the curse of barrenness that my youngest daughter has placed on your wife." The king climbed down the ladder with his men and the ground again trembled. When the tremble stilled, fresh air returned to the longhouse.

None of the fighting men and women returned to their bed. Instead they huddled in groups of twos or threes along the length of the veranda, peering into the blinding darkness around them. The sound of insects and frogs comforted them. Instinctively they learned to recognize the melody of each song, so they would know if there was a break or a sudden change in the symphony to alert them of approaching trouble.

* * *

The morning came bright and warm, but not a single omen

animal could be heard calling in the vicinity. The quiet, however, was soon broken by a shout from one of the young sentries. He pointed his spear downward to the ground, obviously afraid by the way he bent his knees and swung his body from side to side as though looking for a good angle from which to throw the spear. Tawang shouted, "Do not spill blood!"

Though the man did not look up, he nodded to indicate that he had heard but kept his eyes and spear affixed to the ground. Slowly his spear began to inch upwards and he began to inch back. Tawang walked over to the edge of the veranda across from him and looked down. Climbing up one of the pillars was the largest reticulated python he had ever seen in his life. Its girth must be at least as large as the very pillar it was now climbing.

Soon the head of the snake reached their level and everyone saw that it was as wide as the prow of a warboat. The snake slithered along the veranda at an angle, making its way to Nuing. The lozenge-shaped yellow and gold patterns bordered black shone like metal under the glare of the sun.

Nuing was oblivious to the commotion because he was now in a fevered sleep. The snake wound itself around him, inducing a moan and a whimper from Nuing. The sentries circled the makeshift shade, afraid but compelled to watch. Once the snake had covered Nuing's twisted form totally, except for the head and feet, it began to slowly squeeze. They could see its muscles undulating under the scaly skin. Nuing again moaned and his face grimaced. He stretched his neck in an effort to move his shoulders, but to no avail.

The spiralled coil slowly moved Nuing's twisted body and began to straighten it. Nuing's neck arced and he let out a grunt. Then his head fell back and he sighed. The snake started to uncoil and made its way to Nambi, who was now standing at the threshold of the door. It stared at her then hissed, "You are Nambi."

She nodded, her voice stuck in her mouth.

The python rubbed one cheek against the frame of the doorway and dislodged a golden scale. It said, "Boil this in a tube of bamboo filled with water. You must drink all the water before sunset. Anyone else who drinks from the water will die. Tomorrow morning, break the bamboo tube and bury it in your field with the scale."

The snake turned to go. Nambi suddenly found her voice and asked, "What will happen after that?"

The snake turned its face sideways so that one eye was looking at her. "You will begin to bear children and your rice stalks will be sprouting so much panicles that they will bend low enough to touch the ground." Then it continued on its way down the longhouse, climbed down the side, and disappeared into the jungle.

Nuing suddenly woke with a start. He stared about him with surprise for a moment then suddenly realised that he was sitting. He got up stiffly to his feet and his men gave out a shout of joy. Then there was a great shout of victory. Nuing hobbled his way back into the gallery, for though the shaman had healed his back, his other bruises still smarted. He paused to look into his wife's shinning eyes which were now brimming with tears of happiness then took his place as chief in his gallery.

They feasted on the food that they had prepared for the siege and drank to their heart's desire. In the meantime Nambi boiled water which quickly turned as yellow as the scale that was in it. She drank the bitter brew with a happy heart, declaring that it tasted as sweet as the bitter *lalis* palm heart. Before dusk, she finished the last mouthful and when she tapped out the scale from the bottom of the bamboo, she saw that it had become translucent like the belly-scale of a sultan fish.

Nambi did everything according to the instructions of the shaman python and she received all her heart's desire. She bore Nuing six children and her rice field became so abundant that even at times when the harvest was bad for the rest of the longhouse, no one in their community ever went hungry.

Though she had six other younger siblings, Ratai continued to be the balm and hope of both Nuing's and Nambi's spirit because she was a reminder of a life that they had managed to survive together. She was their first-born in spirit, hence Nambi became known as the woman who bore Nuing seven children.

The older he grew, the more Nuing's reputation spread. By the end of his life, people began to account him to be as wise and as strong as Bujang Maias because he was slow to judge, opting to listen to all parties and all facts before coming to a decision. Soon other tribes and other pioneering communities who eventually came to live along the great Lebaan, Rajang and Igan Rivers began to come to him for advice. He became known as a justice who upheld the customary law in proper manner, because all his judgments reputedly brought blessing and prosperity to any community that followed them.

Acknowledgements

The beliefs and taboos mentioned in the book are loosely applicable to the Ibans of all districts in Sarawak, but by no means are they to be treated as the result of an extensive scholarly study. I try to stay as true as I can to the practices of different communities, however, details of the ceremonies mentioned may differ from the actual practices of different districts. This is because Iban ceremonies follow a general guideline but are not set in stone, as the people have to adapt their practices to the environment they live in. Hence in some places the Ranyai, a shrine erected during major festivals, may be built from nipah palms but in others, they are made of banana leaves.

Though I try to keep the taboos and beliefs in the story as accurate as possible, some elements have been added for dramatic effect. One such example is the single fruit that Gunggu eats in Bunsu Bubut's home (the spirit of the greater coucal). I have read Greek mythology obsessively when I was a child, so the idea clearly comes from the myth of Persephone and Hades. Another example concerns the K'lansat demons, which are believed to still roam the jungle and are usually depicted as being alone in Iban superstition, but in this book they are portrayed as living in a group.

I might have found many useful information from printed literature, websites, and museums yet the details would not have been as alive or as localized if I had not talked with the following people during the course of writing both Iban Dream and Iban Journey.

Hence I would like to use this opportunity to give special thanks to Tuai Rumah Mok anak Gelot, a longhouse chief from Julau, for his invaluable advice and insight on hepatomancy, the practice of divination by the reading of a pig's liver. He is also my source of information on paddy planting which is covered extensively in Iban Dream, the first book of this series. If there is any conflict in the story against actual practice, it will be due to my own misunderstanding, and not to his lack of knowledge. This book also owes insight to Dr. Peter M. Kedit, a senior advisor in the Tun Jugah Foundation, who was kind enough to talk about the rituals associated with the Iban traveller during our discussion of his dissertation, 'Iban Bejalai'. Rev. Jerry Rabbu anak Ayun, a retired minister from the Iban Methodist Church of Sibu, has also freely shared his experiences and materials with me. His family continues to be a source of love and encouragement.

Seeing both these books in print is bitter sweet because it saddens me to think that the first person who had shown confidence in my work and supported my aspiration passed away in June 2011, a little under two years before Iban Dream came out in print. Jerome Runggol had gone out of his way to show me Sri Aman and one of the old longhouses in the district, where they still practised the tradition of conversing with guests in poetry. He was proud to be an Iban through and through, and it is my hope that I have managed to capture his spirit in both books.

A few generations from now, this next man I wish to thank will be described as an all-powerful maverick with skin as thick as a rhino's hide and voice as strong as Thor's, but to me he is none other than the mild-mannered and soft-spoken Phil Tatham of Monsoon Books. All my work would have come to nothing if he had not been intrepid enough to give an unknown writer and her strange obscure story a chance. His team of editors, proofreaders, and book cover designers has also done tremendous work.

My love and thanks also goes out to my family and friends. To my cousin Patrick Mowe for instilling in me the belief that it is possible to be published; my three siblings for continuing to love and support me these past years even though two of them believed that I was going down the road of wreck and ruin; my mother who has not stopped worrying; and friends who have cheered me on.

To them all, I dedicate this book.

Iban Dream by Golda Mowe

{ prequel to Iban Journey }

Orphaned as a young boy in the rainforests of Borneo, Bujang is brought up by a family of orangutans, but his adult future has already been decided for him by Sengalang Burong, the Iban warpath god. On reaching adulthood, Bujang must leave his ape family and serve the warpath god as a warrior and a headhunter. Having survived his first assignment — to kill an ill-tempered demon in the form of a ferocious wild boar — subsequent adventures see Bujang converse with gods, shamans, animal spirits and with the nomadic people of Borneo as he battles evil spirits and demons to preserve the safety of those he holds dear to him. But Bujang's greatest test is still to come and he must rally a large headhunting expedition to free his captured wife and those of his fellow villagers.

In this unique work of fantasy fiction, author Golda Mowe — herself an Iban from Borneo — uses real beliefs, taboos and terminology of the Iban (a longhouse-dwelling indigenous group of people from Borneo who, until recently, were renowned for practising headhunting) to weave an epic tale of good versus evil. *Iban Dream* is the prequel to *Iban Journey*.